W9-BLP-232

LEAVE MYSELF BEHIND

LEAVE MYSELF BEHIND

BART YATES

KENSINGTON BOOKS
http://www.kensingtonbooks.com

KENSINGTON BOOKS are published by

Kensington Publishing Corp.
850 Third Avenue
New York, NY 10022

Copyright © 2003 by Bart Yates

All rights reserved. No part of this book may be reproduced in any form or by any means without the prior written consent of the Publisher, excepting brief quotes used in reviews.

All Kensington titles, imprints and distributed lines are available at special quantity discounts for bulk purchases for sales promotion, premiums, fund-raising, educational or institutional use.

Special book excerpts or customized printings can also be created to fit specific needs. For details, write or phone the office of the Kensington Special Sales Manager: Kensington Publishing Corp., 850 Third Avenue, New York, NY 10022. Attn. Special Sales Department. Phone: 1-800-221-2647.

Excerpt from "Sestina," from THE COMPLETE POEMS 1927-1979 by Elizabeth Bishop. Copyright © 1979, 1983 by Alice Helen Methfessel. Reprinted by permission of Farrar, Strauss, and Giroux, LLC.

"Herman Melville," copyright 1939 by W. H. Auden from W. H. AUDEN: THE COLLECTED POEMS by W. H. Auden, Used by permission of Random House, Inc., and Faber and Faber Ltd.

From WINTER OF OUR DISCONTENT by John Steinbeck, copyright © 1961 by John Steinbeck. Renewed copyright © 1989 by Elaine Steinbeck, John Steinbeck IV, and Thom Steinbeck. Used by permission of Viking Penguin, a division of Penguin Putman, Inc.

The author acknowledges Random House Inc. for the use of the quote from Henry David Thoreau's WALDEN.

Kensington and the K logo Reg. U.S. Pat. & TM Off.

Library of Congress Card Catalogue Number: 2002112565
ISBN 0-7582-0348-9

First Printing: March 2003
10   9   8   7   6   5   4   3   2   1

Printed in the United States of America

For Newell Yates
1931-1983.
Wherever you are
I hope they let you read books

Acknowledgments

This book would never have happened without Gordon Mennenga. Period. Thanks, Gordon, for everything.

Thanks as well to Melanie Santos, Angela Strater, and LeAnn Keenan for invaluable help and support. You each get a wet, sloppy kiss the next time I see you—whether or not you want one.

John Talbot is a gifted agent and a good man, and my editor at Kensington, John Scognamiglio, has been a joy to work with. Thanks to both for helping me chase down, painlessly, this particular dream.

Cheers to the Fall River Red Wine Consortium: Tim and Maria Ferreira-Bedard, Kevin St. Martin, Marianna Pavlovskaya, Paul Robbins, and Karen Lehrach. You were all there at the beginning of this book and taught me the true meaning of the word "hangover." I miss you guys. Ditto to Paul and Irene Gross.

Thanks to all my T'ai chi friends, in Iowa City and Madison and Boulder and Minneapolis, especially Pena Lubrica, Dave Dugan and Tonja Robinswood. Moving in slow motion with you is always a pleasure.

Jeff Yates answered dozens of inane questions about law enforcement, and my mother, Lois Yates, has been good-natured and patient with me for forty years. Thanks also to Joel, Debbie, Cheryl, Halley, Chad, Stewart, and Marshall Yates.

Rob and Libby Shannon regularly remind me (through personalized slippers, hot food, and mildly violent games of croquet) exactly what hospitality is all about, and Brad Causey, Karen Levin, Bianca Rigel, Joe Stansbery, Judy Gates, and Brian Pogue help keep life from sucking. And thanks to Marie Von Behren and Thomas Knapp for making me so welcome in their home.

You'd think Michael Becker would wise up one day and stop picking up the phone when I call, but thank God for his relentless stupidity: I'd be lost without him.

Deep appreciation to Sifu Moy Yat Tung and all my Kung Fu brothers at the Moy Yat Ving Tsun Kung Fu Association.

And finally, huge thanks to my adopted family: Brad and Liz Schonhorst, Andrew Knapp, John Perona, Marian Mathews Clark, and Jack Manu. Thank you for your generosity, thank you for your kindness and good humor, and thank you most of all, for your love.

LEAVE MYSELF BEHIND

CHAPTER ONE

've never wanted a different mother. I just want my mother to be different.

Get in line, right?

Anybody who tells you he doesn't have mixed feelings about his mother is either stupid or a liar. Granted, Virginia York is a special case. Living with Virginia is like living with a myth. She's only half-human; the rest is equal parts wolverine, hyena, goddess and rutting goat.

In other words, she's a poet.

But she smells great.

Know the way someone smells when they've been outside on a chilly fall day? That's how Mom smells all the time. Like rain, and wind, and leaf mold, and a faint hint of wood smoke. Hardly the way a woman is supposed to smell, but trust me: if the Glade Air Fresheners people could bottle her scent, you'd have her hanging in your car and your bathroom and your kitchen.

Sorry. I didn't mean to get all Oedipal on you.

Anyway.

Mom and I just moved into this old Victorian house in Oakland, New Hampshire. I grew up in Chicago, but Mom was offered a job at Cassidy College and we decided to get the hell out of Dodge. My dad Frank died last year. The coroner said it was a heart attack but what really happened is a poem got caught in his throat like a chicken bone and he choked to death.

I'm not making this shit up.

He was in his library, listening to Chopin's *Nocturnes* on the stereo and reading poetry for one of his classes. When Mom found him in his armchair there was a book splayed open upside down on his lap; he'd been reading *Herman Melville* by W.H. Auden. Dad hated Auden. He called him "an overrated, pretentious queer with a penchant for sentimental excess."

Mom loves Auden. So do I.

The night Dad died I was in my room, painting. Mom was in her study writing. I thought I heard some odd noises coming from the library but I didn't think much about it. Dad seemed himself at dinner. A little tired, maybe, but cheerful and relaxed. He gently teased Mom for picking the olives from her pizza; he laughed at me for wolfing three slices in the time it took him to eat one. When Mom went to tell him she was going to bed, his body was already growing cold. She came to get me. The two of us stood on opposite sides of his chair waiting for the paramedics. I think I was trembling, but neither of us cried. Real life seldom makes us cry. The only thing that gets to Mom and me is the occasional Kodak commercial.

I'm seventeen. My name is Noah. (Don't blame me; Dad had a thing for biblical names. It could have been worse, I suppose— Enoch, or Amalek, for instance.) I'm going to be a senior this September. That's still a month away. I want to get a job, but Mom won't let me until she and I get the house remodeled. She's probably right. The place is a mess. Plaster dust, nails, boards, spackle, paint cans, caulking guns, and a shitload of boxes. We'll be lucky to have it finished by the time school starts. I keep telling her she should hire somebody to do the harder stuff, but she gets pissed and tells me she's "not going to hire some goddamn carpenter and pay him my firstborn son (and that means you, mister, by the way) to do what any idiot with a hammer and the brains of a squirrel can do, so just suck it up and get back to work."

Like I said, Mom has some issues.

I don't really mind working on the house. It's dirty, sweaty work but fun in a sick puritanical kind of way. By the end of each day I'm filthy—my hair is clotted with dust, my clothes stick to me and when I clean my ears the Q-tip comes out black with crud. But I like doing something where you can see your progress. We've finished a lot of the downstairs and it's nearly livable. The hardest part is stripping the woodwork. Some moron painted over every square inch of wood in the house (except for the mahogany banisters), and most of it is oak and maple. Sometimes I feel like Michelangelo, chiseling away at all the crap until nothing is left but the exquisite thing in the middle that no one else sees until it's uncovered for them. Or was it da Vinci who said that was the way he worked? Whatever.

The house is great. When you walk in the front door it's like stepping into another century. There's an ancient chandelier hanging overhead as soon as you're inside, and even though it looks like it's been dipped in dirt it's still something to see, with hundreds of pieces of glass shaped like diamonds and rectangles. There's an old steam radiator next to the door that Moses himself probably installed, and over that is a window facing west, made with some of that thick, leaded glass that has little waves in it. To the left of the entryway is the living room (with a fireplace big enough to roast a goat), to the right is the staircase leading upstairs, and straight ahead and down a short hall is a massive kitchen with a giant ceiling fan. There's a dining room on the other side of the kitchen, with windows facing east and south, and if Mom owned enough china to host a dinner party for twenty people she'd still have no problem storing all the dishes in the colossal wall cabinet in there. Upstairs are four bedrooms and a bathroom, and as if that isn't enough house for the two of us, we've also got a basement and a full-sized attic.

The best part of the house, though, is the wraparound porch. I love sitting out there at night in front of the house, watching the cars go by. (We live right on Main Street, but Main Street in Oakland is just a two-lane brick road.) There's a porch swing, but I prefer sitting on the steps. I like the solid feel of concrete under my ass.

You can separate people into types by what part of a house they like the most. Mom is a kitchen person. Kitchen people like late nights and early mornings, and they spend a lot of time at the sink, staring out the window at nothing while they wash the dishes. They like cooking for people and don't mind a friendly conversation about the weather, but if you ask them a serious question they hop up to take care of the boiling water on the stove or to get a loaf of bread out of the oven, and by the time they sit back down they've forgotten what you asked them. It's like they're always waiting for someone to come home, so they can't pay much attention to any-body already in the house with them because they're too busy lis-tening for footsteps on the front walk.

I'm a porch person. Porch people also love late nights and early mornings, but we're more likely to answer your questions than a kitchen person is, and we don't mind if someone wants to sit on the steps with us as long as he never mentions the weather. We sit with our chins in our hands and our elbows on our knees until we get uncomfortable, then we lay back and put our fingers behind our heads and let the breeze blow over us, tickling the hairs on our legs. I suppose we're also waiting for someone to show up, but we want to know who it is before he gets as far as the door.

I'm not sure what kind of person Dad was. Maybe a study per-son. Study people are off in their own world even more than kitchen people and seem to be genuinely shocked when they look up and see another human being in the room with them. Not displeased, really. Just shocked. Like they've read about other people but never expected to actually see a live specimen.

Jesus. I am so full of shit. Where was I?

We got the house dirt cheap. A place like this would have cost three or four times as much in Chicago, but Oakland only has two thousand people in it, and thirteen hundred of those are college students. Mom was worried about moving here right before my senior year, but I like it. I hated Chicago. Chicago is dirty and loud, and full of people with really shitty taste in music. Mom thinks I'm a snob, but Mom has a tin ear for everything except language—she even likes rap. I don't mind the lyrics so much (how can you dislike something where every other word is "fuck"?) but the music is mind-numbingly repetitive—it's like a little kid pulling on your sleeve, screaming "notice me, notice me, notice me." It drives me apeshit.

Anyway, Oakland is quieter, and cleaner, and you can walk anywhere you want without worrying about getting beaten up or shot. When Mom is writing I like to go out late at night and walk around town. She never would have let me do that in Chicago even though we lived in a nice neighborhood. Here she doesn't even ask me where I'm going or when I'll get back. Since we moved here a week ago she's been writing every night—she shuts herself in her room (the only room in the house that we haven't torn apart) and scribbles away until two or three in the morning. She's always up before me, too. I think sleep is against her religion, or something.

My current project is my bedroom. It's going to be great when I get it finished. It's the first room on the left at the top of the stairs and it has the most character of any of the bedrooms, with a recessed window seat and a view of the entire backyard. There's a walk-in closet that's almost half the size of the room, and I'm thinking I may eventually put my bed in there so I'll have the bedroom itself to use as a painting studio. Until I get it done, though, I have to sleep downstairs on the couch in the living room. I figure another day or two and I can move upstairs and have a door to shut again. I could have started sleeping up here last week but the wallpaper would have given me nightmares—bulbous purple flowers on a pink background. Godawful. It was so old, the paper had been sucked into the wall. When I tried to get it off, big chunks of plaster came with it, so we decided to tear the walls down and start over.

"Don't be so dainty."

I turn around and Mom is standing in the doorway watching me work. I'm tearing down plasterboard with a hammer. She walks over and takes the hammer.

"Hit it like this." She smacks the wall and uses the claw to rip out big chunks around the hole she made. She spent a couple of summers when she was in college working for some carpenter guy and now she thinks she's Mrs. Fix-it. Granted, she's pretty good at this kind of stuff, but I grew up helping her with various projects and I'm not bad with a hammer myself.

"Go away, Mom. This is my job, remember?" I try to take the hammer back and she swings again; plaster explodes from the wall and peppers us both with white dust. A big clump gets caught in her black hair and she yanks it out and grimaces when it snags. She swings again.

Christ. "Don't you have some other wall you can beat up on?"

She pauses. "Just don't be so delicate." She hands the hammer back and walks out of the room.

Mom almost always wears jeans. If she's not barefoot she wears sneakers. She likes tank-tops and flannel shirts, and almost everything she wears is either blue or white, except for when she's feeling daring and puts on something bright red. She's about five-foot-four, thin and tough and restless. Dad was a lot taller than either Mom or me. He was six-three, and I'm only five-seven. He had big shoulders and meaty hands, but I take after Mom. I'm thin and small, like her. But I act a lot more like Dad than like my mom. He was quiet, mostly, and even-tempered. Mom is kind of high strung—funny and wild, but easy to upset. When she got a bad review for her last poetry collection she called the reviewer and told him she didn't know that buttholes could read poetry, let alone critique it. Dad tried to get the phone away from her. He should have known better. After she finished with the newspaper guy she went after Dad and screamed something about whose side was he on anyway and he could just go to hell if he didn't like her attitude. As usual Dad didn't say anything, which just made her madder.

She's gotten worse since Dad died. She's always been unreasonable when somebody hasn't liked her work, but lately she even gets insulted when her name is misspelled on junk mail. She got a letter from some credit card company last week addressed to 'Virginger Yirk' and instead of laughing it off she went ballistic. She ripped the letter into shreds and threw the pieces all over the kitchen. I told her she was acting like a spoiled brat and she yelled "Shut up and clean up this goddamn mess," then stomped out of the room like an autistic five-year-old.

Sometimes I set her off without meaning to—like when I interrupt her when she's working or when I forget to wash the dishes when it's my turn. But sometimes I do it on purpose, just for fun. I mean, come on, what are my options? When she takes herself so seriously, what can I do but fuck with her? Some salesguy came to the door the other day peddling cleaning products and I introduced Mom to him as 'Mrs. Vagina Pork.' The poor bastard took one look at Mom's face and scurried away like a rat with diarrhea. I thought she was going to kill me. She stood with her hands balled into fists at her sides and glared at me until I mumbled an apology, then she finally tore out onto the porch and slammed the door behind her hard enough to make the whole house shake.

If Dad were alive, she still would have been pissed. But she eventually would have laughed, too.

*   *   *

"Hey. Take a look at this." I'm holding an old mason jar, crusted with dirt and dust and cobwebs. It's rusted shut and it feels empty, but when I shake it I can hear something inside, clanging lightly against the metal lid.

She takes it from me. "Where'd you find it?"

"It was sitting on a little shelf behind the wall I just tore down in my room. I can't get it open."

Finding it was the weirdest thing. I ripped out a chunk of wall and once the dust settled there was this jar sitting all by itself, framed perfectly between two wooden spars, like somebody anal had gone to the trouble of making sure it was smack in the middle. I tried to get it open but my hands were too slippery.

She fights with it for a minute, then whacks the lid a couple times on the door frame and tries again. It opens with a pop. I reach for it to see what's inside, but she holds it away from me.

"Come on, Mom. I found it."

"Big deal. I bought the house." She pulls out a piece of paper, neatly folded. She unfolds it and I can see typewritten words on it. How cool is that?

"What is it?"

She laughs. "A poem! Of all the houses we could have bought, we find one with a poem in the walls."

Phoenix

Sunset was an orange ball
rolling down the sky
it struck the trees without a sound
and tumbled off the earth to die.

I watched it go and felt undone—
as if I'd lost a friend.
I wish I'd held it in my arms
and burning, rose again.

Mom snorts. "An Emily Dickinson wannabe." She folds the paper, puts it in the jar and hands it back to me. "Next time find something more interesting. Like a lost Blake poem."

"What's wrong with it?"

"The grammar, for one thing. It should be 'risen,' not 'rose.' "

"Whatever happened to artistic license? I like it."

She raises her eyebrows but doesn't say anything. I hate that.

We're in the room she's working on, the one that's going to be her study. One wall is a floor-to-ceiling bookcase painted a hideous shade of yellow; Mom's been stripping the paint off to get at the dark wood underneath. "Do you think any more poems are lying around?"

She stares at the walls for a minute, then shrugs like she doesn't care. But I know better. One of my mom's guilty pleasures is mystery novels. She reads one or two of them a week and then has the balls to make fun of me for reading science fiction and fantasy.

"Who do you think wrote it? The old fart?"

"Mr. Carlisle? I doubt it."

Stephen Carlisle was the former owner. We never met him, but the realtor told us horror stories about him. Apparently he used to throw rocks at the street lights because they kept him awake at night, and he was known to chase dogs off his lawn with a BB gun, running after them for blocks, swearing his head off. He lived in this house for at least fifty years, but he had no family to leave it to, so after he died last January the city got it and put it up for sale.

He'd been dead for a week when they found him in the bathroom. The neighbors complained about a cat yowling in the house all night long and the police came to investigate. Carlisle's pants were around his ankles and he was sprawled out beside the toilet. His cat, Hoover, an ugly old orange tom with an unbelievably foul disposition, had been lunching on his eyes and nose. Hoover was taken to the pound and snatched up by an old woman who lived on the other side of town, but he found his way back here every time she let him out of her house. Eventually she gave up trying to keep him, and he became the neighborhood stray, fed by everyone but sleeping every night under our porch until we bought the place and moved in. Mom hates cats, but she got tired of him sneaking into the house every time we left the door open, so she finally let me keep him. He sleeps with me most nights, but when he sniffs at my eyes I send him flying.

Someone's knocking at the door. I raise my head from the pillow and blink at my watch on the coffee table; it's only eight o'-clock in the morning. I listen for Mom, but I don't hear her so I push the sheet off me and onto Hoover, who's curled up against my legs. More knocking. I sit up, rub my eyes, and put my feet on the floor. My back hurts. Stupid-ass couch. More knocking.

"All right, goddamnit." I stumble to the door and only when I'm opening it do I realize all I'm wearing is boxer shorts with Mickey Mouse and Goofy all over them.

There's a skinny kid about my age standing on our porch dressed in a T-shirt, ratty cut-offs and sneakers without socks. He's got short blond hair, a big nose, and a sunburned neck. I lean against the door and blink at him.

"Hi. I'm J.D. I live there." He points at a small white house a few doors down on the opposite side of the street. "Did I wake you up?"

"Yeah."

"I'm sorry. I thought you'd be up by now."

He waits for me to say something, but I just stare at him. If all New Hampshire people are like this then there's been way too much inbreeding going on around here.

He starts to fidget, glances at my shorts and looks away, embarrassed. What's he embarrassed about? He's not the one wearing stupid fucking Disney shorts.

"Noah?"

I jump. Mom's coming down the stairs behind me, fully dressed and with her hair pulled back into a sloppy ponytail. Her hair is a lot longer than most women her age keep it, but I kind of like it.

"Who is it?"

"Some neighbor kid."

"Well, don't just stand there. Let him in."

Oh, for Christ's sake. "Come in."

I stand back and the kid steps past me. He smells like Right Guard and Crest. I smell like dirty socks and last night's pizza.

Mom offers her hand. "I'm Virginia York. This is my rude son Noah. He's more civilized when he's awake."

"That's okay. I didn't mean to get you up. I'm J.D."

"Don't apologize for me, Virginia." I stick out my hand. "I wake up slow."

"That's okay."

Mom flicks my head with her finger. "Don't call me Virginia." She turns back to J.D. "What can we do for you, J.D.?"

"My dad sent me down to ask if you guys want to come to dinner at our house tonight."

No way. Come on, Mom. Tell him no fucking way.

"We'd love to. I'd forgotten how friendly small towns are. In Chicago we didn't even know the names of our neighbors."

"Yes we did," I mutter. "Sleazebag and Shithead were on one side, and Mrs. Fat Ass was on the other."

Mom ignores me. "Do you want some coffee, J.D.? I was just getting ready to put some on."

"Sure. That sounds great."

"Come on back to the kitchen with me. Noah, go put on a shirt and join us."

"*Sieg heil.*" I goose step past them, my feet slapping the tiles of the entryway. J.D. laughs. Mom tells him not to encourage me.

God forbid.

Our kitchen is the most impressive part of the house. It's gigantic. Epic, even. If Beowulf could have had a kitchen, this is the one he'd have chosen. The sink is long and deep enough to take a bath in, and the ceiling is so high I can't reach it standing on the counter. There's an island in the middle of the room that's part stove and part counter, and there's a breakfast nook with a table by the back door that could comfortably seat eight people around it. The ceiling fan, turned up to its highest speed, is like having a helicopter in the house.

When I walk in Mom is filling the coffee pot with water and J.D. is sitting on a bar stool at the island. I pull up a stool and sit beside him.

He glances at me and reads my T-shirt. " 'Shiitake happens.' What's shiitake?"

I roll my eyes. "It's a kind of hemorrhoid."

Mom glares at me. "Noah."

"I'm just joking. It's a mushroom."

"Oh." He blushes and looks at his hands.

What can I say? Sometimes I'm an asshole. I come by it honestly. But I feel kind of bad about being mean to him.

Mom leans on the other side of the island and studies us. I'm a lot darker than J.D. Mom is half-Portuguese, so my skin is olive, like hers. In the summer I usually turn dark brown, but this summer I haven't been outside much.

"What year are you in school this year, J.D.?"

He looks up at her. "I'll be a junior."

"Noah is going to be a senior."

The coffee pot starts to spit and hiss like Hoover when he's coughing up a hairball.

Mom goes to the refrigerator and pulls out eggs and milk and cheese and veggies. She glances at J.D. "Are you hungry? I make a killer omelette."

"No, thanks. I already had a bowl of cereal."

I can see he wants one but he's being polite. "You should have one. I'll eat whatever you can't finish."

"Okay. Thanks." He looks at me shyly. "If you have time later I'll be glad to show you around town. If you want to."

I start to say no but Mom catches my eye behind his head and mouths yes. God, she makes me mad. But she's got that "don't fuck with me" look on her face. I tell him yes.

We sit in silence and watch Mom make breakfast. She's an artist in the kitchen. Besides poetry, cooking is her only other love. She slices up an onion, some garlic, a red pepper and a tomato in the time it would take a normal person to get the knife out of the drawer. J.D. watches her with open wonder. Great. Another admirer. Mom is good at a lot of things and people are always oohing and ahhing over her. It gets old.

While the butter melts in the saucepan she whisks the eggs in a bowl with one hand and pours the coffee into three mugs with the other. I get up and get J.D.'s and mine. Just as I'm sitting down again he asks for milk and sugar. What a baby.

The vegetables are sautéeing in olive oil and my mouth waters. Mom chitchats casually with J.D. about the town and his family and the school, politely pumping him for information. His last name is Curtis. His dad's an accountant, his mom's a housewife, his little sister is ten. He's lived here his whole life. Jesus, he's boring. I pretend to pay attention.

"How's the band at the high school?" Mom asks. "Noah plays trombone."

"Really? I play trumpet." He swivels toward me. "Maybe we can play some duets or something this summer."

And maybe I'll eat a nice bowl of pigshit before bed. I nod.

"Are there any music teachers in town? I want Noah to take lessons."

"Mr. Bixell is pretty good, except he's got a drinking problem. He used to go house to house until people got tired of him showing up drunk. Last year he came to our place for a lesson and in the middle of it he ran outside and threw up on the sidewalk." J.D. laughs. "My parents weren't very happy."

I smile in spite of myself. When he laughs his whole face changes and he almost looks like he has a personality.

Mom gives him an omelette and tells him to start eating before it gets cold. I watch him take a bite and the look on his face makes me smile again. You'd think he'd been eating clay all his life and only now discovered food.

"This is wonderful. I didn't know eggs could taste like this." He turns to me. "Maybe you guys shouldn't come to dinner tonight. My mom's cooking tastes like dog food."

He says it so matter-of-factly I can't help but laugh.

Mom thanks him modestly but I can tell she's pleased. No matter how much praise she gets it's never enough. I suppose I should tell her more often how good she is, but she wouldn't believe me anyway.

"Hey, Mom, why don't you tell J.D. about our mystery poem. Maybe he knows who wrote it."

"What mystery poem?" he asks.

"I found a poem in the wall in my room yesterday and we don't know who put it there."

"I'm sure he won't know, Noah. It was there a long time before either of you was born."

"Why do you say that?"

"Because, honey, that wall had to be at least forty years old. You saw the wallpaper."

She only calls me "honey" when she's irritated. What's her problem?

"It won't hurt to show him."

"I'd like to see it," J.D. says quietly.

I go upstairs and get the jar. There's a light layer of sawdust on the top stairs; on the way back down I see that my feet have left prints, all toes and no heels. When I get to the bottom I hear Mom and J.D. talking through the swinging door. Mom's telling him "how nice it is Noah will have a friend his own age in the neighborhood" and not to be "put off by his weird sense of humor, he's just prickly with strangers."

Sometimes I could just fucking kill her.

I walk back in and pretend I didn't hear them. I hand the jar to J.D. and he opens it like it's a bomb. He reads the poem, refolds it neatly and hands it back with a shrug. He's got long fingers and he chews his nails.

"I guess Mr. Carlisle could have written it, but I doubt it. Writing poetry doesn't seem much in character for him."

"You knew him?"

He swallows a bite before answering. "Some. He was the neighborhood troll. We all kept about as far away as we could get." He grins. "When I was little I always thought of this house as the witch's cabin in *Hansel and Gretel*. I used to pitch a fit if Mom tried to make me come here on Halloween for trick-or-treat. I was sure he'd eat me."

"Who'd you go as?" The words are out of my mouth before I can stop them. "Gretel?"

I see Mom's spine stiffen, but before she can say anything J.D. turns to me.

"That hurts a lot coming from such a snappy dresser," he says mildly, with a pointed glance at my boxers.

Mom is as surprised as me, but after a few seconds we both laugh.

"Good for you, J.D.," she says. "And Noah is sorry for being such a jerk."

That pisses me off, of course, and I stop laughing. But J.D. looks me right in the eye and smiles. I have no choice but to smile back; any idiot can see that, unlike me, there's no meanness in him.

And because of that, I like him.

After breakfast we go for a walk. Mom tells me to be back in a couple of hours. I can't believe she's letting me go when we've got so much work to do. I ask her if we can take the car and as usual she says no. I put on a pair of khaki shorts and some sandals, and we take off down the sidewalk toward town. Neither of us knows what to say so we're both quiet, which is fine with me. I hate people who yak just because silence bugs them. I once read something about the measure of a man being how much silence he can bear. Most people my age can't be quiet for more than two seconds. If they're not babbling about this or that they're blasting their stereos or zoning out in front of the television or playing loud games on their computers. I can't stand that shit.

I don't really need to be shown around; I already know where everything is. Oakland's not exactly a metropolis. Mom and I live on the far side of town, less than a block from open countryside. Past our house to the west there's nothing but a few houses, a water tower, the Rose Hill Cemetery, and a bunch of farms. Some nights I wander down the road that way and I can't believe how quiet and dark it is. The nearest town, Cody, is about fifteen miles away and Mom says it's even smaller than Oakland.

Everywhere you turn there's a waist-high wall of rock. "What is it with New England and stone walls?"

J.D. shrugs. "It makes sense on farms, I guess. The soil is really rocky and they have to clear the land somehow. But in town we do it because it looks cool."

He waves at someone driving by but doesn't tell me who it is. A few people are mowing their yards but mostly it's just us on the street. It's hot, even though it's early in the day. The back of my neck starts to sweat so I peel my shirt off and tuck it through my belt loops. He waits a minute or two, then says "Good idea," and pulls his shirt off, too. He's got freckles on his shoulders and a few stray hairs on his chest.

We walk for a minute, listening to the sound of our feet on the sidewalk, then J.D. stops all of a sudden and squats down to look at something on the sidewalk. I squat next to him and ask what he's doing, and he points at an ant carrying a piece of bread five times its size. He glances over at me and grins. "Hercules with six legs."

I wait while he watches the ant struggle across the sidewalk, which sounds like a stupid waste of time, but I don't mind. The sun feels great on my back. Mom says it's bad for me, but when something feels this good, who cares?

We're already almost 'downtown.' In Chicago it used to take nearly a half an hour by car to get into the city; now my house is only six blocks from what passes for the business district. We stand up after the ant disappears into the grass and within a couple of minutes we're cutting across the parking lot of the laughable little grocery store, Edgerton's, and heading through town. All the shops are within a two-block perimeter, but with the college out of session, Oakland is dead. On our side of the street there's a drug store, a flower shop, a coffee shop and the public library, and on the other side there's a video store, a hardware store, a bank and a pizza place. A few cars are parked here and there but for the most part nothing's moving. We walk past the drug store and there's a couple of old men sitting on a bench in front. Their eyes flit over us and one of them says hello but thankfully J.D. doesn't stop to chat. Old people creep me out. Every once in a while you'll meet one that's kind of cool, but most of them look at you like you've stolen their youth and they want it back. It makes my skin crawl.

J.D. points down a side street. "The school's down there about half a mile. There's an outside track by the gym, if you like to run."

"Sometimes. I get shin splints, though."

"Do you like to swim? The town pool's pretty good."

"I hate chlorine."

"It's only about a hundred miles to the ocean. I might be able to borrow Dad's car sometime and we could drive over."

I've never seen the ocean and that kind of sounds like fun. But why's he being so nice? Doesn't he have any other friends? I shrug and he stays quiet for another block.

"Do you have a dad?" he blurts out at the street corner.

My throat tightens. "Of course not. Mom just woke up pregnant one morning after spending the night with a turkey baster." I'm trying to make my voice sound light but it comes out bitter and harsh. He chews his lip.

I start to step off the curb and he catches my arm as a car I didn't see goes by. The car is full of girls about our age and they whistle at us. One of them screams out "Marry me!" and they all howl with laughter before disappearing down the street. J.D. looks after them but he's still holding onto my arm. His hand is warm. I say thanks under my breath and he lets go. We start walking again, heading east toward Cassidy College. We pass the movie theater, the lumber yard, and a couple of gas stations, and by the time we're crossing in front of the weird little combination hospital/nursing home, for some reason I'm telling him about Dad. About what a good man he was. About how he died. About how Mom gets this awful, vacant look in her eyes sometimes.

J.D. listens and doesn't say anything. He walks close, and once in a while our forearms or our shoulders touch.

I remember one morning in Chicago when I had an early jazz band rehearsal at the school and got Dad out of bed to take me to it. He waited too long to get up so I was going to be late, and I was mad at him. For some dumb reason he didn't put on his glasses before we left and he was half-blind without them. He squinted at the road all the way to the school and drove about five miles an hour. I nearly went nuts and did my level best to make sure he knew how stupid he was. He never said a word until we got to the school, where he ran into the curb before dropping me off. All he said was "Have a good rehearsal, son." I stormed off without saying goodbye, but I turned at the top of the steps and watched his car crawl out of the parking lot, narrowly missing a parked van and panicking a paper boy in the crosswalk.

"Jesus, Dad. Get a clue," I whispered, and suddenly my anger vanished, and I was laughing and shaking my head.

I don't know why it seems important to tell you this.

*   *   *

I say good-bye to J.D. back at the house and tell him I'll see him later for supper.

When I get inside Mom is upstairs pulling the floor of the bathroom apart. Her back is to me and I can see the knobs of her spine through her t-shirt. She barely glances over her shoulder.

"Look at these floorboards. I thought we might get by with new linoleum, but some of this is rotten."

"I thought we were going to wait and do the bathroom later."

"I changed my mind."

"Well, don't tear it up too much. We'll both need showers later on today unless you want to go to J.D.'s looking like that."

She doesn't say anything. I watch her dig at a patch of glue with a scraper; she tears into it like a hen protecting its young from a fox. I catch a glimpse of the side of her face and see tear tracks in the dirt on her cheek. Seeing tears on Mom's face is like watching the Statue of Liberty sit down and bawl its eyes out. I can't even remember the last time I saw her cry. I want to ask what's wrong but I know she won't tell me, so I just stand there like an idiot.

"Don't you have some work to do?" she asks roughly.

I stare at the back of her head for a minute and turn away.

Mom yells "Noah" from the bathroom.

I'm putting up drywall in my room. "What?" I yell back.

"Come here!" She sounds excited.

I wipe my hands on my shirt and wander down the hall. Mom is sitting on the floor of the bathroom holding another old mason jar in her hands. She points to a space between floorboards, showing me where she found it. "I can't get it open." She shakes it before giving it to me. It rattles. "Something besides a poem this time."

I wrestle with it for a minute, then try her trick of smacking the lid on the doorframe. It won't come off. Mom stands up and takes it back. Her fingers turn white as she fights with it. "Kind of makes you wonder how many more of these might be buried around the place, doesn't it?" She drapes a corner of her T-shirt over the lid and tries again, grunting. "Maybe we'll eventually find Jimmy Hoffa."

"Who's Jimmy Hoffa?"

She doesn't answer, of course, and when I try to take the jar again she shakes her head and takes a metal bucket from under the sink. She puts the jar on its side in the bucket, covers it with a rag, picks up her hammer off the counter, and shatters the jar with a solid whack. She lifts the rag like a magician unveiling a dove. We both stare into the bucket.

A silver chain necklace with a small locket stares back at us from a mound of broken glass.

Mom cuts herself getting it out, swears, and reluctantly hands it to me while she sticks her hand under the tap to wash her cut.

The locket is also silver, with a putrid flower engraving on the front. Mom watches from the sink as I turn it over in my palm. "Does it open?" She shuts off the water and immediately more blood seeps from her finger. She wraps a Kleenex around it. "Give it to me."

"Get away. You'll bleed all over it." I find the catch and pop the locket open, holding it up so both of us can see what's inside. Where a photo usually is there's nothing. The other side says "To N.M. from S.C. All my love."

"Oh, that's original." I give it to Mom. "Just once I'd like to read a locket that said 'To N.M. from S.C. Fuck off.' "

" 'S.C.' Stephen Carlisle." Mom fools with the chain for a minute, then opens the clasp and puts it around her neck. The locket hangs loosely in the sweaty hollow of her throat. She fingers it absently, stares right through me and walks out the door without a word.

She almost never wears jewelry. She hates earrings, and I'm pretty sure she hates necklaces, too. Even when Dad was alive she was always losing her wedding ring because she didn't like wearing it, either. I follow her down the hall to her room.

She's standing by the window with her forehead pressed against the glass. I stop in the doorway. Her bed is between us, still un-made; the sheets and blankets are twisted and scattered like she's been humping a tornado.

"Mom?"

Nothing.

"Are you okay? You're acting like one of those guys in *Invasion of the Body Snatchers.*"

"You don't remember your grandfather very well, do you?"

I can barely hear her. She's talking about her dad, I know, be-cause Dad's father died before I was born. "I remember him mak-ing me raisin-bread toast with peanut butter. That's about it. What was I? Three?"

She turns around and leans against the window frame, smiling wanly, and touches the locket again. "He gave me a necklace like this, once. I'd forgotten all about it."

She never talks about her mom and dad. The only stuff I know about them I learned from Dad: her mom was a housewife who died a long time ago, her dad was a manager in a grocery store who raised Mom and my aunt mostly by himself. He died when I was a little kid. I don't think Dad knew much more than that, either, but he always told me not to pester Mom with questions about her folks because she wouldn't like it.

"Do you still have the necklace?"

Another scary, tired smile. "I threw it into Lake Michigan one night after too many glasses of red wine."

"Oh." I blink at her stupidly. "That's nice."

She faces the window again. "I'm fine, Noah. I just need to rest for a minute. Go back to work."

Like I told you earlier, I paint. Portraits, I mean, and landscapes and murals. Everybody calls my stuff surreal; Mom says I make Salvador Dali look like Norman Rockwell. But I don't paint weird stuff on purpose. It just comes out that way.

I painted Mom once. She was in her study writing and I asked to set up my easel behind her. I was surprised when she let me. She usually doesn't like having anyone around when she works, but she knows I don't make any noise when I'm painting, and besides, she was flattered.

It was late afternoon. The sun lit the left side of her body and brought out red highlights in her hair I'd never seen before. I remember the sound of her fingers on the computer keyboard; it was so quiet I could hear both of us breathing. She probably forgot I was there.

What came out on my canvas was a woman with half of her body on fire. The other half was ice.

CHAPTER TWO

J.D.'s dad opens the door after Mom rings the bell. When he shakes my hand I can smell beer on his breath. His name is Tom, he's tall and fat, and J.D. doesn't look a thing like him. "Come on in. Welcome to the neighborhood."

Mom thanks him and I follow her into the house. She's wearing a sky blue summer dress and sandals, and she's still got the necklace on. She made me wear long pants and a shirt and tie even though it's almost ninety degrees outside. I asked her if she wanted me to put on a parka and mittens too and she told me to knock it off because she wasn't in the mood to put up with my shit.

J.D.'s ten-year-old sister, Heather, is sitting in front of the television watching a *Gilligan's Island* rerun. Tom makes her turn it off and come over to meet us. She says hello then sits on the couch and sulks. J.D.'s mom comes out of the kitchen.

"Hello, I'm Donna Curtis." She shakes Mom's hand and then mine. Her skin is clammy. I guess J.D. kind of looks like her. They both have blond hair and blue eyes and that same big nose. But her face is out of proportion in a way that his isn't. She's got enormous nostrils and her eyes are too far apart. J.D.'s kind of handsome. Donna's not.

She tells us to sit down and goes back in the kitchen. Tom offers

Mom a drink and she asks for a gin and tonic. He asks her if I can have one too and she says no, he'll have a soda. While he's in the kitchen Mom asks Heather the usual stupid-ass questions grown-ups ask little kids ("What year are you going to be in school?" and "Are you enjoying your summer?") and Heather answers in surly monosyllables. Tom comes back with her drink and a can of Pepsi for me. I ask where J.D. is.

"He just finished mowing the lawn and needed to take a shower. I think he's out now if you want to go upstairs and find him." He talks really loud.

I stand up quickly and start walking out of the room with my soda and Mom tells me not to take it with me because I might spill it. Tom tells her it's fine. Mom tells him I shouldn't because I'm a klutz and you know how clumsy teenage boys are. They have a good laugh. I remind her that she spilled coffee all over her blouse two days ago. Her eyes narrow. Tom tells me to go ahead. I get out before Mom can say anything else. She hates it when I "talk back" in public. Tough shit.

I should probably apologize for how much I swear, but fuck it. I've read that some people think swearing shows a lack of imagination and a limited vocabulary, but sometimes "darn" and "poop" and "oh heck" just don't cut it. Besides, swearing is kind of fun. It's not like I have a trash mouth all the time, but I like the way the words feel on my tongue, how they roll off the teeth, how they kind of blister the air. "Fuck" and "shit" may not be polite words, but they're succinct as hell and they let me blow off steam without hurting anybody. And if you're the kind of person who gets offended by gutter language you should probably get your thumb out of your ass and smell the goddamn roses.

The Curtis's house is way too clean and orderly. The magazines on the table at the bottom of the stairs are perfectly lined up and look brand new and unread; the pictures on the wall of the staircase (mostly school photos of J.D. and Heather) are hung so straight it's all I can do to keep from turning them upside down. There's one of

J.D. when he's probably six or seven that catches my eye for a second. He's sitting on a swing with Donna standing behind him, and they're both laughing at something. They look a lot more alike in the picture than they do now. I guess J.D.'s one of those rare kids who gets cuter as he gets older. I go to the top of the stairs and wander down the hall until I get to the open bathroom door.

He's shaving at the sink with a towel tied loosely around his waist. He doesn't see me at first and I get a little flustered for catching him without clothes.

"Hey."

He jumps about four feet. "Jesus Christ, Noah. You scared the hell out of me."

"Sorry. Your dad said I could come find you."

"That's okay. I just didn't hear you." He smiles a little. "It's a good thing I don't use a straight razor. I could have cut my head off."

He turns back to the mirror and I lean on the doorframe and watch him. He's got more of a beard than I do even though he's a year younger. I only have to shave once a week or so, and then it's just four or five hairs that need it.

"Did you meet everybody?"

"Yeah. They seem nice." Actually I think his dad is fat, his mom is ugly and his sister's a brat.

His eyes find mine in the mirror. "They're okay, I guess." He looks away.

J.D.'s in pretty good shape. You can see all the muscles in his stomach and his arms look really strong. I can see his legs from the knee down and he's got good shin muscles too. I'm too fucking skinny. My ribs stick out and my legs look like matchsticks.

He shaves another stripe of lather off his cheek and as he rinses the razor his towel starts to slip. Before he grabs it I see part of his butt and a patch of dark hair under his navel. We both blush and I stare at the floor while he awkwardly rewraps the towel.

"J.D.?" Heather comes up behind me and it's my turn to jump.

She ignores me. "Mom says hurry up. Dinner's almost ready." She looks at her brother with distaste. "Gross. Put clothes on."

He doesn't even glance at her. "You're just mad because my boobs are bigger than yours."

She glares at him. "You're mean. I'm going to tell."

"Go ahead."

She stalks off.

J.D. washes off the rest of the lather and pats his face dry with a hand towel. "You're lucky you're an only child." He brushes past me, smelling of Ivory soap. "Come see my room."

I like his room. It has personality, unlike the rest of the house. There's clothes on the floor, piles of books with mangled covers— I see *The World According to Garp* and a mangled copy of *The Once and Future King*—and a bulletin board over his desk covered with pictures of famous people—Janis Joplin, Buddy Rich, Leo Tolstoy, Albert Einstein. The one of Einstein is great. He's sticking his tongue out like a five-year-old and his eyes are crossed. "Why does every genius have bad hair?" I take a swig of my Pepsi and keep my eyes on the pictures as J.D. dresses behind me.

He laughs. "Probably because the jocks at their high schools gave them too many noogies when they were kids."

He walks over and stands next to me. He hasn't put on a shirt or socks yet but he's wearing pants. He points at Tolstoy. "There's a homeless guy downtown that looks just like that."

"He probably smells the same too."

"I hope not." He touches a picture in the bottom right corner. It's a school photo of a girl about our age with long brown hair, freckles and big teeth. "This is my girlfriend, Kristin."

She looks like the kind of moron who'll spend four hours putting on her makeup and brushing her hair just for one dumb picture. "How long have you been together?"

"We've only gone out a couple of times. But she's really nice."

He asks me if I had a girlfriend back in Chicago and I tell him no one special, just someone I went to prom with last Spring. He nods and tells me there are "a lot of hot chicks" at the high school and he'll be sure to introduce me around.

We stare at the pictures together until his mom yells from downstairs.

"This is wonderful, Donna," Mom says.

What a liar. The chicken is dry and rubbery, the asparagus has had the shit boiled out of it and the potato salad is the basic color and consistency of vomit.

Donna thanks Mom with a prim little smile. I chew in silence. J.D. and I are on one side of the table with Mom and Heather across from us and Tom and Donna at the ends.

Tom eats with his mouth open and talks through his food. "So, Virginia. When does school start for you?"

"At the end of this month. I'll have to go in soon and get my office in order, but there's a lot of work to do at home first."

Mom's already told them she's a poet with a couple of published books and of course Tom and Donna are impressed. Now whenever she says anything there's a respectful silence after she finishes talking, like she was God and they've just been given the meaning of life.

I guess I should be proud of her but I don't get her poetry at all. Her last collection was called *Midnight Musings* and every stanza is stuffed with obscure references and words like 'cunctuation' and 'tenebrosity,' so you need a PhD and a brain the size of a beach ball to figure it out. She's always telling me to write like I talk but she sure as hell doesn't bother to practice what she preaches. Thank God. If she talked like she writes my head would explode. I've never had the heart to tell her that her poetry leaves me cold. Auden and Yeats are hard to read too, but there's always enough on the surface to make you want to dig deeper. Mom's stuff is too smart for its own good. The only thing of hers I've ever liked was something she wrote when she was fourteen, and even that only has a single fragment I can remember: *'Sick of being/prose/she be-*

came/poem.' Ever since then she's made a career out of being unintelligible.

Tom is playing with a mole on his forehead. "Well, you and Donna should get along great. She was an English minor in college."

Donna winces. "Tom, don't insult our guest. Comparing me to Virginia is like comparing an accountant to a physicist."

Tom's fork freezes midway between his plate and his mouth. "And what's wrong with being an accountant?"

"Nothing, dear. It's just apples and oranges, that's all." Donna wipes her lips with a linen napkin. "Don't be so sensitive."

"I'm not being sensitive," Tom snaps.

I glance at J.D. from the corner of my eye. He's staring blankly at his plate.

The only sound for a while is Tom chewing his food and Heather trying to hack through her chicken breast with a steak knife. Good luck, kid. Buy a chain saw.

Mom starts chatting brightly about the weather and how hot it's been lately and Donna says oh, yes, it's just been miserable, hasn't it? and Tom says maybe all this stuff we've heard about global warming is really true and Donna says she can't believe how outrageous their electricity bills have been because of having to run the air conditioner so much. Mom nods enthusiastically, like this is the most fascinating conversation she's ever been privileged to be part of.

Donna and J.D. are seated close enough together that I can compare them without being too obvious. Donna's a little taller than he is, and the extra inches are all in her face, stretching it too far apart, like God used her for a Gumby doll or something. Her fingers are longer, too, but they've got the same thin wrists and the same big veins on the backs of their hands, and even though she's wearing bright red nail polish, I can see where J.D. learned to bite his fingernails.

Heather interrupts something Donna is saying. "This is good, Mommy."

Donna smiles indulgently and says thank you and for the first time all evening the smile looks real. She runs a finger through Heather's hair, tucking some of it behind an ear, then she picks up where she left off, rattling on about how hard the heat is on her flower garden and how much she hates the city ordinance restricting when she can water to once a day.

Tom belches softly and puts about a pound of butter on his asparagus. He's got jowls and his face is kind of sweaty and glistening. Donna waits until he says excuse me before resuming her monologue. I zone out for a while and push a piece of chicken around my plate. The next thing I know everyone is staring at me.

Mom sighs. "You'll have to forgive Noah, Donna. I don't think he heard your question. I don't know where his brain is these days." She fixes me with the evil eye. "Donna asked how you were adjusting to life in Oakland."

"Oh. I like it." They all keep staring at me. What do they want me to say? *Sorry I spaced off, Donna, but you people are the most fucking boring human beings I've ever met in my life. And by the way, your food sucks.* I try again. "It's a nice town."

"I imagine it's difficult to get used to the slower pace here after living in Chicago." Donna smooths the tablecloth around her plate and puts a sympathetic look on her face. "You must miss all the excitement."

I guess we've officially reached the 'Let's patronize the teenager' part of the evening. It's a parlor game along the lines of 'pin the tail on the donkey.' I hate it. She couldn't care less about what she's asking, but I have to play along or else she won't get to feel good about including me in the conversation.

I tell her living with Mom is more excitement than I can stand and everybody chuckles, even Mom. It's a stupid joke but at least everybody stops gawking at me.

Sometimes I make myself want to puke. I'm just as much of a phony as Tom or Donna or Mom. When I get uncomfortable I make people laugh, which fools them into thinking I'm enjoying their company. What I wish I'd do instead is just stare right back at them and not give a rat's ass what they think of me.

Tom offers me a plate with celery and carrots on it and I take a couple of carrots and pass it on to J.D. Out of the blue Tom asks me if I've ever gone fishing and when I say no he tells me he'll take me fishing some time with J.D. and him because "there's nothing better than a trout you've caught all by yourself." I tell him that sounds like fun and I even kind of mean it, but when I glance at J.D. all he does is roll his eyes.

Tom's hair is the color of a mud puddle, and he's got it combed to try and hide his bald spots. He leans his elbows on the table and shovels another mouthful of food into his face, and even though I look away I can still hear him chewing. Nothing grosses me out like listening to a fat person eat.

Mom asks him if he goes fishing very often. "All the time," Tom says.

"Almost never," Donna says in a stage whisper intended to be cute.

Tom bristles. "It's true that I haven't gone in a while, but I used to go almost every weekend during the summer."

"That was years ago, dear." She says 'dear' the way I'd say 'asshole.'

Tom looks like he wants to argue with her some more but she's not even looking at him so he just gets this sullen look and stares at his plate.

Heather is playing with her silverware, sticking the knife blade between the tines of her fork, but she's watching me the whole time. "Where's your daddy?" she asks.

There's a sudden stillness at the table. "He died last year," I tell her.

"Oh." She accidentally drops her fork and it bounces on her plate with a clatter. "How'd he die?"

I keep waiting for her mom or dad to tell her to shut up, but Donna just watches me like I'm being asked about my favorite football team and Tom's still making pouty faces at his food.

Mom steps in. "He had a heart attack last year. It was a very sudden thing."

Donna and Tom both make all the right noises. Mom thanks them and casually changes the subject, asking Donna if the art teacher at the high school is any good because Noah likes to paint.

Donna says she doesn't know for sure because J.D. doesn't have any artistic talent whatsoever and even though Heather shows promise she of course is still in elementary school. J.D. doesn't react at all to his mom trashing him; it's like he's heard this all before. But his fingers are tight around his glass as he takes a drink of milk.

A brief frown passes across Mom's face but she tries to smooth over what Donna just said. "I don't know where Noah gets his talent. I can only draw stick figures and his father wasn't much better."

Donna asks if I inherited Mom's writing ability but before I can answer her she's telling us all about the wonderful story Heather just wrote about a magical puppy who could fly. Tom looks as bored as I am.

Mom waits until Donna is through and then asks J.D. if he likes to write, too.

"No, not really. I'd like to learn how to compose music, though."

"Oh, that's right. You told us this morning that you play the trumpet."

Donna makes a weird dismissive sound, like she's trying to blow out a candle with her nose. "He never practices. I don't know why we bother to keep paying for his lessons when he's so lazy."

"I'm not . . ." J.D. starts, then closes his mouth and fiddles with his plate, turning it slightly one way, then the other.

There's a tense silence until Tom starts telling us about the neighborhood and who lives in what house and who's related to who. He's slurring his words a little and I can't help wondering how many beers he had before we got here.

"Did you know Stephen Carlisle very well?" Mom asks when he takes a breath.

Donna shakes her head. "Not much. He was a bit of a recluse."

Tom snorts between chomps. There's a string of asparagus caught in his teeth. "He was a bit of an s.o.b., you mean."

"You're exaggerating, dear."

"No he's not," J.D. says quietly.

Donna glances coldly at J.D. "Don't argue with me." She keeps her eyes on him for at least ten seconds like she's daring him to say something else. J.D. calmly takes a bite of vomit salad but his breathing gets faster like he's mad or scared.

It doesn't take a rocket scientist to see that something is fucked up between these two.

Tom takes a drink from his beer. "We were neighbors for almost twenty years and I can count on one hand the times he said 'hello' when we saw him. Usually he just ignored us."

"Did he always live alone?" Mom asks.

"I think he used to be married but that was before we moved here. I don't know what happened to his wife."

"Do you know what her name was?"

Jesus, Mom. Just put him under bright lights and attach electrodes to his nipples.

Tom says no. Donna says she thinks the wife's name might have been Nellie or Nettie or something.

J.D. asks for the butter which is next to Donna. She ignores him and asks me if I want some more chicken. I tell her no thanks. J.D. asks for the butter again. She acts like she doesn't hear him and tells Mom she likes her dress.

"Mom." J.D.'s voice is tight. "Can I please have the butter?"

Donna snatches up the butter and slams it down in front of him. The knife on the serving dish slides off the table onto the floor. She doesn't look at it or at J.D., and her face doesn't change. Instead she asks Mom who her favorite poet is.

J.D. picks up the knife and his hands tremble as he butters his bread. I try not to look at him. Heather has a smirk on her pointed little face and Tom takes another drink.

I can see Mom is uncomfortable but since she's being consulted in her role as the goddess of poetry she puts on a polite smile and says "Myself, of course." And, predictably, Donna and Tom laugh right on cue. J.D. and I don't. Me because I've heard it before, him because he's just been run over by his psycho mother and a stick of butter. I steal another glance at him. He's trying to act like nothing's wrong but he looks like he wants to cry. All of a sudden I start getting mad. I want to tell Donna to go fuck herself and I want to tell Mom to get some new material for her stand-up routine. And of course I don't have the balls to say a word.

I gently bump my leg against J.D.'s under the table. He looks up at my face like he's wondering if I meant to do it, then he smiles a little and bumps back.

After dinner Mom stays in the kitchen with Donna and Tom, Heather goes to watch television and J.D. and I go to the rec room in the basement. I know Mom won't want to stay long but she has this thing about eating and running so she'll stay and chat for at least a half hour. I don't mind staying now that J.D. and I are off on our own.

There's a piano in the rec room. I go over and plink a few notes then sit at the bench and show off a little with a blues thing I learned once. We had a piano when I was a kid but we sold it when I refused to keep taking lessons. J.D. sits beside me and when I'm done I ask him if he plays anything. He tells me to scooch over a little and when I do he rips into some classical piece. Beethoven, maybe. He plays the shit out of it. When he's finished I gape at him.

"You didn't say you played piano. You said you played trumpet."

He looks away, shy.

"That was great. Play something else."

"Show me that blues piece you were doing."

He watches my hands and in a couple minutes he's playing it better than me. I give him a playful shove and call him a show-off. He shoves back and in a second we're both on the floor. He's bigger and stronger than me so it doesn't take long before he's sitting on my chest with my arms pinned under his knees. We're both breathing hard and laughing.

"Get off. You smell like overcooked asparagus and leather chicken."

This gets him laughing so hard he falls off me. "I told you she was a crappy cook."

We sit up and get our breath back. His smile fades. "I'm sorry about that butter thing at dinner. "

I shrug. "Wait till you see my mom get mad. Dad pissed her off one time and she chucked a plate of eggplant parmesan across the room like a football."

"Really?" He fingers a small hole in the knee of his jeans. "What was she pissed about?"

"I don't remember. Nothing big. Dad probably forgot to flush the toilet or something. When she's in a bad mood it doesn't take much to push her over the edge."

"Is she in a bad mood a lot?" He looks up quickly at me. "Sorry. It's none of my business."

"That's okay. No, most of the time she's only mildly psychotic." I put the soles of my feet together and try to do a butterfly stretch. I'm about as limber as a pine cone. "How about your mom? Does she do stuff like that very often?"

He shrugs and puts his legs in the same position as mine, except he can almost touch his nose to his toes. If I tried to do that I'd snap in half. I watch him and wait for an answer, but before he says anything Mom yells from upstairs and tells me it's time to go.

"Jawohl, Frau Commandant," I yell back. I grin at J.D. "She hates it when I call her that."

He shakes his head and stretches his legs out in front of him. "Imagine that."

I start to stand up but he gets a shit-eating smirk on his face and he reaches over and pushes me down again.

"Moron," I grunt.

"Retard."

Mom bellows for me to hurry up. J.D. lets me get up this time and when I say good night he says he'll see me in the morning. I tell him I have to work on the house and he just nods. "I know. I'll help."

Mom waits until we get in our own door before she says anything about the evening. "Thank God that's over."

"What do you mean? You seemed to enjoy yourself."

She kicks off her shoes. "I've had more fun getting a Pap smear."

Sometimes she is funny, but never in public.

I sit on the stairs and take off my tie. "J.D. volunteered to come over tomorrow to help us. I think he just wants to get away from Donna."

She sits beside me. "You two seem to have hit it off."

"I guess so."

"Good. I've been worried about you. You haven't had any friends in a long time."

She's one to talk. The only friends she has are pen pals. "That's stupid. I had a lot of friends in Chicago."

"Yes, but this is different. I can tell."

What's that supposed to mean? I get uncomfortable and tell her I'm going upstairs to bed. My room really isn't ready to sleep in yet but I can't stand another night on that couch. She says she'll be going to bed soon too but I know better. She'll be awake for hours. Even before Dad died she was a night owl, but now I doubt she gets more than four hours of sleep a night. She says she's writing but one time she left her door open and when I walked by to go to the bathroom she was just sitting at her desk with her hands in her lap, staring at the blank screen of her computer.

I wake up with an erection. That's probably more information than you want, but I think it matters. You're probably wondering if I've been "sexually active." Only once, really. That girl I went to prom with. Colleen. What a disaster. She was nice enough, I guess, but things didn't go as planned. Her braces kept touching my tongue, and her body kind of grossed me out. I kept going limp and could barely keep the rubber on. It was bad for her too, I think, because she was really dry inside. We eventually gave up on screwing and resorted to a handjob; it took me forever to cum and I could only do it by closing my eyes. Poor Colleen. The muscles of her forearm must have ached for days. But we were both determined to do what we were supposed to. I feel bad because I didn't try and do anything for her. I couldn't make myself, even though I knew I should.

Maybe she was just the wrong girl.

Or maybe, well, you know. I hope not. Life is hard enough without that.

It's not that the idea of being gay bothers me. Not really. Mom and Dad have always had a lot of gay friends so it's not like I think there's anything wrong with it. Dad had a few hang-ups, I guess, but nothing serious. It's just that if somebody's going to be gay, I'd rather it's somebody else and not me. I've seen what happens to gay kids at school and on the streets.

It's not just that, either. It's a shitty thing to say, but I don't want people looking at me like I'm some kind of freak. Even in so-called liberal places like Chicago, two guys walking along holding hands or kissing still raise a lot of eyebrows. I mean, who in his right mind would want to deal with that kind of crap on a daily basis? I guess I'm as brainwashed as the next person about what society expects and endorses; every other fucking image on TV is of some deliriously happy heterosexual couple and the implicit message is that "this is the way things should be." Sure, there are gay people on sitcoms and in the movies, but the last thing I want to be is one of those hapless, one-dimensional fuckers who lives his life as the token queer guy surrounded by understanding straight people.

Maybe that's what bothers me most about the idea of being gay. I'm not worried about AIDS or bigotry or all of the rampant stereotyping that goes on. But no matter how you slice it, if you're gay you're always on the outside of 'normal' human experience, even if you're lucky enough to be loved or at least left alone by those on the inside. I like to think of myself as a rebel who doesn't give a fuck what other people think, but the truth is I don't think I have the guts to find out just how cold it is on the outside. I've never really looked at the future and seen myself living with another man. Give me a smart, pretty wife and two babies and a bungalow surrounded by a white-picket fence, and if I happen to be gay I'll hide out in the bathroom, whacking off to fantasies about Brad Pitt and Keanu Reeves.

Shit. I don't know if I mean that or not. I hate thinking about this kind of stuff. It's too fucking complicated.

I did have one "gay" experience. When I was thirteen, I went to a sleepover at my friend Ben's house and our hands somehow ended up in each other's underwear, but nothing much else happened and we never did it again, and I never did that with anybody else either. I guess I liked messing around with Ben a lot more than with Colleen, but that doesn't necessarily mean I'm gay, does it?

I try to keep my hand away from myself but it goes down there anyway. I stare at the ceiling and try not to want what I want. But there's a face in my mind I can't get rid of, a body wrapped in a towel I wish was here next to me. I bite my lip as I cum on my stomach.

Two hours later I wake up from a dream of J.D. kissing me. I've got another hard-on.

Goddamnit.

Mom won't get out of bed this morning. After breakfast and a cup of coffee she still wasn't up, so I went upstairs and knocked on her door. She told me she'd get up in a while. That was about seven-thirty. Now it's almost ten, so I try again.

"Mom?" I knock harder. "J.D.'s coming over in about half an hour. You better get up."

Nothing.

I open the door. The shades are pulled and she's got her head under her pillow. The room is hot and stuffy, with harsh bars of sunlight poking through the blinds. Dust gets caught in the light and spins slowly, suspended in the air like some artsy-fartsy mobile.

"I made you a cup of coffee." I sit on the corner of the bed and she shifts away from me. "Come on, it's good. I only spit in it twice."

"Go away, Noah," she mumbles. "Let me sleep."

"What time did you go to bed last night?"

"I don't know. Late."

"It's ten o'clock. What's up with that? You never sleep this late."

She pulls the pillow off her face and blinks at me. The skin of her face is slack and sweaty and her eyes are puffy. She's wearing one of Dad's v-neck T-shirts and the locket is still hanging around her throat.

"Are you sick?" I hold out the mug and she finally sits up and takes it.

"I'm fine."

"You look like shit."

"I'm fine." She sips the coffee and makes a face. "This is awful."

"J.D. said he might be able to borrow his dad's car this weekend so we could go to the beach."

"There's too much work to do."

"With his help we'll get a lot more done and be ahead of schedule."

"No."

Whatever. I'm going. "You'll get the house to yourself for a while. With me out of the way you can run around the house naked and make sacrifices to Robert Frost and stuff."

Silence. The kind you drown in.

J.D.'s wearing jeans, work boots and a faded white T-shirt with the sleeves torn off. We're in my room painting the walls. Even with a fan in the doorway we're already drenched with sweat.

Mom's finally up and ripping apart the guest room next to the bathroom. About five minutes before J.D. got here she rolled out of bed looking like the swamp creature and immediately went to work. I told her she should put the bathroom back together first but of course she's not going to do that. It's much more fun to destroy the whole fucking house than be organized about it and complete one room at a time. We can hear her smacking the wall and grunting.

"Where'd your mom learn to do this kind of stuff?"

"I don't know. She probably slept with a construction crew somewhere."

He tries to frown but I can see he thinks it's funny. "That's terrible. I can't believe you talk about her like that."

I'm shy around him today and have a hard time making conversation. He keeps talking about his girlfriend and how they're going to a movie tonight and how maybe she has a friend and all of us can go together. "That'd be great," I tell him.

I'd rather put my testicles in the toaster.

I lift my shirt and wipe the sweat off my face. His eyes flick to my stomach then away. White paint is spattered all over his arms.

There's a particularly loud whack from down the hall, then a sound like a dog chewing apart some nasty old carcass. It's quiet for a minute and all I can hear is the sound of our rollers.

Mom's in the doorway. She's got cobwebs and plaster dust in her hair, and she's holding another mason jar.

When I was five I fell down the stairs and broke my arm. I also drove my teeth pretty far into my lip and made a pretty good mess of my face. Mom was at work and I was home with Dad. He took me to the hospital and got me fixed up, and I was trying to eat some ice cream when Mom got home. She took one look at me and then turned to Dad. Her eyes scared the shit out of me. I thought she was going to kill him. At the time I figured it was because she thought he hadn't been watching me closely enough. But a couple of years ago she told me she thought he'd beaten me up. I laughed my ass off when she told me. Dad was the mildest man imaginable. I reminded her about the time I'd been fooling around with an electrical socket and she caught me and was about ready to spank me when Dad picked me up and carried me to my bedroom and wouldn't let her in until she'd calmed down. He never was anything but good to her and me, but I don't think she ever really trusted him. I don't know why.

This time the jar has a marriage license in it. It's dated June 20, 1952, and says Stephen Carlisle and Nellie Mitchell are lawfully wedded. The words are printed with that old-fashioned, over-wrought type peculiar to certificates and diplomas, and the paper has been folded several times and is a dull, yellowish white, like an old man's teeth.

Mom, J.D. and I read it. J.D. doesn't know about the necklace yet so I tell him. He reaches out and touches the locket on Mom's throat. I can see she's surprised but she doesn't pull away. I bet if I did the same thing she'd flinch.

"It's pretty," he says.

"Would you two like to be left alone?" I ask.

J.D. turns scarlet and drops his hand. Mom gives me her "what a piece of dogshit you are" look.

There's an uncomfortable silence that Mom finally breaks. "Well, at least now we know who N.M. is."

J.D.'s looking at the floor. I guess I shouldn't have embarrassed him.

"This is fucking weird." My voice comes out too loud. "Why would anyone hide stuff in jars all over their house?"

Mom studies the license. "There was a poet I read in grad school whose name was Nellie Mitchell. She wrote in the Forties and Fifties, then she stopped publishing." She looks up. "I'm sure it's just a coincidence, but I'm going to the library this afternoon and see if I can find what happened to her." She laughs like a little girl. "Wouldn't it be something if it turned out to be the same person?"

"You said you hated the poem we found."

"I do. But a lot of other people would be thrilled to find more of her work."

J.D. smiles at her but ignores me. Shit. He's mad.

I try to get him to look at me. "Maybe if we're really lucky we'll find her bones lying around. Maybe Carlisle pulled an Edgar Allan Poe and walled her up in the basement."

Mom pushes her hair off her face. "Why don't we work for another hour or so then I'll make us some lunch?" She walks out.

J.D. picks up his roller without a word and keeps his back to me.

"What's wrong with you?"

He stays silent. Jesus, if he can't take a little teasing maybe he should just go home.

I get my roller and start to paint, but I keep glancing at him until he finally meets my eyes.

"That was a shitty thing to say, Noah. You made me look like a jackass in front of your mom."

I try to think of something funny to say and can't. My eyes sting and I quickly turn away. "Sorry," I mumble.

We work in silence. "It's okay," he says after a while.

After lunch I talk Mom into taking me to the library with her instead of making me stay home and work. J.D. goes home but says he'll call me later about the movie if Kristin can come up with a friend to be my date. Whoopee.

I've always liked libraries and Oakland's is surprisingly good for a small town. It's an old building that's been recently revamped so it's clean and bright inside, with lots of windows and big oak desks and tables. Mom grabs a computer and starts interrogating it with her fingers and I wander off into the stacks. I run my fingers across the spines of books I've read and reread—*The Grapes of Wrath, Franny and Zooey, The Fountainhead, One Hundred Years of Solitude.* It's like walking into a room full of strangers and all of a sudden seeing someone you love. The only problem with library books is the covers. Too many hands have touched them and they feel like they have boogers on them. It doesn't matter if the book is by Virginia Woolf or Agatha Christie—the booger monster doesn't discriminate between literature and pulp fiction. But all my books are still in boxes, so boogers or no I'm taking a truckload home to get me through the next few weeks.

Mom snaps her fingers to get my attention and of course everyone in the library stares at us as I walk over to her. The librarian is a caricature of a librarian—short white hair, horn-rimmed glasses, a bosom you could hide Christmas presents under and a New England–tight-ass face that looks like she hasn't taken a shit since her family came over on the Mayflower.

Mom's writing down call numbers of books and she tells me to go find them. She wants to fish around on the Net and see what else she can turn up. I tell her she can do that at home but she says run along and get the books and stop bothering her while she works.

All the books Mom wrote down are poetry collections. I thumb through the table of contents of some of them and each has one or two poems by Nellie Mitchell. All the poems I find are short with one or two rhyming stanzas, like this one:

> *What matters is the letting go,*
> *the moment of release.*
> *The rest is potent prelude—*
> *love, and rage, and grief.*
>
> *It's not that life is pointless—*
> *every day's a feast.*
> *But in the end we give it up*
> *screaming with relief.*

I take the books back to her and show her this. She sniffs dismissively. When I ask her why she doesn't like it she says it doesn't have images, or imagination, and that the language is too simplistic to convey emotion. Whatever. I knew she'd hate it before I showed it to her. To Mom a poem that any idiot can figure out isn't a poem. Sometimes I think she's the biggest fucking snob in the world.

She sees I don't agree with her but I change the subject before she can get into full-blown lecture mode. "Did you find out if it's the same lady?"

"No. So far I haven't found any record of her at all since she stopped writing. For all we know she could still be alive and well."

I tap the books. "Are these the same style as what we found?"

"Maybe." She squints at the screen. "Here's something. This article says the last poetry collection she published came out in January of '51. When did Stephen and Nellie get married? July of '52?"

"June, I think."

"So, if it's the same Nellie Mitchell there's a year and a half be-tween when she stopped writing and when they got married."

"Is she from around here?"

She shakes her head. "She grew up in Chicago."

"Really? The rude bitch never even had us over for dinner."

I guess my voice is too loud. Several people glare at us, includ-ing the dragon at the check-out desk.

Mom tells me to keep my voice down and watch my language, but she's trying not to smile. Sometimes she thinks I'm funny but she won't admit it. She pulls at her lower lip. "Where's Carlisle from? And for that matter, what did he do for work? Where did he and Nellie meet?"

"Yeah. And what did he eat for breakfast? What was his favorite color? How many bowel movements did he have a day?"

"You're being ridiculous." A laugh gets away from her before she can stop it. The librarian scowls and Mom waves an apologetic hand at her.

I really like Mom's laugh. It's husky and rich and full of gravel. I just wish she'd let it out more often.

She says we'll have to come back another day and hunt through county records and stuff. She also wants to talk to some of the old-timers in town and see if anybody knows anything about the Carlisles.

I pick up a few books and we get ready to leave. At the check-out desk Mom chats the librarian up for a minute then gives her the third degree about Stephen and Nellie, but the lady says she doesn't remember Nellie and she barely knew Stephen. I expect Mom to be disappointed, but on the way home she's cheerful and relaxed and fun to be with. She hasn't been like this in a long time. Not since Dad died.

The problem with death is that it kills so much more than just the person who actually dies. Dad took a big part of Mom with him, and probably great big fucking chunks of me as well. Sometimes it makes me pretty bitter. Before Dad died, the three of us were like the points of a triangle—separate (and maybe a little warped), but still connected. Now it's like Mom and I can't figure out what shape we're supposed to be. Everything we try has a side missing and neither of us has a clue what to do about it. I mean, we get along fine, and on the surface not much has changed. She's still a volatile pain in the ass and I'm still a smart-assed little shit, but every conversation we have has holes in it—like we're in a play where every third line of dialogue has been deleted and we're always waiting for something or someone to fill in the missing part.

I've heard that the death of a loved one can bring the surviving members of a family closer together, but so far I haven't seen any evidence of that with us. Our routine, such as it is, hasn't changed much. We still eat together most of the time like we always did when Dad was alive, and we still pretty much do our own things in the evening—she writes, I paint. There was a brief period, right after the funeral, when we tried to hang out in the same room together after supper, but we'd never done that before and it didn't feel right. I think we were both trying to be there for the other one, but neither of us are built for that much togetherness with each other and we soon went back to the way it used to be.

But it's only an act. Neither of us is okay, and I think both of us are terrified of losing each other. I get really pissed at her now when she drives like a maniac and comes home with yet another speeding ticket—one time I yelled at her to just keep it up if she wants to make me a fucking orphan—and I've caught her standing outside my bedroom door twice since Dad died, with this wild look on her face like she was afraid I'd been kidnapped or something while she was taking a crap or brushing her teeth.

We need each other, but the fucked-up truth is that we drive each other bugshit when we spend too much time together without Dad around.

Erosion

It seems the river doesn't care
about the sand along its banks—
the water rudely eats the earth
and never stops to mutter thanks.

I'd like to see one grain refuse
to leave its home for no good reason
the river might be forced to speak
and grant the sand another season.

Okay, so John Donne doesn't have to worry about Nellie Mitchell usurping his place in the pantheon of poets. But I like it.

I'm sitting in my room on the window seat, reading through one of the poetry collections we brought home today. This is how I like to read poems; with big breaks after each one for better digestion. If you read too many poems at once without properly chewing them your brain can start feeling bloated and before you know it you're farting out your ears and drooling all over your shirt.

I've got the windows open and it's hot, but there's a strong breeze now and then that ruffles the blue curtains by my head and dries the sweat on my face and chest. I've got a pillow behind my back and I'm leaning against the wall, and when I look up from reading I can see the shadows shift in the backyard as the sun slogs toward the west.

Mom is somewhere downstairs, messing around in the dining room or the kitchen. I'm supposed to be working on the house, but I need a break before supper. J.D. called a while ago and said he and Kristin found a date for me for the movie tonight and I need something to take my mind off that. I've only been on one other blind date and the girl I got trapped with that time had a luxurious zit beard on her chin and a scab on her elbow she kept picking at all during dinner.

Anyway, I'm trying to figure out what made Nellie Mitchell

tick. Who was she? There's a thread of sadness running through all her stuff, a wistfulness that quietly twists your heart. It's not like she's wallowing in self-pity or anything, but why is she so pensive? (Mom hates it when people assume things about a poet simply because they've read a few of his or her poems. She says the biggest disservice a reader can do to a poem is to wonder who the poet was or why or when or how the poem got written, and she says it pisses her off when someone presupposes that the "I" in a poem is one and the same as the poet herself. As usual, I don't have a clue what the fuck she's talking about. To me, works of art can't be severed from the artist. It might be impossible to know the details of Beethoven's life just by listening to his music, but any idiot who pays attention to his symphonies can hear his anger and his quirky sense of humor and his passion and his sadness. I might not know the name of his barber or what condiments he liked to put on his hamburger, but I know his soul as well as I know my own.)

This is my favorite Mitchell poem so far:

Lost

One day I will not be
this soul, this flesh, this mind—
I'll melt into another form
and leave myself behind.

My name will quickly disappear: resolve itself
into a dew—
I'll feel no loss for anything
except the Me that knows of You.

Like I said, wistful. So much for happy endings and love lasting forever. I guess it doesn't matter who she's talking to, but I can't help wondering about the specifics. For all I know, she could be swooning over a parakeet, though more likely it's some hairy gardener or a grizzled old lesbian. But whatever, she seems to be hurting, even though she has the decency not to whine too much about it.

Hoover sticks his head in the room and mews when I say hello, but when I put my hand out to entice him over to me he turns around and runs down the hall like I just threw acid on him. Carlisle must have treated that cat like shit. He wants attention all the time but flips out whenever he gets it.

I'm in a strange mood. These poems are bugging me for some reason, but I can't seem to concentrate enough to figure out why. Somebody's mowing the yard next door. I hear it but I can't see the mower. Every now and then it gets snagged on something and the engine revs a notch or two higher while the blades mangle whatever they get hold of. I have to do our yard soon; it's my turn. Mom and I take turns with all the chores—laundry, dishes, mowing, trash—because neither of us can stand doing any of that stuff. I guess I should be glad I have a mom who doesn't make me do everything while she sits around on her ass eating Fritos and watching Jerry Springer.

A bead of sweat runs down my face and drops on the first line of the next poem.

> *When I owned a younger soul*
> *I loved one person at a time—*
> *I had no room for more than one,*
> *and then the next in line.*
>
> *Older now, and far more torn,*
> *I may have grown too much.*
> *Now I love the world at once*
> *and none of it enough.*

I think what's bugging me is the overall sense of resignation. It's like she's given up and is trying, without much luck, to put a brave face on it. Every single poem of hers I've read has that same tone; I guess I'd like to read something with a little hope in it.

"So this is why your room is taking forever."

I jump a little and drop the book. Mom is standing in the doorway.

"Christ. Don't sneak up on me like that." I reach down and snag the book by its cover. "I'm just taking a break for a few minutes."

She waves a hand like it doesn't matter. "That's fine. You've gotten quite a bit done today." She points at the pile of stuff I've been reading. "Finding anything interesting?"

"Not really. Just that Nellie Mitchell could have used some Prozac."

She smiles a little and stares off into space like she's trying to remember something. *" 'There is an in-between time/when nothing sticks to me/there is no pain or pleasure then/there's just anxiety./And in this in-between time/I start to think of death/It isn't life I want to lose/it's the tightness in my chest.' "* She focuses on me again. "That's the only poem of hers I remember. I never liked it but it got stuck in my head just the same. Simple rhymes are deadly that way."

I've always been astonished at Mom's memory. She can quote hundreds of poems, beginning to end, word for word, even really hard stuff like Pound and cummings and Eliot. But if she walks into a grocery store needing three things she'll forget two of them.

She walks over and takes the book from my hands, then stands there and starts to thumb through it. I reach for it but she steps away without looking at me.

I clear my throat loudly. "You might not have noticed, but I was reading that."

"Break's over," she says, and shuffles out the door, flipping pages.

J.D. and I are at the movie. Kristin and a girl named Melissa are here too. The movie is a dumbass comedy starring people I've never heard of and with any luck will never hear of again. I feel the same about Melissa and Kristin. We're all in a row, lined up like bottles on a fence. I'm on the right, Melissa's next to me, then Kristin, then J.D. Melissa and Kristin started giggling and whispering during the previews and haven't stopped since. J.D.'s got his arm over Kristin's shoulder and now and then he touches her hair.

Melissa is sort of cute, I suppose, if you like your women fat and homely. She's got long greasy blonde hair, bad skin, and the body of a Sumo wrestler. Kristin probably keeps her around to make herself look better. Still, I like Melissa a lot more than I like Kristin. When we were in line I asked both of them what they were going to do after high school. Melissa said "Go to college and become a nurse." Kristin said "Have a party!"

I catch J.D.'s eye and he gives me a goofy grin and a little wave. I turn back to the movie when I see Kristin put her hand on his leg. Melissa leans closer to me and I know I'm expected to put my arm around her. I ask her if she wants more popcorn. She says no but I go get some anyway. Kristin is starting to stroke J.D.'s thigh.

I take my time in the lobby. It's the kind of movie theater that only gets one movie at a time a month or two after it's been everywhere else. I stare at the posters of coming attractions: some stupid horror movie and yet another rip-off of *The Big Chill* are due in Oakland at the end of the month. More riveting intellectual fare. I pick pieces of popcorn from the bag with my tongue, then remember Melissa will probably eat some of it. What she doesn't know won't hurt her.

J.D. comes out of the movie looking for me. "There you are."

I glance at him then back at a poster, pretending to be engrossed by it. "Here I am."

He gives my shoulder a playful tap with his fist. "Sorry about Melissa. We'll find you somebody better looking next time."

All of a sudden I feel hot blood in my face. I don't need their fucking help to get a date and if he thinks Kristin is a catch with her beaver-sized teeth and her cheap make-up and her skanky clothes I don't fucking need him either.

"Melissa's fine," is all I say and I walk back into the theater, leaving him to trail behind.

Through the rest of the movie he glances at me a lot but I don't look at him. From the corner of my eye I see him holding hands with Kristin and then I see her rest her hand briefly on his lap. Right on his fucking crotch.

Melissa turns to me and tilts her face up like she wants a kiss. I say something stupid about the movie and she laughs like a horse.

J.D.'s driving but I tell him I want to walk home and I quickly say good-night to everybody and tear off down the sidewalk. J.D. calls out "See you tomorrow," and I act like I don't hear him.

When I get home every light in the house is on and Mom is walking around knocking on walls with her fist. In her other hand is a hammer. Her hair is a mess and she barely acknowledges me.

"Mom? What are you doing?"

"I don't know, really. I thought I might be able to find another jar."

"By playing 'Knock knock, who's there?'"

"I was thinking maybe there's a pattern to where they are."

"What pattern? There was one behind the wall in my room, one under the bathroom floor, and one behind the guest room wall."

She nods. "I know. But maybe if we find one or two more we can start to make some sense of it."

"So you're going to stroll around punching holes in things until you find more?"

Her eyes are too bright, and her voice is higher than usual, like someone screwed her head on too tight. "Why not? We have so much work to do, what's another wall or two?"

She's out of her fucking mind. "That's the stupidest thing I've ever heard. I'm not going to waste my time fixing what you tear apart just because you want to go on a treasure hunt." I'm almost yelling. I'm not in the mood for this shit.

She stops pacing and looks at me. Maybe she's actually listening. Or maybe she's thinking how that hammer would look sticking out of my forehead.

"You're right," she finally says. "There's got to be a better way. How about a metal detector? The lids on those jars are metal."

Why can't I have a normal mother? One I could come home to and tell how much the movie sucked and how much I hate Kristin and how Melissa grossed me out and how shallow J.D. is. Instead, I get a nutcase who needs to be disarmed before I can go to bed.

She puts the hammer down and watches me. She looks worn out but almost human. "I'm going to make some tea. Want some? You look like you've had a rough night."

Hoover rubs against my legs and I push him away. I don't know why but I almost start to bawl. I take a deep breath and follow her into the kitchen.

CHAPTER
THREE

J.D. calls while I'm having breakfast and says his dad is staying home from work today with the flu and that means if we want to we can take his dad's car and go to the beach. I ask him if Kristin and Melissa are coming and he says it'll just be us because Kristin's mom won't let her out of town with him unless somebody's parents tag along. That's too bad, I tell him, but unless he's dumber than a house plant he must hear the relief in my voice.

He says I should come over to his house as soon as I can and we'll leave from there. I hang up the phone and my heart starts pounding fast. I run upstairs and find Mom spackling the walls in the guest room.

"Hey, Mom. J.D.'s dad is sick today so we can have his car and go to the beach. J.D. wants to leave right away."

She looks over her shoulder at me and there are dark circles under her eyes. "I already told you we've got too much work to do. The beach will have to wait."

"Come on, Mom. I've never been to the ocean. I'll never leave the house again after today, how's that?"

She turns back to the wall. "No."

"Goddamnit, Mom, I'm not your fucking slave."

"Don't swear at me." Her voice has ice in it. "I need you here. That's final. Now get dressed and get to work."

I know better than to push, but I'm pissed. "So what if I don't work for one day?" I hate my voice when I'm mad. It goes high and whiny. "Is the world going to come to an end?"

She keeps her back to me. She's applying the spackle with one of those flat metal knives with a wooden handle. She does it slow and smooth, but I can see the tension in her shoulders. "Not another word, Noah."

"Or what? You'll spank me and send me to my room? See how much work gets done then."

She pivots on her heel and heaves the knife at me. It gouges a chunk out of the wall about a foot from my head and splatters spackle everywhere. "No means no, you little shit!" she screams.

Both of us stand gawking at each other, then I start to shake. I run to my room and as fast as I can grab a tank-top, cut-offs, sandals and a towel. I charge down the stairs and out the front door, stopping only for a second on the porch to slip the cut-offs on. I expect Mom to yell for me to come back or worse yet chase me across the lawn, but by the time I get to J.D.'s there's no sign of her.

J.D.'s putting a cooler in the car when I run up. He smiles at my bare feet and starts to make some smartass remark, then sees my face. "What's wrong?"

"Nothing. Let's get out of here." I'm trying not to cry and my voice is trembling.

He glances over at my house, then back at me. "Okay. Go on and get in. I've got to grab a couple more things."

He goes inside and comes out carrying a towel and some sunblock. He's wearing bermuda shorts and a short-sleeved button-down shirt with the top three buttons undone. His mom follows him out to the car.

She says hello to me, her eyes flicking over me like a lizard's tongue, then rests her hand on the open car door after J.D. gets into the driver's seat.

"Make sure you're home by five. Your father may be feeling better by then and want his car back."

J.D. says okay. Donna turns to go back inside, then stops and looks at me. "Is everything all right, Noah? You seem upset."

Her face is surprisingly kind. I tell her I'm fine, I've just been running, that's all, and I'm out of breath. She nods but she knows I'm lying. She looks at J.D and the kindness drains away. "Five o'clock. Hear me?"

"Yes, ma'am," he says out loud. "Whatever," he says under his breath.

Donna hears the phone and heads for the house without saying good-bye or anything. I start to panic, thinking it's probably Mom calling, and I tell J.D. to hurry. He pops the car into reverse and we pull out into the street. I look through the rear windshield and just as we pull away from the stop sign at the end of the block I see Donna come running out the door, yelling and waving her arms. J.D. doesn't see her. I pretend not to.

About three months after Dad died, Mom brought a guy home with her one night. She'd been out late and probably hoped I'd be in bed by the time they got there. I was up watching an old movie, *The Lion in Winter,* on television. They walked in during the middle of the great scene where Peter O'Toole and Katharine Hepburn are in the dungeon trying to figure out how everything got so fucked up.

I barely looked up at Mom and her boy toy when they came into the room. His name was Carl and he had frog eyes and a potbelly. Mom reluctantly introduced us, then they excused themselves and went to her room. He was gone by the time I got up in the morning, and we never talked about him or any of the other half dozen one-night stands she brought home the rest of last year.

I tried to be mad that she was fucking other guys so soon after Dad died, but I couldn't really blame her. She was probably lonely and needed to be touched.

What can you say about loneliness except that it sucks? Most of the time I'm okay, but every once in a while I wake up in the morning and I'm so lonely I can't stand it. I can hug Hoover till hell freezes over and it helps some but it doesn't take away the ache of wanting another human being to hold.

I don't know why it's gotten so much worse since Dad died. We were hardly ever physically affectionate with each other—neither of us seemed to need or want that kind of thing from each other—so it's not like I'm going through a sudden withdrawal of hugs and kisses or anything. Mom may be missing that, but I don't know what my problem is.

Maybe physical intimacy isn't always about touching. Maybe it's also about being able to sit next to someone at dinner and not care if he takes something off your plate or reaches across you for the salt. Maybe it's about being able to sprawl out on the floor and read a book in the same room with someone who's grading papers and muttering about 'incompetent boobs who couldn't write a good paper if their lives depended on it.' Maybe it's about sharing the same space with another person and not going fucking crazy because you can't get away from them.

That's it, I guess: true intimacy is really just the run of the mill, day to day stuff that happens without thinking—thousands of simple, meaningless, comfortable ways you can be close to someone, never dreaming how shitty you'll feel when you wake up one morning with all of it gone.

The first part of the drive we don't talk. J.D.'s watching me out of the corner of his eye but he lets me get myself under control before he says anything.

He clears his throat. "Are you all right?"

I nod and sit up in my seat, wiping my eyes. "Mom and I just had a bad fight. She chucked a spackling knife at my head."

"She did what? Why'd she do that?"

"I don't know. We were arguing about going to the beach and

then she just snapped." I feel like crying again and look out the window so he won't see. "She's never tried to hurt me before."

He doesn't say anything for a minute. His dad's car is a Ford Taurus with an ugly red interior. It smells like sour milk. J.D. has the air conditioning cranked and I put on my tank-top when I start to shiver.

He passes another car. There are little kids in the backseat and one brat sees me watching her and sticks her nostrils against the window.

J.D.'s voice is so soft I can barely hear it. "My mom slaps me all the time."

I turn back to him. His eyes are straight ahead, watching the road. "How come?"

"She hates me." He says this calmly, like he's discussing what color to paint his house. "She didn't used to, but the last couple of years something changed, and now she hates my guts."

"What changed?"

"Fuck if I know."

"Does your dad try to stop her from hitting you?"

He snorts. "That would cut into his drinking time." He glances in the rearview mirror then over at me. "He doesn't have the flu today, by the way. He's just got another hangover." He flushes a little, like he's just said something he's ashamed of. A few miles roll by before he looks at me again. "Will you be able to go home tonight or will your mom still be mad?"

"I can go home, but she'll be mad. Especially because she told me I couldn't go today and I went anyway."

His hands tighten on the steering wheel. "Jesus. If she tells my folks you weren't supposed to go I'll get killed."

I feel like a heel, but I have to tell him the rest of it. "It's worse than that."

"What do you mean?"

"I saw your mom chasing after us, trying to stop us."

He jerks his head toward me and the wheels on my side of the car slide off the road for a second until he gets control again. "Are you kidding?"

I shake my head.

"Christ, Noah, why didn't you say something?"

"I had to get away from there." I am such a piece of shit. "I'm really sorry. I wasn't thinking clearly at all."

He studies my face for a minute and his expression softens at something he sees there. "It's okay."

I make myself ask. "Do you want to go back?"

He hesitates and I'm sure he's going to turn the car around, but he surprises me. "No. Fuck it. Let's go to the beach and forget about them for the day. What are they going to do? Castrate us?"

"Don't joke. The next owner of our house just might find my balls in a mason jar."

All of a sudden we're laughing like fools.

I can't get used to these puny New England states. Mom and Dad and I once drove from Chicago to Colorado and spent a whole day just trying to get across Nebraska. J.D. and I are on the road for less than two hours and we go all the way through New Hamphire and southern Maine.

There's a line of traffic waiting to get into Potter Beach. J.D. turns off the air conditioning and we roll down the windows. By the time we get to the lady taking the money at the booth we're both drenched with sweat. I tell J.D. I'm sorry I don't have any money because I ran out of the house so fast. He tells me not to worry about it.

It's a gorgeous day. There's a slight breeze, no clouds, and the sun is just the right kind of hot—not enough to broil us, but perfect for a long, slow bake. I carry the towels, a beach blanket, the sunblock and a frisbee, and J.D. carries the cooler. We walk through some dunes and all of a sudden there's the ocean. I should be more impressed, I guess, but it looks a lot like Lake Michigan.

The beach is crammed. It reeks of suntan lotion and seaweed.

There are little kids everywhere screaming and running around, and a lot of fat people sprawled out on the sand frying themselves, like maybe they think a sunburn will make them look thinner or something. We decide to walk as far away from the noise and the crowd as possible, and about fifteen minutes later we have a stretch of water and land to ourselves. I spread out the blanket and we plop down on it, taking off our shirts and sandals.

We stare at the surf coming in, and in a minute J.D. starts putting on sunblock. He coats himself up pretty good then asks if I'll do his back. He lays flat on his stomach and hands me the bottle.

His skin is warm and his spine is bumpy. There's a scar under his left shoulder blade and a small mole at the base of his spine, right next to the waistband of his shorts.

After I'm done with his back I do my legs and arms and chest. He watches me and then sits up and offers to do my back. I lay on my stomach. The sunblock is a little cold but he works it in with his fingers. Neither of us talk while he's doing it, and I close my eyes and hear gulls crying above us and the waves washing against the shore a few feet away. He lets me know he's done with a playful slap between my shoulder blades and for a second rests his hand on my neck. After he lies back down beside me, I don't dare turn over for a minute. I've got an erection the size of Florida. It's a wonder it doesn't drill through the earth and put someone's eye out in China.

"Too bad we don't have some chicks with us," he says. He's face up, eyes closed against the sun.

I don't know what's a bigger turn-off: Him wanting girls here or calling girls "chicks." Whichever, it works like magic: no more erection. I turn over. "Yeah. Too bad."

In a while we play frisbee, about waist deep in the ocean. I can't believe how cold it is. Then he teaches me how to body surf. We crawl out shivering after a few good waves and have lunch on the blanket—peanut butter and jelly sandwiches, apple juice, potato chips. We talk about music for a long time—he listens mostly to jazz and classical, but he seems to like just about everything else, too, from Tom Waits to Black Sabbath. He keeps asking if I've heard this or that and sings snatches of stuff when I tell him I'm not sure. He's got a decent tenor voice and he's not self-conscious at all about singing. I sing something with him and he looks startled.

"I didn't know you could sing."

I shrug. "I don't very often. Every time I sing around the house Mom tells me to stop before she slits her wrists."

"She's nuts. I like your voice."

I mumble thanks. In spite of the sunblock he's getting a bad burn on his shoulders. I touch it lightly and my fingers leave a stark white print.

He grimaces. "I guess we should get going while I still have some skin left." He scowls at me. "You're not burned at all."

"Real men don't burn."

He grins, stands up, grabs my ankles and drags me back to the ocean, where he proceeds to dunk me several times. I accidentally swallow a little water and he holds me upright while I'm coughing, his arms wrapped loosely around my chest. A couple of joggers run by and he immediately lets go and heads back to the blanket to pack up our stuff. I trail in behind him, my feet and shins gunked with wet sand.

We stop at the changing room to wring out our shorts. Neither of us brought swimsuits so it'll be a damp ride home. The room is full of people changing clothes, but J.D. unceremoniously pulls off his shorts and underwear and stands naked at the sink while he wrings them out. I do the same thing and try not to look at him, but I can see his penis in the mirror, a little shriveled from swimming in cold water. His pubic hair is a lot darker than the hair on his head. He gives my body a surreptitious glance, then quickly pulls on his shorts and tells me he'll wait for me outside.

During the ride home I fall asleep watching his hands on the steering wheel, wishing I could reach over and touch them, trace the veins in his forearms with my fingers, rest my head in his lap.

Donna's waiting for J.D. on the porch when we pull into their driveway.

"Shit." J.D. turns off the engine. "We're fucked."

"I don't care. It was worth it."

"Yeah." He tries to smile but can't quite manage it.

Donna stands up as we get out of the car. She walks over to within a foot of J.D. and glares coldly at him. He starts to say something but before the words come out her arm comes flying up and she backhands him across the mouth. All of us stand there not moving; I think she's as shocked as we are.

"Jesus, Mom!" J.D. touches his lips and his eyes go wide when he sees blood on his fingers. "What the hell are you doing?"

Her mouth twitches and for a second I think she's going to cry but then her face hardens again. "As if you weren't aware that Noah's mom didn't want him to go today. As if you didn't see me trying to stop you before you left this morning."

Shit. I hurry around the car. "It's not his fault, Mrs. Curtis. J.D. didn't know I was in trouble with my mom." The least she could do is look at me when I'm lying to her.

The tendons in her neck are sticking out. "Tell your little friend to go home."

J.D.'s expression says it's no use. "Bye, Noah," he says.

"Bye, J.D."

As I walk away I hear her order him into the house, and when I look over my shoulder she's grabbed him by the arm and is almost dragging him toward the front door. He pulls away from her but she grabs him again and says something I can't hear and this time he doesn't try to get away. They disappear into the house but before the door slams shut she's yelling.

Great. Just fucking great. Way to go. Maybe next time I can

manage to get him shot. I take my time walking home, not in any hurry to see if I'll get the same kind of reception that J.D. just got from Donna. Christ. It was such a good day and now it's all gone to shit. I don't get it. What part of Donna's fucked-up brain tells her it's okay to treat her son that way?

It's not quite five o'clock and my neighborhood looks like an advertisement for small-town America. The lawns are perfectly manicured (except for ours, of course), and people are out messing with flower gardens and herb pots in front of their perfectly painted houses. A goofy-looking dog missing half an ear comes running up to me, followed by a little girl about Heather's age on a pair of rollerblades. She's wearing a purple helmet with the words *No Evil* scrawled in big green letters on the side, and she smiles and says hi when I stoop to pet the dog. Right after that I pass a guy playing catch with his kid in front of their house, and both of them look up and wave.

All of a sudden I get this weird lump in my throat just because strangers are being nice to me. For all they know I could be a terrorist or a drug-dealer, but they're willing to give me the benefit of the doubt. It seems strangers are the only people who know how to get along with other human beings. Familiarity may not breed contempt but it sure as hell breeds bad manners.

I climb up our porch steps, take a couple of deep breaths, and force myself to open the door and go inside. It's cooler in here because all the shades are pulled and several fans are going full blast. The floor of the entryway looks freshly mopped; I can smell Murphy's wood soap.

Virginia is waiting for me in our kitchen. She's wearing the same jeans and T-shirt she was this morning. I wait for her to say something but all she does is stare at me. This morning her eyes were wild, murderous. Now they're just sad and I can't stand to look at her.

"I'm sorry," I mumble. "You scared me this morn . . ."

She stands and I shut up. She walks over, puts her hands on my shoulders, and kisses my forehead. She says something about needing a nap, then she pushes through the swinging door and goes upstairs, her footsteps heavy and slow. The bathroom door closes and I can hear running water in the pipes above my head. I stumble over and sit on a bar stool until she comes out of the bathroom and shuts her bedroom door.

Maybe I should let her throw sharp tools at my head more often.

I go to the refrigerator to get something to eat, but before I open the door I see a mason jar on the counter, its lid upside down beside it. Inside the lid is a woman's gold wedding ring. I pick it up and put it on my ring finger. It won't go past the middle knuckle, so I know it's not Mom's. Mom's hands and mine are pretty much the same size. This one has a small, elegant diamond set on it and I hold it up to the light. It glitters fitfully in the shadows made by the ceiling fan.

I look in the jar and find a clipping from an old newspaper. It's one of those awful wedding photos where the bride and groom are trying to appear happy and relaxed but instead look like their lips have been stapled to their cheekbones. The caption reads, "Stephen Carlisle and Nellie Mitchell wed." Carlisle looks about thirty-five. He's got a crewcut and a ridiculous caterpillar mustache, and he's tall and thin. The tux he's wearing makes him look like a starving penguin. Nellie is tiny beside him. The photo is black and white, of course, but it looks like her hair was black. She's younger than him, and she's got a delicate, fine-boned face and enormous eyes, and she's wearing a long-sleeved wedding gown with too much lace.

I think of something and walk over to the breakfast nook. On the table are the poetry books Mom and I got at the library. Inside one of the collections I remember seeing small snapshots of all the contributing poets. I find Nellie Mitchell the poet and compare that picture to the photo of Nellie Mitchell the bride.

It's the same lady. Fuck me running.

*   *   *

Mom wakes up from her nap around sunset. I'm sitting on the steps of the front porch when the screen door squeaks open and she comes out to sit beside me. She looks a little better now. Some of the strain has left her face. She's got her hair pulled back in a bun and she's wearing a sleeveless blue-and-white cotton dress.

It's hot but not too bad. I'm drinking iced tea, and I've been reading *The Remains of the Day,* by Kazuo Ishiguro. It's about this emotionally repressed butler who needs to get laid in the worst way and never will. I started an hour ago and even though I've read it before I can't put the damn thing down. My fingers are damp from sweat or from condensation on the glass, and the pages of the book stick together when I try to turn them.

Neither of us knows what to say. I know she feels bad about going nuts and I feel bad about pissing her off and disobeying her. She tucks a stray lock of hair behind her ear and yawns. "Did you see the jar I found today? I left it in the kitchen."

Good for you, Mom. Act like nothing happened. Let hell freeze over before we discuss anything important. She's always been good at avoidance, but since Dad died she's turned it into an art form.

I tell her I saw the ring and the clipping, and that I compared the two photographs.

She nods. "I have colleagues who would give anything to get their hands on this stuff."

"Hard to believe. You said she was just a second-rate poet."

"Yes. But in some obscure academic circles she's been quite the mystery for the last fifty years. No one knew where she went or why she stopped writing, and now we've not only found where she ended up, we've also unearthed a poem no one's ever seen before. If word of this gets out we'll have a pack of salivating grad students beating down the door." She stares at her bare feet on the concrete steps, picks up a pebble with her toes and puts it down again. (We have the same toes, long and thin and absurdly flexible. Mom won a bet with Dad once when he didn't believe she could write with her feet. She put a piece of paper on the floor, stuck a pen between her toes and signed her name quite legibly, with a flourish.) "But I suppose I'll have to see if she has any surviving family members who might want anything we've turned up."

I look down the street at J.D.'s house. I can see Heather playing in the yard and Tom sitting on his lawn chair, but no sign of either Donna or J.D.

Mom sees where I'm looking. "Did you have fun today?"

I listen for sarcasm or reproach in her voice but don't hear any. "It was great."

"You got a lot of sun. Your back is really dark."

"J.D.'s fried." One of Oakland's two police cars crawls by. "I imagine Donna's happy. It'll make him easier to torture."

"Is he in trouble?"

I tell her what J.D. told me about Donna hitting him, how I saw her slug him. She doesn't say anything. I can't blame her. What's to say? Because I pissed her off today and she lost her temper and I ran off and she called Donna to try and stop me from leaving for the beach, the wicked witch of New Hampshire is likely using J.D. as a punching bag tonight. Courtesy of us. Plus Mom is probably not feeling like she can judge someone for hitting a kid when she tried to replace my brains with spackle this morning.

It's getting darker. The sun is almost down. I wish I'd brought out my easel to paint it. The sky is a glorious fiery orange.

I slap at a mosquito. "Where'd you find the jar?"

It seems I'm my mother's son. Neither of us can talk about what matters.

"The ceiling in the pantry."

The pantry? Why the hell was she messing around in the pantry? There's nothing wrong with the pantry. Or there wasn't until today.

I'm too damn tired for another fight. I don't say a word.

The sun disappears and soon after that the stars start coming up. Within an hour the sky changes from mostly black into a glittering, dazzling mess. Scorpius is too close to the horizon and is mostly hidden behind houses and trees, but the brightest star in it, Antares, is right next to a neighbor's chimney. I look overhead for Vega, my favorite star, and find it immediately, stuck in Lyra just like always.

Dad loved the stars and made me love them too. Living in Chicago it was hard to see much except the brightest ones, but here the sky is so packed I have a hard time picking out individual constellations. I know there's millions of miles between each of them, but from here it looks like one gigantic clot of light. The coolest thing about the stars is that thousands of years ago people were looking up at night and seeing basically the same damn thing I'm seeing right now. This star or that one might go supernova, but for the most part not much changes. You can count on the sky to hold still and be what you need it to be.

Mom goes in for a minute and brings out a bottle of red wine and two glasses. I've had wine before but tonight it actually tastes good. We chat about stuff like we used to when Dad was alive, and neither of us makes any move to go in when it starts to get cooler.

I don't remember the last time the two of us sat together like this. We talked a lot before Dad died, but Dad was always with us. It's not that we don't sometimes enjoy each other's company, but Dad was the one who knew how to draw Mom out of her head and keep her involved in a conversation. She gets frustrated with me because she thinks I'm too young and too full of shit to take seriously. She's never said that, but I know it's what she thinks. Most of the time when I try to talk to her she either looks bored or irritated. She may be a fucking genius, but Jesus Christ, she should hear some of the coma-inducing diarrhea that comes flying out of her pie-hole sometimes.

I point out Sagittarius and show her how to find Arcturus and Spica by following the handle of the Big Dipper. She acts impressed and says she didn't know I knew so much about the stars. I tell her I learned everything I know from Dad, and she seems genuinely surprised, like she had no idea her husband was a star freak. I can't believe she didn't know, but I guess most of the time when

Dad and I were watching the sky Mom was someplace else, usually scribbling in her room.

I have two glasses of wine to Mom's four, and presto, the bottle's empty. We eventually fall silent, just listening to the night, and I start getting sleepy. I shift a little, knowing I need to go to bed but not wanting to. The Milky Way is a vast smear across the sky, like a white brush stroke on a black canvas.

We haven't said anything in so long that when she starts to talk it startles me, even though her voice is quiet, almost a whisper. "Did I ever show you a picture of your granddad when he was young?"

I can't see her face very well. "I don't think so."

"That wedding photo gave me a bit of a shock today. There's an uncanny resemblance between my dad and Stephen Carlisle."

"I only knew him when he was in his sixties. I don't remember him looking anything like Carlisle."

"He did, when he was younger."

"What was he like?" I ask, then could kick myself because she stands up and says good-night.

I broke the spell. If I'd kept my mouth shut, she might have actually said something real.

The week after Dad died was a miserable fucking week. I kept going over in my head what would have happened if I had only gotten off my ass and gone into the library when I heard Dad making those weird coughing noises. It was killing me to think that while he was probably holding his chest and fighting for air, I was happily squirreled away in my room, dabbling away at a canvas.

But I know I couldn't have saved Dad even if I'd walked in right when he was just starting to feel the pains in his chest. The doctor who did the autopsy told us the heart attack had happened so quickly that even if Dad had been in a hospital at the time it probably would have ended the same way.

But it still hurts like hell. At least I could have held his hand. At least he could have seen my face, and known how much I wanted to help him.

I tried to talk to Mom but she just told me not to worry about it and then she changed the subject. We still haven't talked about it. It used to piss me off, but now I guess I don't blame her. It's not like she's some kind of ditzy Pollyanna who can't stand dark thoughts; I think it's more like she's got this big fucking bomb in her chest waiting to go off and she's doing everything possible to avoid lighting the fuse.

Mom holds the door for me as I struggle with a box of books. We're up at Cassidy College on the way to her office; she insisted I come with her this morning and help her carry all her teaching junk. No doubt she'll be pissed later that I wasn't home working on the house at the same time.

Her office is in a big square building in the middle of campus, wedged between the administration building and the fine arts center. There are only a few cars in the parking lot because everything is still closed up for the summer, except for a few administrative offices. I suppose it's a pretty campus; it's got a lot of oak trees and big stretches of green grass, and the buildings are all old brick and half-covered with ivy.

She closes the door behind us and relocks it, then I follow her up the stairs. This building is called Harris Hall, most likely named after some tedious old guy no one remembers. It smells like mildew and dust even though the floors look clean and waxed, and it's pretty dark in spite of a lot of windows.

I'm panting by the time we get to the top of the staircase. "Jesus. Haven't they ever heard of elevators?"

Mom glances over her shoulder at me. "There's an elevator at the other door. This way's quicker though."

"Great. When my heart explodes make sure the ambulance guys carry me out the same way."

Her face darkens and I feel like a clod. It's weird how easily I forget that Dad is dead and how he died. It's like part of me still thinks he's waiting at home for us, trying to find the pork chops in the freezer or mucking around with the electric can opener.

"Don't be such a baby," is all she says.

We come to her office door. There's a big tag on it with her name in capital letters that wasn't there the last time I came up, and it's obviously new to her, too, because she taps it with a finger and smiles. "How about that?"

I swear to God. She's like a little kid when it comes to this kind of stuff. "That's great, Mom. You've officially arrived. You've got a door named after you."

She fiddles with her keys in the dark and my arms are starting to quiver by the time she finds the right one and lets me in. She turns the light on as I drop the box on her desk, then I get out of her way and plop down in a stuffed chair in the corner as she bustles about unloading the books. The office is small but cozy, with a good-sized desk, floor-to-ceiling bookcases, and a big picture window looking out over a pond surrounded by pine trees.

"Hey there, stranger."

We both jump a little. There's a guy in his thirties standing in the doorway beaming at Mom. He's dressed in a T-shirt and shorts, and he's so pale his arms and legs look like sticks on a birch tree. I suppose he's moderately good-looking, though, if you like tall thin guys with big gray eyes and fragile faces.

"Oh, hi, Walter." Mom puts on her best smile and comes around the desk toward him. "You startled me."

"Sorry about that. I was on my way home when I saw your light on and I just thought I'd come say hello."

Mom introduces me and I stand up to shake his hand. His name is Walter Danvers, and his palm is cold and wet.

"Mr. Danvers was on the search committee when I flew out here for my interview last spring. He's also a fine poet."

He smiles at me. "That's very flattering, but I'm nowhere near being in your mother's league, I'm afraid."

"Don't be silly," Mom says. "I saw your piece in *Harper's* last month. It was lovely."

They gab for a while and I sit back down again and thumb through Mom's copy of *The Collected Works of Pablo Neruda*. I tune in and out of their conversation, but Mom's doing her usual spiel, and by the time Walter says good-bye and leaves us alone I'm shaking my head.

Mom waits until she's sure he's far enough away not to hear us. "What?"

"Nothing."

"Don't play games, Noah."

"I just can't believe what a flirt you are."

She goes back to putting her books on the shelf. "I was not flirting."

"'Oh, Walter,'" I mimic, "'Your last piece in *Harper's* was lovely.'" I put down the Neruda book. "I seem to remember you talking about him when you were telling me about the other poets on the faculty. 'Ick' was the word I think I heard you use about his stuff."

She flushes. "Just because I may have been less than forthcoming about his work doesn't mean I was flirting."

"Do you think he's cute?"

"What? Of course not." She's not looking at me.

"Whatever." I guarantee that Walter will be her next fuck-buddy.

I don't see J.D. for a week. The one time I try to call, Donna answers and politely tells me he's grounded and has "lost his phone privileges" and she'll make sure to have him call me when he gets them back. I want to ask her, equally politely, how it feels to have a corncob up her fat stormtrooper ass but figure that won't help anything. I try to talk Mom into calling someone about Donna hitting

J.D., but Mom says J.D. is old enough that we should ask him before we do something like that.

Great. What if he's dead and buried in the backyard?

Mom and I are normal again. She tears things up and I put them back together. My room is finished and the bathroom will be done as soon as I get the wallpaper up. Mom bought some really cool Oriental paper—dark green with gold Chinese symbols. I asked her what the symbols mean and she said something about prosperity and peace but for all I know (or her either, I'm pretty sure) they could be saying "Die, imperialist pigdogs."

Mom's been trying to find out about Stephen Carlisle. She met some old guy at the college who used to know Carlisle, and she's invited him over for lunch today so she can pick his brains and try to figure out what happened between Nellie and Stephen and why our house has more jars per square foot than your average Victorian home.

I'm in the basement. Mom sent me down here to "clean it up" but I haven't got a clue where to start. It looks like Dresden after the fire bombing. There's no room to move. Boxes are piled everywhere, plus bikes, lawn chairs, and bookcases full of tools and shit that don't even belong to us. When the city cleaned out the house after Carlisle died, they pretty much ignored the basement. Christ. It's only nine in the morning and I'm already covered in dirt and cobwebs and sweat.

I hear the doorbell ring, then Mom's footsteps coming from the pantry through the kitchen on the way to the front porch. She woke up in a foul mood but now her voice sounds almost cheerful. Relieved maybe.

"J.D.! We've missed you."

My heart skips a beat or two. I start to go upstairs then decide to wait for him. They chat for a minute and I hear him say he missed us too, then he's standing at the top of the stairs calling my name.

"Hey." I force myself to sound nonchalant. "Come on down."

He clumps down the stairs and grins at me. He's got on white painter's pants, sneakers without socks, and a black t-shirt with holes in it. He looks great.

I step toward him but stop about a foot away, wanting to hug him but not sure he'll let me. "It's about time you got out of jail. Any scars?"

"Just a few. You?"

I shake my head. My arms are glued to my ribs. "I'm sorry I got you in trouble."

He shrugs. "You're a mess." He reaches out and brushes some dirt off my shoulder.

My heart is hammering violently against my ribs. I pull him toward me and give him an awkward squeeze. He squeezes back for a second then pulls away. We're both embarrassed and start talking at the same time about stupid stuff—the weather, the house, his sister. He asks if we found any more jars and I tell him about the ring and the clipping.

"No kidding? Mrs. Carlisle was a poet?"

"Not a very good one, according to Mom. But Mom thinks Shakespeare is an overrated hack, so who knows?"

"I heard that." Mom comes down the stairs. Was she listening the whole time? She ends up next to us. "And the only negative thing you've ever heard me say about Shakespeare is he's too clever for his own good." She gazes glacially at me. "There's a lot of that going around."

Teasing is a nice change from browbeating, but I wish she'd get more sleep. She looks like crap. Her shoulders are slumping and her eyes are so red it hurts to look at them.

"I have to go to a dinner at the dean's house tonight, Noah, and I probably won't be home until late. Why don't you ask J.D. if he wants to have dinner with you and stay the night?"

What's she up to? She's never before suggested I have someone over for a sleepover. In fact, I usually have to beg to get a friend in the house. Maybe she just wants a chance to talk to him about Donna or something.

I look at J.D. and try not to seem too eager. "Want to?"

"I can't." He sees how disappointed I am even though I try to hide it. "I wish I could, but I'm supposed to have dinner with Kristin tonight. We haven't seen each other all week."

"Oh. That's okay." Kristin. Goddamn her.

His eyes search my face and he looks unhappy at whatever he finds there. "But that's at five and maybe I could still come over later and spend the night."

Before I can help it I'm smiling like a village idiot, but I shrug like it doesn't matter if he comes over or not. "Only if you want to."

Mom looks pleased. "Good. That's settled, then." She checks out the basement. "You're doing a good job down here, Noah."

Someone call an exorcist. Mom's been possessed by a nice person.

Donald Elliott's nostril hairs have a life of their own. When he talks they move about on his upper lip like spider legs. He's bald and paper thin, his skin is pasty and almost gray and he's older than Yoda. When Mom introduces him to J.D. and me at lunch, she tells us she met him a few days ago in the government documents section at the college library. I guess when she found out he'd lived in Oakland his whole life, she asked him if he'd known Stephen Carlisle. He told her yes, of course, but he was in a hurry so she invited him to our place today.

We're sitting at the table in the breakfast nook. J.D. and I are next to each other and Mr. Elliott is across from us beside Mom. Mom has outdone herself on lunch with some kind of a spicy tofu thing with sun-dried tomatoes and pesto on sourdough bread. J.D. and I both smell pretty bad. We've been moving boxes around for almost three hours. Every once in a while Mr. Elliott catches a whiff of us and wrinkles his nose, making his nostril hairs do a stately little dance.

Mom tells him about all the stuff we've found. He listens to her quietly, nodding when she tells him about who Nellie really was.

"I knew she was a poet, but I've never read any of her work. Poetry isn't really my cup of tea."

"How did you know Carlisle?" Mom isn't eating. Her eyes are boring into the side of Elliott's face.

"We both were hired at the college about the same time. I was in the business office and he was the Chair of the English department. We weren't exactly friends, but it's a small college and you get to know everyone on campus, whether or not you want to."

He's got bad teeth. Right now there's a moist glob of pesto stuck between two of his incisors. That grosses me out, so I watch J.D. instead. J.D. eats delicately, with a napkin in his lap. He keeps his elbows off the table and his mouth closed while he eats. I study the muscles in his face as he chews until he catches me watching him. He touches the corners of his mouth self-consciously, like he's checking for crumbs.

"What is it?" he whispers while Mom and Elliott talk. "Have I got something on my lips?"

I shake my head and turn back to Elliott, my face flushing.

Mom asks if he knows how Carlisle met Nellie.

"I don't recall. Maybe she came to do a reading or something. Stephen was always trying to get money in his budget for bringing in writers and guest speakers."

"What was she like?" J.D. asks. He seems genuinely interested.

Elliott glances at him dismissively, then focuses on Mom to answer the question. Apparently he's of the 'children should be seen and not heard' genus, *Gigantis Assholis.*

"I only met her once at a faculty and staff get-together. She was very quiet. I never saw her more than a foot or two away from her husband. She seemed pleasant enough, I suppose."

Mom's looking irritated, like she's not learning anything she didn't already know. "How about Stephen?"

Elliott frowns. "He was a bastard. Pardon my language, but that's what he was. Just a bastard."

"Why do you say that?"

"There were dozens of stories about him. But as an example, one time he came into my office to pick up his payroll check. The girl I had working for me was new, so there was a line waiting. Carlisle started complaining loudly to anyone who'd listen that he was glad to see the mentally retarded getting hired, but did they have to be in charge of his paycheck? and so on and so on, until by the time he got to the desk the girl was in tears. Her crying just seemed to make him madder. He told her 'I don't appreciate being made to wait and for God's sake stop sniveling and hurry up.' "

I want to ask what he was doing when Carlisle was abusing his assistant, but I'm afraid his nose hairs might reach across the table and rip my tongue out.

"Why would Nellie have married him?" J.D. asks. He's really into this.

Again, Elliott acts like Mom asked the question. "I'm sure I don't know. But a funny thing about Carlisle was that he never pulled anything like that on a man. He was only hateful to women. Men he just ignored."

Gosh. Imagine ignoring someone.

For some reason Mom's looking really upset. Elliott doesn't notice. "Everybody hated him, including his students, but he got tenure somehow, and you know how that goes."

Mom nods, distracted. "Do you have any idea how Nellie died?"

Elliott stops to think. "A heart attack, maybe. I know they were only married for a year or so when it happened." He pauses. "I didn't go to her funeral, but I heard that Carlisle wept like a baby all the way through it. I saw him a day or two later and tried to give him my condolences but he was back to his usual self by then and said something like 'Yes, well, these things happen.' He said it like we were discussing the loss of a stuffed toy."

Mom asks about the jars. He says he doesn't have any idea. She asks if there's anyone he can think of that might have known the Carlisles better. He tells her everybody's long gone.

J.D. shows up on the porch around seven, carrying his trumpet case and a paper bag ("Clothes and a toothbrush," he says). Mom left for the dean's house about an hour ago.

He steps inside and sets the trumpet on the floor. "I figured we could play some duets later."

I ask him how dinner was at Kristin's house. He says fine but changes the subject. We go into the kitchen where I'm making fried egg sandwiches for supper. He says he's too full to eat but I make him one anyway and he eats it.

"What'd you think of that guy who was here for lunch?" J.D. asks, taking a swallow of milk.

"Elliott? Not much. His teeth are going to give me nightmares, though."

He laughs. "No, I mean what he was talking about. I think it's kind of funny that no one has anything good to say about Carlisle. He must have had some redeeming qualities. Maybe he was different with Nellie than with other people."

"You're getting as bad as Mom. All she talks about is dead people."

He grins. "Maybe if she lived with someone interesting she'd stop doing that."

Everybody's a comedian.

After dinner we play duets for a while. He's a lot better on trumpet than I am on trombone, but it's kind of fun. It doesn't even sound too bad, considering I haven't played in a couple of months. When we get bored with that I make popcorn and we watch television, both of us sitting on the floor with our backs against the couch and our legs out in front of us. We squabble over the remote until I find *The Poseidon Adventure* on some old movie channel and he says he's never seen it before. Halfway through it he sniffs, then sniffs again, louder. I look up and he's grinning at me. He sniffs again, making a face.

"What's your problem? Did you fart?"

"Nope. But somebody's feet smell."

Our feet are lined up in a row and both of us are wearing white socks. His are hanging loosely off his toes. I shake my head. "Not mine. Mine smell like roses."

He sits up and leans over my legs, snuffling at my feet like a hunting dog. He looks back at me and waves a hand in front of his nose. "Pew."

"You're just jealous because my feet smell better than your breath."

"That's it. These have to go." He grabs my legs and starts yanking at my socks.

"Are you nuts?" I try to get away but he's got one arm wrapped tightly around my shins so all I can do is flail around. I poke him in the ribs and he yelps and both of us start laughing. He gets hold of one sock at the top and peels it off, then tosses it away and starts on the other foot. "One down, one to go!" he shouts. I grab a handful of popcorn and squirm forward to stuff it down the back of his shirt. He tries to fight me off but I get my fist under his collar and let go, smashing the popcorn against his skin.

"Gross," he yells, tearing off my other sock. He throws it toward the fireplace, then he rolls away and sits up, panting. I lean back against the couch and catch my breath, watching as he takes his shirt off to shake it out. He starts to put it back on, then says "Screw it" and tosses it aside. He settles next to me. We're both breathing hard.

I wiggle my feet in the air. "Happy?"

"Yeah. I've never smelled anything worse in my life."

I pretend to watch the movie, but out of the corner of my eye I'm looking at his stomach, noticing how the sparse hair around his

belly button gets thicker near his waistband. I cross my legs and try
to concentrate on Gene Hackman and Shelley Winters swimming
underwater in an upside-down ship.

Before the movie's over both of us are yawning. It's only ten
o'clock and I'm usually up till at least midnight, but ever since we
got this house and started working on it I've been falling asleep
early. I ask him if he wants to watch anything else and he says no,
he's kind of tired, so we clean up our mess and head upstairs, leaving the porch light on for Mom.

He goes to the bathroom first to get ready for bed. I wander
around my room nervously, eyeing the bed we'll be sharing. My
heart's going about twice as fast as normal and my palms are
damp. I try to force myself to calm down because he's got a girlfriend for God's sake and they probably fuck like bunnies every
chance they get and he would likely beat me to a pulp if he knew
what I'm thinking.

I hear the bathroom door open and he comes into the room. All
he's wearing is a pair of blue nylon gym shorts. He glances at me
shyly, then drops his clothes on the window seat and gets into bed.
I go to the bathroom to brush my teeth.

Have you ever looked in a mirror and studied yourself like you
were someone else? The guy in the mirror has thick black hair
that's getting too long in back, almost touching his T-shirt collar.
He has big green eyes and a small nose and thin lips. His neck is
thin with an average Adam's apple; his shoulders are narrow. I
smile experimentally and he smiles back. Objectively, I guess he's
kind of cute, in a lost-puppy-who's-just-peed-on-your-lap sort of
way. This sounds fucked-up, I know, like the worst sort of narcis-
sism, but for the first time I'm looking at myself and don't mind
what I see. Why is that, I wonder? It's the same damn face I see
every day, but today it looks different to me.

I finish brushing my teeth, then I take a piss and flush the toilet.
I wash my hands and check one last time for stray zits or boogers

before going back to the bedroom. J.D.'s lying on his back with the sheet pulled up to his neck.

"Your room is weird," he says.

"How come?"

"It looks like a monk's cell or something. There's no pictures or anything."

"Everything's still in boxes. I've got a bunch of stuff to put up when I get the chance."

He watches me strip down to my boxers, then I shut the door, turn off the light and crawl under the sheet. Neither of us says anything for a minute. I can hear him breathing, and we're close enough I can feel heat from his body. My penis twitches against my leg and I make myself think of something else so it will go to sleep again.

"Who do you hang out with when you're not with Kristin or over here?" I ask.

"I've got some guys I run around with sometimes but they're kind of boring. All they talk about is sports and chicks and all they want to do is get drunk and smoke pot." He shifts and his knee bumps into my thigh. "But they're okay, I guess. Maybe we could all go to the pool sometime this week and you could meet them."

"Maybe." I roll onto my side so I'm facing him. "Have you smoked pot?"

"A couple times. I don't like it. It hurts my throat. How about you?"

"No. I kind of want to see what it's like, but I don't want to smoke it with people I'm not comfortable with. Everybody I knew at my old high school who was into it was a moron."

There's enough moonlight coming through the blinds to see his face turned toward me. "Maybe I can get some and the two of us can smoke it by ourselves." He pushes the sheet down past his navel. "It's kind of hot in here."

"Do you want me to get a fan?"

"No. It's okay."

His nipples are the size of dimes and surrounded by ten or twelve hairs each, like little kids standing around a campfire. I put my hand a few inches above him and watch the shadow of my fingers on his chest and stomach. He laughs a little when he sees what I'm doing but it doesn't sound like his usual laugh.

"Don't be a queer," he says.

I pull my hand back. "I'm not." I turn over with my face away from him.

He's quiet for a few seconds. "I know you're not."

I fake a yawn and tell him good-night. He doesn't say anything for a while but then I feel him prop himself up on an elbow.

"Noah?"

"Yeah?"

"Are you mad at me?"

"No. Why would I be mad?"

"I wasn't calling you a queer. I was just teasing."

"I know."

He settles back down. I lie awake for a long time and I think he's awake, too, but I finally drift off when I hear him start to snore.

I wake up when the bedroom door opens. Mom's head is silhouetted against the hall light.

"Mom? What time is it?"

"I don't know. One-something."

Something's wrong with her voice. It's tight, like someone is choking her. We're both whispering, trying not to wake J.D., even though I'm pretty sure he's awake by now.

"How was dinner?"

"Fine. Have you boys heard anything strange tonight?"

"What do you mean?"

"I thought I heard someone crying downstairs when I got home. It sounded like a woman."

I try to think of something to say but she's scaring me. One hand is pulling at her hair, over and over. I can't see her face but I can see she's still wearing the dress and shoes she had on when she left the house earlier tonight.

"Mom? How much did you have to drink?"

I can barely hear her. "Not nearly enough." She closes the door without another word.

I stare at the closed door for a long time. If J.D. is awake he doesn't say anything, which is fine with me. I don't feel like talking.

When I wake up in the morning, J.D.'s back is pressed against mine. I can feel his shoulder blade along my spine and our butts are touching. His breath is slow and heavy so he must still be asleep. It's hot in the room and we're both sweating. I don't move. I breathe when he breathes. I lay awake and feel him next to me, his skin sticking to mine like wet Velcro.

CHAPTER
FOUR

chool starts in a week. Mom's been going up to Cassidy College every day for a little while to prepare for her classes and she leaves me to work on the house. J.D.'s spent a lot of time here the last few days and nights. Now and then he goes to dinner at Kristin's or takes her to a movie but most of the time he's with me. He almost never goes home, and his mom and dad don't seem to care where he is as long as he isn't with them. That's fucked up. But it works for me.

I was sitting on the porch a couple of days ago when J.D. pulled into the driveway to drop off a shirt he'd borrowed. Kristin was in the car with him. I've only seen her one time after we all went to the movie, but J.D. tells me she's a "little jealous" of our friendship. She waved at me like she was shooing a fly and I made my finest "eat shit" face and didn't bother to wave back. J.D. saw the exchange and I don't think he'll be bringing her over again anytime soon.

I finally worked up the courage to ask him if they were screwing. He said yes. He asked me if I'd had sex with anyone and I lied like Pinocchio and bragged about multiple conquests. Why do guys do that shit with each other? I mean, I'm sure he and Kristin are sleeping together but why did he have to get that hornier-than-thou look on his face when he told me about it? And why did I feel like I had to compete?

The house is coming along okay. I'm still working in the basement but it's a lot better. Mom wants me to transform it into a family room but that means laying down linoleum and some carpet, tearing down a wall or two and putting up paneling. I've finally got it cleaned up enough to do some of that but there's no way in hell I'll have it all done before school starts, not even with J.D.'s help. Meanwhile, Mom charges about like a hummingbird on acid, leaving piles of rubble all over the house. She's been in the attic the last couple of days. She wants to make it into a guest room.

We haven't found any more jars. Mom keeps the ones we've found in her room and she's been calling people she thinks might know something about Nellie. She's still wearing the necklace and she fingers it all the time like it's a worry stone.

She's at the school this afternoon and J.D. will be here in a few minutes. He actually ate lunch at home today instead of with us but he's planning to spend the rest of the day over here. I'm sitting on the basement stairs trying to come up with a plan of attack for tearing down a dividing wall when I hear the front door open and him yelling hello.

"I'm down here."

He finds me and plops down beside me. "Hey."

"Hey, yourself."

He stares at his feet. He's wearing sneakers with holes in them and, as usual, no socks, so I can see his big toe on his right foot and part of his heel on the left one.

"Where's your mom?"

"Up at Cassidy. She'll probably be there until dinner time."

He nods but I don't think he's listening. Hoover comes down the stairs and bumps his head into J.D.'s back, purring loudly, but when J.D. turns to pet him he hisses and charges back upstairs to hide.

"That cat is whacked out."

"What do you expect?" I scratch at a spider bite on my elbow. "He lived with Carlisle for who knows how long and now he lives with my mom."

"Your mom's not so bad."

"Tell that to the cat. You've seen that little porcelain bowl he eats out of? Mom has a whole set of those, but all different sizes. She keeps changing them to see what Hoover will do. One day she puts out the tiny bowl, then the next she puts out the one that looks like a trough. She does it on purpose, just to fuck with him."

J.D. laughs. "At least she has a sense of humor. My mom . . ."

I wait but he doesn't say anything else. What I can't figure out is why he never says anything bad about her. If my mom treated me like Donna treats J.D., I'd tell the whole fucking world.

Mom had "the talk" with J.D. about whether he wanted her to call somebody about Donna hitting him. J.D. got this horrified look on his face and begged her not to. I want to tell him the next time his mom hits him to knock her on her ass but I know he won't ever do that. For some unfathomable reason he loves her. And I guess it's not my place to tell him I think his mom makes Stalin look like Florence Nightingale.

I lean into him and he leans back. Our faces are about two inches apart and his breath is warm on my face. His eyes are beautiful. "So," he says, uneasily breaking the silence. "Are we doing any work this afternoon or what?"

I stand up and he holds out a hand for me to pull him to his feet. We argue about who gets what hammer and who gets to hit the wall first and where the best place to start is and which of us is the better carpenter, and he makes some dumb joke about him doing carpentry when I was still in diapers. I tell him to shut up because I've been doing this kind of stuff so long I did my apprenticeship with Jesus and he laughs so hard that snot comes flying out his nostrils.

Within an hour we're both filthy, spattered with plaster dust and sweat. Our shirts are off and we're wearing them wrapped around our mouths and noses to keep from breathing all the crap in the air. The wall is only about a third of the way down.

I put my hammer on the floor and pull off the makeshift mask. "Let's get a drink and get out of here until the dust settles."

He follows me up to the kitchen, grabbing at my ankles near the top of the stairs and almost making me fall. I tell him to grow up and he blows me a kiss and tells me to lighten up. We wrestle around for a minute near the refrigerator until he puts me in a head lock. I wrap my arms around his waist and squeeze, my face against his ribs. He smells pungent but good and his skin is warm. My hands are trembling when I pour us both some iced tea. He gulps his down and refills it, then stands next to me at the sink.

I watch a bead of sweat trickle down his forehead through the dirt. The ceiling fan is going full blast but it's still hot.

He's studying me, too. "You got a cut."

"Where?"

"Here." His finger lightly traces around a small scratch on my shoulder. My heart starts pounding and my breath catches in my throat.

I'm scared, but he's still circling the cut like he's hypnotized, so I reach out and touch a thumb-sized black-and-blue spot on his chest. "You've got a bruise." My voice is shaking.

He watches my finger outline the bruise then slowly his eyes lift and meet mine as my hand drifts to his collar bone. He stands frozen for a second, then he reaches up and touches my cheek, running his knuckles gently along my jaw line. He swallows hard, and his hand drops to feel the tendons in my neck. I move closer to him and he touches my chest, my ribs, and finally my nipples, one at a time. When he looks back at my face he's biting his lip like he's trying not to cry.

I put my arms around him and we hold each other. His heart is racing, drumming a furious counterrhythm to mine. I massage his back for a minute then pull away enough to unbuckle his belt. He glances at the windows to make sure the curtains are closed, then unzips my fly and reaches in. I moan when he pulls my penis out and starts playing with it. I lean forward and kiss him on the lips. He looks shocked, then he smiles and kisses me back. I push his shorts down until they fall around his ankles, and he does the same to me.

Every night he's spent here this is all I've wanted to do. I kiss his neck, his breastbone, his navel. When I'm on my knees, I look up at him. His eyes are huge. I take him into my mouth, cupping his balls with my hands. His fingers are in my hair the whole time, and finally he cries out. I swallow once, then again. He leans against me for support, his stomach against my head, and I travel the backside of his legs with my hands, kneading the soft flesh of his butt.

He pulls away abruptly, and without looking at me, yanks his shorts up and rebuckles his belt. "I gotta go," he mumbles, and runs out the door like God was waiting for him on the other side. I sit on the floor with the bittersweet taste of him in my mouth and stare down at my retarded penis, pulsing madly in the open air. I ignore it until it falls.

Most of the wall is torn down when Mom comes home. I don't hear her until she's standing right behind me, coughing in the dust.

I glance over my shoulder. She's wearing a white cotton blouse and blue jeans. "When did you get home?"

"Just now. How's it going?"

"Dandy. Couldn't be better. Fabulous." I punctuate the words with hammer blows to the remaining wall.

"What's the matter with you?"

"Nothing." I walk over to the makeshift workbench in the corner. "Look what I found."

I hand her a mason jar. She tears into it like a wolf ripping into the belly of a lamb, and pulls out a piece of bright pink and red fabric. She holds it up in front of her and gives me a puzzled look. "It's a dress for a baby girl."

"No shit. I thought it was the Confederate flag."

She stares at me hard. "What's eating you?" Her face changes. "Have you been crying? Where's J.D.?"

I turn away. "He had to go home."

"Did you two have a fight?"

I feel like I'm six years old and she's asking if I had a scuffle on the playground. "No, Mom, we didn't have a cute little fight." My voice is harsh, mimicking. "And I haven't been crying. It's just the dust. Maybe I'm pissed off because you're leaving me alone every day and I'm having to do all the fucking work by myself."

I want to make her mad, but all she does is look at me. There's concern in her eyes, and love, but no anger. My throat tightens and my eyes burn.

"What is it, Noah? What's wrong?"

Where do you start? *Well, see Mom, it's like this. I gave J.D. a blowjob this afternoon and he wouldn't even look at me afterward and he tore out of here like I was a serial killer and I don't think he'll be coming back.* So I shake my head. "I'm just having a bad day, that's all. Can we not talk about it?"

For once she's at a loss for words. She studies my face, then finally gives up and inspects the dress again. "This is so odd. Didn't the real estate agent tell us that Stephen didn't have any children?"

I shrug.

She looks at me one more time then turns to go upstairs. "Dinner will be ready in about forty-five minutes."

What I hate most about Mom's poetry is that something is always something else. I enjoy a good metaphor or simile as much as the next person, but Jesus Christ, sometimes a rose is just a rose. In my mom's poems, even an asterisk is suspect. She once told an audience at a reading that the asterisks were meant to signify campfires on a hill. The two or three people in the room who had a clue what she was talking about were mouthy academic gasbags you wouldn't want living in your town, let alone eating at your table. I suppose gasbags need soul mates too, but they've mistakenly adopted Mom as their patron saint. In her heart she isn't like them. She'd never admit it, but I think if she wrote what she really wanted to she'd ditch all the intellectual pyrotechnics in favor of clarity, and simplicity, and raw emotion. But for some reason she always hides behind her brain and her education.

I wake up when Mom starts screaming. I kick the covers off and stumble down the hall in the dark, and the screams keep coming when I open her door and turn the light on. She's flailing around on the bed with her eyes open, but she's not seeing anything in the room.

"Mom!" I run over and try to grab her shoulders and she lashes out at me. Her fingernails gouge my arm and blood wells up.

"Ow! Goddamnit, Mom, wake up!"

The screams stop suddenly and she quits thrashing. Her eyes are still wild but at least they're starting to focus. I stand back from her, cradling my forearm and dripping blood on the wood floor. I watch her gradually calm down, her breaths slowing. She sits up, stares at me, at my arm, then drops her head on her knees.

"Jesus, Mom. One too many anchovies on your pizza tonight or what?"

She takes a deep breath and barks out a muffled laugh. The laugh scares me more than anything else. It sounds unhinged, wretched. I wait until she stops before I get a Kleenex from her nightstand to put on my cut. I can't believe how much I'm bleeding.

She raises her head. "I'm sorry." Her voice is strained and I can barely hear her. "Nightmare."

I sit on the bed. "What was it about?"

She shakes her head. "It doesn't matter."

"It doesn't matter? You were screaming so loud we'll be lucky if the neighbors haven't called the cops."

"Will you get me a glass of water? Better put a bandage on that arm, too."

I go to the bathroom. There are three deep slices in a row close to my wrist, and even though they're small I'm still bleeding pretty fiercely, like my arm is a ketchup bottle someone keeps squeezing. I wash them out and get a Band-Aid. The only kind I can find is one of those gigantic things the size of your palm. I put it on and pour a glass of water.

When I get back to her room, Mom's on the floor, wiping up the blood. Her Kleenex is more red than white. I must be a hemophiliac or something. I give her the water and she takes a big swig, then another.

"It was about Stephen." She's not looking at me.

"Stephen Carlisle?"

She nods. "He was . . . doing things to me. But the worst part was when he talked. It sounded like Dad."

"My dad?"

"No. Mine."

I don't know what to say. I stare around the room. There's a breeze coming through the north windows, playing with the curtains. I glance at the bed. Her sheets are dark blue, but next to the pillow, balled up, is a pink and red baby's dress.

The doorbell rings. We both stare at each other, then at the clock. It's almost three in the morning. She stands up and puts her robe on over her nightshirt. I follow her downstairs to the door.

A policeman is on the front porch. He's got a big gut and a police-issue mustache. His uniform is trying to choke him. He introduces himself as Officer Ganski and says his office received several phone calls reporting a woman screaming.

"That was me, Officer. I apologize. I'm afraid I had a bad dream." She tells him our names.

His eyes search her face, then drop to her hand. She's still holding the Kleenex she was using to clean up the blood. He looks at me and sees the ridiculous industrial-size Band-Aid.

"What happened to your arm, son?" He rests a beefy paw threateningly on his truncheon. "What's going on here?"

What's he going to do? Beat the answer out of us? I know that Chicago cops are paid to be assholes, but this is New Hampshire for Christ's sake. Mom and I are about as dangerous as a pair of titmice. "She accidentally cut me with her fingernail while I was trying to wake her up."

"Uh-huh."

It's three in the morning and my Looney-Tunes mother just woke up the neighborhood screaming. Thinking about the neighbors reminds me of J.D., and all of a sudden I'm tired and sad and frightened and I don't need this suspicious shit of a yokel cop waddling around on our porch questioning us. I open my mouth to say something really stupid but Mom puts her hand on my shoulder and stops me.

I turn to her. She looks like I feel. Maybe worse. My eyes fill with tears and she puts her arm around me.

Officer Ganski watches us for a minute and his face softens. He clears his throat. "You folks have a good night," he says finally and goes back to his car.

Alert the media. The police department accidentally hired a human being.

It's the first day of school. Mom doesn't start classes at the college until tomorrow, so she's already messing with insulation in the attic when I leave to walk up to the high school. We got a lot done this week but it hasn't been any fun. Mom is up every night walking the floors like a zombie until she passes out for an hour or two before sunrise. I asked her if she's still having nightmares and she said yes but she won't tell me about them. I can't sleep either. J.D.

hasn't been back. I could call him, I suppose, but I don't want to risk it. I saw him drive by a couple days ago and he kept his face turned away from our house.

Oakland High School is an old brick building with a tacky red and black gymnasium added to one side. There's a giant oak tree in front of the main door and some of its roots are busy chewing up the cement walkway by the stairs. The junior high is on the other side of the road, and the elementary is a block away. When I get there all the kids are milling around outside waiting for the bell to ring. I don't know anybody so I squat beside a flower bed and toss pebbles at a spider.

"Hi, Noah!"

I look up. It's Melissa. She's standing with her back to the sun so I have to squint to see her. "Hi, Melissa."

She's wearing a billowy yellow sleeveless dress and her chubby triceps jiggle as she shifts her purse. "Where have you been hiding? J.D. and Kristin and I went out for ice cream last night but J.D. said you were too busy to join us."

I mutter something about the house. She babbles on about this and that until the bell rings and everybody starts going inside. I stand up and try to think of a way to ditch her so I don't have to sit with her during the assembly. All of a sudden I see J.D. He's with Kristin and they're holding hands. He doesn't see me yet.

"There are the lovebirds, now," Melissa crows. She calls out to them. J.D. gets a sickly smile on his face and they come toward us as we step inside.

"Hey," he says. "Long time no see." He's trying really hard to be casual but he looks nervous enough to pee his pants.

"Hey."

Kristin and I nod at each other and she takes J.D.'s arm and puts her head on his shoulder. I get in front of them on the staircase that descends into the gymnasium. It's already hot. My shirt is sticking to my back. Melissa sees another friend and moves toward her, chattering. People are sitting on bleachers and I climb up quickly, trying to get as high as possible, next to the open windows. I'm a little claustrophobic and I hate crowds, but mostly I want to get the fuck away from J.D. I sit down in time to see him arguing with Kristin about where to sit. He's pointing up at me and she's pointing to a spot closer to the floor. She gets a pouty face and of course he sits where she wants him to, but then he turns and looks at me and gestures for me to come join them. I shake my head and mime that this is where I want to sit. He frowns, then gestures again and mouths "Come on."

"Bite me," I mouth back. He doesn't get what I said. I say it again, exaggerating the syllables. He looks flustered and turns away.

A boy with long greasy hair sits on one side of me and a girl with dimples and thick glasses sits on the other. We smile fake smiles at each other but we don't bother to introduce ourselves. Fine by me.

The principal stands at a podium facing us and says the same dumbass things every principal in the country says on the first day of school—where to get lockers, where to find our first classes, what a good year we'll all have if we just stick to certain rules blah blah blah. J.D. keeps looking over his shoulder at me the whole time and I ignore him as much as I can but once in a while our eyes meet.

You know what's sick? The second our eyes meet I get an erection. Okay, he's an asshole for trying to pretend that nothing's happened between us, and he's an even bigger asshole for not talking to me for a week. But while I'm thinking what an asshole he is I'm also remembering how his body felt against mine, and how I'd give anything to touch him again. Anything at all. I cross my legs in case Grease-boy or Dimple-girl should happen to glance at my lap.

I don't see J.D. until third period, which is right after lunch. We're in the same gym class. Fortunately we don't have to do anything today except get our gym lockers assigned. I've always hated

P.E. I hate the gang showers, I hate the stupid games, and most of all I hate the cruelty that goes on in the locker room. You know what I mean: dickhead jocks strutting around, snapping towels at the poor fat kids with zits on their backs. They usually leave me alone, but I fucking hate it anyway. Besides, there's the stench. Does anything smell worse than a boys' locker room?

J.D.'s talking to a couple of kids when I walk in before class starts. I can't avoid him without being too obvious, so when he waves and says hello I have to stop. He introduces me as his neighbor and "a really good guy." One kid is named Riley and the other is Paul. I shake their hands. Riley's a big boy, taller than J.D. by several inches and quite a bit meatier. Paul is just as tall but ludicrously thin.

Riley asks how I like Oakland.

I can see J.D. out of the corner of my eye and suddenly I'm as nervous as he is. I start to babble. "Is this Oakland? I thought this was Cleveland. I told my mom we should have bought a map but she never listens."

They all stare at me blankly then Riley and Paul start to laugh like I'm the God of Really Funny Jokes. I can see J.D. relax a little. What did he think I was going to do? Tell them what his semen tastes like?

Mrs. Chapman, the phys. ed. teacher, comes in and tells everybody to sit on the bleachers. J.D. sits beside me and for a minute no one is close enough to hear us. He leans close. "What are you doing after school?"

I shrug. "Working on the house."

"How's that coming?"

I sigh. "Look, J.D. I don't want to talk about the goddamn house."

He makes a quick, frustrated gesture. "I know. I just don't know what to say." He stares at his legs. "I'm pretty confused right now. Can we talk?"

I tell him I'll meet him out by the parking lot later and we can walk home together. He nods.

Paul and Riley come sit beside us and Mrs. Chapman prattles on for half an hour about what clothes we'll need for gym and mandatory showers and other equally riveting bullshit. All I hear is J.D.'s breathing. All I see is his hand, an inch from mine on the bleacher seat.

The last period of the day is Creative Writing. The teacher's name is Billy Otis. He's probably forty-five, with wire-frame glasses and short blond hair. He's not very tall but he's built like a wrestler or a gymnast, and he can't sit still. He paces around the room as he tells us about the class. We're all supposed to write a story and a poem per week, etc., etc.

I look at the other students. There are only twelve of us and, oddly enough, I recognize two of them from this morning's assembly. Dimple-girl's name, I find out during attendance, is Shannon Farnum, and Grease-boy's is Scott Something-or-Other. I nod at them but I'm having trouble concentrating on anything because all I can think about is getting together with J.D. when class is over.

Otis writes a sentence on the board: *"Else another light might go out."* He turns back to us and says, "Does anybody know what this is from?"

Silence. I raise my hand tentatively and I'm impressed when he doesn't have to look at his list to remember my name. "Noah?"

"The Winter of Our Discontent."

"Very good. Do you read a lot of Steinbeck?"

"Not much." I'm lying. I read a lot of everything. I know that sounds like bragging, but it's true. Besides, I've heard Mom and Dad talking about literature my whole life. I know books like other kids know sports statistics.

"What did you think of this one?" He holds up a battered copy of the Steinbeck.

"It was okay. Parts of it were weak, I guess. The narrator's voice was too chatty, or something. But that's the coolest last line I've ever read in any book."

Everybody's staring at me. I just set off every geek alarm in the building. I turn crimson.

Otis smiles warmly, like he wants to adopt me. "I think so too."

He tells us to use the sentence as the first sentence of a story or a poem and turn in whatever we've got done at the end of class. Surprisingly, nobody grumbles. Pens scritch on notebook paper and pretty soon I'm writing a stupid story about a monkey caught in a chandelier, throwing shit at blue-haired ladies suffering from chronic eczema. I can't help smiling and several times when I look up, Otis is watching me. It makes me uncomfortable, because he doesn't seem to be watching anybody else.

At the end of class he asks if I can stay for a minute. I tell him yes, but only a minute because a friend's waiting for me outside.

I'm standing in front of his desk and he comes around and sits on the corner of it. "Your mom is Virginia York, isn't she?"

Goddamnit. No wonder he remembered my name. I nod.

"I'm a great admirer of hers. I was very excited when I heard she'd been hired at Cassidy. I have no idea how they got someone of her caliber."

I tell him we wanted to move out of Chicago and Mom liked this part of the country. He sees me glance at the clock and he frowns.

"Do you suppose there's any way we could get her to come to class sometime and talk to us about her work?"

This happens every fucking time with every fucking English teacher I've ever had. I want to ask him how he'd like it if his mommy came to talk to our class, but I politely tell him I'll ask and let him know.

As I say good-bye and leave, I'm having a psychic premonition: Mom's going to say no. I won't ask, of course, but her answer will still be no.

* * *

Kristin's with J.D. when I come out of the building. They're in the parking lot sitting on the front of her car. When he sees me he stands up, bends down to kiss her, then comes over to me. We walk about a block before we say anything. Kristin drives by and honks and J.D. waves gaily at her.

"Did you tell her what happened?"

He shakes his head. "Of course not." We walk another few steps then he puts his hand on my arm and we stop. He jabbers what sounds like a prepared speech. "Look, Noah. I really like you a lot and stuff but what happened shouldn't have happened. I mean, I'm not gay and it's cool if you are but I'm not. I like girls." He's watching me closely, trying to read me. "I want to be friends but just friends and what happened can't happen again, okay?"

I look down at his hand on my arm, then back up at his face. I feel a knot in my chest and I can barely talk. "You're a coward." I pull out of his grasp. "You wanted something to happen as much as I did the other day and now you want to act like it was my fault or something." I start walking away fast. He comes after me.

"Wait." He grabs my wrist. "Noah. Wait." He glances around to make sure no one is watching. "I'm not saying it was your fault. But it's not for me."

"Right. I don't recall you saying anything about it not being for you the other day. I guess I just imagined your dick in my mouth."

He lets go. "Don't talk about that."

"Fuck you. I'll talk about it all I want. I loved it. I'd do it again in a second if you weren't such a fucking pussy." I'm getting angrier with every word. "You're all over Kristin in public but I bet sex with her sucks."

His lips tremble and he looks away.

"I mean, look at her. Just look at her. She's got the I.Q. of a brain-damaged earwig. How in God's name can you want to be with that?"

"Jesus, Noah, keep your voice down."

I turn away. "Nice meeting you."

He grabs me again. "Stop walking away from me."

"Look who's talking, Mr. Spooge-and-Run."

An old woman comes out on the porch of her rickety house, carrying a broom and dustpan. She says "Hello, boys" as she dumps her dirt in the rosebush and we wait until she goes back inside.

"I freaked," he whispers. "I've never done stuff like that with another guy."

"It's not exactly an everyday occurrence for me, either. It made me feel like shit when you took off."

We start walking again. He puts his hands in his pockets. "I'm sorry. I shouldn't have done that." He says something else I can't hear.

"What?"

"I said, 'I didn't even let you cum.' "

"Yeah, I noticed," I mumble. "Thanks. And in case you're wondering, blue-balls is everything it's cracked up to be."

Our feet fall in step: left right left right. I watch J.D. out of the corner of my eye and he watches me. A squirrel charges in front of us like a kamikaze then panics when it sees us and leaps onto the nearest tree, chittering obscenities once it's out of reach. Both of us smile in spite of ourselves.

If the world weren't such a fucked-up place I could hold his hand. I tell him that.

He gets mad. "I told you, I'm not into that."

"Whatever."

We're getting close to his house. I see Donna in the yard with a pair of lawn shears, hacking up a bush. J.D. stops again before we get to her.

"So what do we do?"

"Nothing, I guess." I'm tired. I want to go home. "You keep on banging Kristin to your heart's delight and I'll keep whacking off, and we stay the hell away from each other." I move away from him.

"Don't be like this. We can still be friends."

"Sorry. Chickenshits make lousy friends."

Before he can say anything else we're in front of his house. Donna waves and asks how I am and where I've been. I tell her I'm peachy keen but just too darn busy these days. I can't help noticing she doesn't acknowledge her son at all. Who gives a shit? I head for home, trying to feel good about the miserable look on his face.

There's a note from Mom on the refrigerator.

Noah,

Up at Cassidy. Back soon. Take a look at the article on the counter. I pulled it off the Net this morning. —VY

Why does she initial her notes to me? I know who writes the damn things. Other kids have moms who actually sign their notes "Love, Mom." But the great Virginia York wants to make sure everything she writes is properly attributed.

I open the fridge and take a few swigs from a bottle of apple juice as I hunt around for something to eat. There's part of a left-over pepperoni pizza and I grab two slices and some hot sauce and sit at the counter.

Hoover got to the article first and, not to be outdone by Mom, left equally distinctive initials: a corner shredded by his small, sharp teeth. It's a newspaper clipping from *The Boston Globe,* dated February 13, 1951, and it's a review of Nellie Mitchell's last book. The author of the review is Stephen Carlisle. I scan it without paying much attention because it's written in Academese, the only language known to man uglier than German. But there are a lot of words like "trite" and "banal" and "naive." It concludes with "Let us fervently hope that Ms. Mitchell has other interests besides writing poetry. If she feels she must write, then perhaps she will do the reading public the enormous favor of refraining from publishing."

That must have been a fun marriage.

Mom and Dad weren't a perfect couple but they respected the hell out of each other. Dad was the only person in the world Mom ever deferred to (albeit rarely), and Dad was always asking Mom for her opinion on this or that. According to Mom, Dad was a great teacher. She said he got tons of thank-you notes and gifts from ex-students, and kids were always hanging around his office after class. I don't know how Mom is as a teacher. She's not exactly the most patient person in the world, and she doesn't suffer fools gladly. But she knows her stuff and she's passionate about it, and she gets a lot of requests from people for recommendations.

I finish my pizza and go upstairs to change clothes before starting to work on the attic. My room finally looks like a room. I've got a giant poster of Yeats on one wall, looking very professorial, and on the opposite wall are Frost, and Emerson, and Virginia Woolf. My books are stacked on boards resting on milk crates and take up an entire wall; I've got the collected works of Dickens, Shakespeare, Wilde, Faulkner, Melville, and Austen.

Jesus. I guess I really am gay.

I strip off my shirt and open my chest of drawers to get another. Lying on top of the pile is J.D.'s Sierra Club T-shirt. He left it here last week and Mom must have finally gotten around to doing the laundry. I pull it out and hold it to my face. I can still smell him in the fabric. Damn him. I toss it back in the drawer and get one of my own.

God damn him.

I run down the stairs when I hear Mom come in the door, but I stop when I see her. She's in the entryway. Her hair looks like she's been riding a motorcycle and her eyes look like she's been poking needles into her corneas. She's carrying a bag of groceries in one arm and a gallon of milk and some books in the other. She pushes the door shut with her foot and glances up at me, and when she sees the small metal box I'm holding she runs over and plops everything down on the stairs.

"What is it?" She grabs for it and I pull it away from her, taunting.

"A treasure trove. What'll you give me if I let you see it?"

"I'm not in the mood for games, Noah. Give it to me."

"How about cooking me some lasagna?"

Without warning her face turns purple and she erupts. "Just give me the goddamn box!"

I stare at her numbly and she tears it out of my hands.

"God, Mom, I was only teasing. What's wrong with you?"

She ignores me and sits down to open the box. It's made of tin and has 'DiCamillo Bakery' printed on the top of the lid in small red letters and down at the bottom in flaking gold is 'Hand-crafted Biscotti.' It's about the size of a shoe box, but all that's inside are four loose photographs and two scraps of paper. The photographs are just simple snapshots, probably taken by a portable camera. They look a little dog-eared, like they've been handled too much.

The first is of Nellie standing on the front porch of this house. The picture is black and white but she's wearing some kind of bright frock, yellow maybe, with a wide frilly belt, and she's got on a huge bonnet that leaves a shadow across most of her face. What I can see of her expression looks a little grim, her lips pursed tightly together. The porch looks exactly the same, the stairs still flanked by the same two stone pillars and the swing still hanging from the same heavy chains. There's some kind of wild vine growing around the railing, climbing all over it like a skinny kid on a jungle gym. Scrawled across the bottom of the picture is the date, June 27, 1952.

"June 27 . . ." Mom looks up, thinking, and she's all sweetness and light again, as if she's forgotten she just pulled a scene straight out of *Long Day's Journey Into Night*. "That's only a week after they were married." She pats the stair next to her. "Sit down, Noah.

I'm sorry I yelled at you, but sometimes you can be a little irritating."

Half a dozen funny things to say pop into my mind but I don't say a word. She makes room and I sit beside her.

The second photograph is dated August 19, 1952, and it's a casual shot of Nellie and another woman. Both are in their thirties and look so much alike they must be sisters or at least cousins. They're sitting on a bench in the backyard, next to the pin oak that's still back there, only now the tree is at least three times as big. Neither seems to be aware of the photographer; Nellie's head is thrown back in laughter and both have drinks in their hands. She looks a lot different when she's laughing. The serious photos make her seem mousy, but here she looks confident and relaxed. Both women are wearing light summer dresses and no shoes, and the one I don't know has a hand across her forehead, shading her eyes from the sun.

I point at something in front of the women. "Take a look at that."

Mom nods. "A fish pond. A big one."

"Yeah. I went poking around in the backyard after I saw this. There's a concrete rim under the grass out there. It's easy to see once you know where to look. Maybe we can go digging sometime and see if the foundation for the whole thing is still there."

I can tell she doesn't care, but I think it's pretty cool. I felt like an archaeologist this afternoon, rooting around in the grass for signs of some dead and buried civilization.

The third photograph is out of focus. Nellie's coming down the stairs and she's standing almost exactly where Mom and I are sitting. She's heavier than in the other photos, but part of that might be the bulky sweater she's wearing. She's got a skirt on that clings to her knees, and some kind of fuzzy slippers on her feet. Her hair is longer, too, and she looks several years older even though the date is only three months later, November 14, 1952. She's carrying a book in one hand and resting the other on the banister, and she's smiling one of those "Say cheese" smiles that doesn't reach her eyes.

Do the things someone touches hold a memory of them? Something beyond the sweat of their fingerprints? I reach up and touch the spot on the banister where her hand was. It's smooth and warm, and the mahogany is worn to a dull shine. I lay my palm flat against the wood like hers is in the picture and all of a sudden I get weirded out. It was almost fifty years ago when she stood here. Now she's dead and I'm feeling the same piece of wood she did, like I'm standing behind her in line or something. I yank my hand away as fast as I can but the hairs on my arms are standing up and a chill runs across my back.

The last photograph is of Nellie holding a baby girl on February 6, 1953. Nellie looks haggard and frail, and the baby doesn't look much better. The baby's hair is curly and sticking straight up, but Nellie's hangs lifelessly to her shoulders. They're sitting in a rocking chair in what's now the living room, but it seems Stephen and Nellie used it as a study because there are books everywhere and a massive Edwardian desk next to them. (I'd love to have that desk, but the bank must have decided to steal it before they put the house on the market. It's probably sitting in some vice-president's office now, its drawers stuffed with mortgages and loan agreements.) Nellie's eyes are barely open and look puffy, like she's been crying.

The girl is very small, and I think she's wearing the dress Mom has in her room.

Mom holds this picture the longest and her hands are trembling when she lays it on top of the box. Her face is bone white.

"Where'd you find this?"

"The attic. I was poking around in that little cubbyhole where you found the croquet set." Mom stumbled across an old croquet set last week. There are six mallets and five balls, all badly discolored, plus a bunch of wickets and a couple of stakes. We made a course in the backyard a couple of nights ago but we haven't gotten around to playing yet. "I was trying to find what you did with the paint I was using around the skylight and I noticed a loose floorboard. It was under that."

She's not really paying attention. She's counting on her fingers. "February is only eight months after they were married, and the baby in the picture is at least two months old. Anything seem funny about the math?"

"It could explain why she married such a butthead."

"What if Stephen wasn't the father?" Her hand goes unconsciously to the locket at her neck. "Maybe he was doing her a favor."

I shrug. "Maybe it's not even their baby. Who's the other lady? Nellie's sister?"

"There's no mention of a sister in any of the biographical information I've found so far."

Seeing the baby's picture seems to have done something to her. She looks like she just drank a quart of bleach. She pulls out the scraps of paper and unfolds them, her fingers trembling. Both fragments have words scribbled on them; the handwriting looks like a woman's, but it's hard to read because the letters are faint and shaky, like whoever wrote them didn't have much strength. One says: *'Oceans gone and so the sky: Who will watch the world die?'* The other says: *'Cradle me, then, within this earth/I'll stay in the soil/ until I find/the strength for a rebirth.'*

Mom flinches and drops the paper back in the box.

"What's wrong, Mom?"

She swallows several times, then covers her mouth with her hand. "It was all so long ago."

"What was so long ago? Stephen and Nellie?"

She shakes her head and starts to say something else, but before the words come out there's a knock at the front door. Mom jumps up and runs upstairs, carrying the metal box and leaving the groceries on the staircase. I stare after her and almost follow, but then I think it might be J.D. at the door so I answer it.

Perfect. It's two Jehovah's Witnesses. Great timing, guys. One of them asks me if I've accepted the Lord Jesus Christ as my personal savior. I tell him that Jesus and I go way back, and He prefers to be called by His middle name (which, by the way, is Hubert), and He's coming over later to help me with my homework. For some reason that makes them mad and I close the door before they decide to crucify me in the name of the Lord.

By the time I get upstairs, Mom's locked herself in her room and won't answer when I knock.

Not that you care, but Christianity pisses me off. I mean, look at it. Just look at it. Have you ever seen such arrogance? Everyone thinks he has the answer for how everyone else should live and if you don't agree, he'll beat you to death with his Bible. The only Christian sect I can stand is the Quakers. They're as fucked-up as everybody else but at least they're quiet about it.

Mom's a lapsed Catholic, Dad was a resentful ex-Mormon and I'm a quasi-Buddhist. I like the Buddhists because they seem to trust that people from other faiths will somehow manage to find a way to God without physical coercion.

What kind of a crackpot hides stuff in the walls and floors of his house? What goes through his head while he's doing it? Is he thinking at all? Or is it just an impulse, a kind of poison ivy on the soul that he can't help but scratch?

When I was eight I wrote a note on a piece of paper and hid it in a cranny between the wall and the baseboard in my room. The paper was some of that wide-lined crap they make for kids (because hands at that age are too retarded to write small) and I used a pencil and carefully shaped each letter, probably sticking my tongue out of my mouth in concentration. My plan was to never tell anyone about the note, because I wanted someone in the distant future to find it, someone that had no clue who I was. I could picture this person seeing a tiny corner of the paper jutting up above the baseboard and wondering what it was, then bending down to pull it out and gawk, dumbstruck with reverence when they read the words: *"In 1991, Noah York inhibited this house."*

I managed to not say anything about the note for about a month, but the secret was much too good not to share, so one night I temporarily extracted it from its hiding place and took it to the kitchen to show Mom and Dad. They read it together and burst out laughing. I got pissed and demanded what was so damn funny (even then I had a potty mouth), and they explained that the word I'd really meant to use instead of 'inhibited' was 'inhabited.' I snatched the paper back and stalked out of the room, mortally embarrassed, and when I got to my room I tore it up. I thought about making another, but was too humiliated to go through with it.

I'm still not sure why I wanted to leave something like that behind. I don't think it had much to do with taking a stab at immortality or anything like that; I think it just sounded like a cool thing to do. It never occurred to me that the graphite from the pencil would eventually fade, or that the paper would yellow and fall apart. In my eight-year-old mind, that note would have lasted forever, maybe as much as a thousand years. Maybe even a million.

But I was a kid and didn't know any better. What lame-ass excuse did the person have who stuffed our house with jars and biscotti boxes?

I eat supper by myself and decide to go outside before it gets completely dark. I grab one of the croquet mallets and a ball from the kitchen pantry and head out to the backyard.

It's getting chillier in the evenings and the grass is cool and wet under my feet. I'm wearing long pants and a button-down shirt, but I'm not putting on shoes until I absolutely have to. I smack the ball around for a few minutes, just screwing around since I don't know the rules. Mom does but she's still playing hide-and-seek and can't be bothered with a different game.

Our backyard is big and really private because it's lined by trees and bushes, strategically placed to block out the rest of the world. The neighbors can't see us and we can't see them. We haven't spent a lot of time out here yet, but maybe when we get the house done we'll get around to it. I aim for a wicket and miss by at least ten feet.

The voice comes out of nowhere. "Good shot."

I look up, startled, and J.D. walks out of the shadows toward me. He stops a couple feet away. "I knocked at the front door but nobody answered. I was coming to try the back door."

"What do you want?"

"I don't know. Just to talk." He points at a stone bench under the trees, next to a ridiculously ornate Victorian birdbath. "Please?"

I shrug and follow him. We sit down a few inches apart, facing the back of the house. The sun set a while ago but the sky is still orange and red to the west, fading slowly to black.

J.D. clears his throat and starts talking, not looking at me. "I went over to Kristin's tonight."

"I don't really want to hear about it."

He rests his forearms on his thighs and leans forward with his fingers laced together between his legs. "Will you shut up for a minute and let me talk?" He waits until I nod before he says anything else. "We had dinner with her folks and then she and I went for a drive out by the old dairy."

A dog barks down the street and a truck goes by in front of the house. He rubs at his nose and waits a while, like he's trying to figure out what to say. "We parked behind the barn and started to fool around a little." He glances at me as if he's getting ready to tell me to shut up again, but I don't say anything and he looks back down at his hands. "I didn't really want to and she got mad and wondered what was wrong. I lied and told her I didn't feel good."

There's a half-moon tonight. I watch it and listen to J.D.'s voice, quiet and steady, and I feel a little like that moon—floating in space, getting higher and higher by the second.

"I dropped her off about an hour ago and I've been walking around the neighborhood, trying to get the guts to come over here and talk to you."

He meets my eyes fully for the first time since we sat down. "I figured out that I'd rather be with you than with her." His voice drops to a whisper. "I'd rather be with you than with anybody." The words come spilling out. "Ever since we . . . well, you know, all I think about is you. I know it's queer but I wanted to die when you walked away from me this afternoon. I feel stupid talking like this to a guy but I can't help it."

It's almost dark now and we're alone and no one can see us. I can barely make out his face and I can't believe what I'm hearing. But I also can't stand to sit here next to him any longer without touching him, so I do. I put my hand in his hair, stroke his cheek, touch his lips. He reaches out and undoes the buttons of my shirt, one by one, and he leans over and kisses me. Before I know it his tongue is touching mine, and we're on the ground, wrapped around each other on the grass under the trees. Then poof like magic I'm naked and so is he and his hands are everywhere and we hear a door slam somewhere close by and we wait tensely until we're sure we're still alone and he's asking me a question and I say yes and then and then somehow he's inside me and it hurts a lot but it feels better than anything else I've ever felt, too, and he starts to pant and finally stifles a cry and collapses on me and lets me hold him and I stroke his back while he kisses my neck and after a while he kisses my chest and my ribs and my stomach and then I'm in his mouth and there's grass and tree roots under my back and I'm watching the stars through the branches and his head is going up and down really fast and I can't even believe how good this feels I can't even believe this is happening to me I can't believe can't believe can't oh God, oh Jesus, I never knew, I never had any idea I could feel like this.

*   *   *

We wait a while, and talk a lot, and hold each other. It's cold so we get dressed and go inside, and J.D. calls his folks to ask if he can stay the night. Mom is still shut in her room when we go upstairs. He follows me quietly to my bedroom and I close the door and turn off the lights. In darkness we undress each other before crawling under the sheets.

Whatever comes after, I will have had this one night.

CHAPTER
FIVE

I get in the tub after J.D. is finished and he uses my razor while I'm showering. He borrows a pair of boxers and a T-shirt so he doesn't have to go home before school, then we go downstairs to get some breakfast. Mom is sitting at the table in the corner, sipping tea and looking at the pictures I found yesterday.

She glances up when we walk in and says hi to J.D. "I didn't know you were here until I heard you boys talking this morning."

You know the color of tomato paste? That's the shade J.D.'s face is, and mine feels the same. Mom raises her eyebrows.

I open the refrigerator door and talk with my back to her. "He came over last night after you went to bed."

"I see."

I sneak a quick look at her but she's not watching us anymore. She's got her nose in the pictures. She looks like she hasn't slept at all. I remember all of a sudden that she was trying to tell me something yesterday when we were interrupted by Jehovah. I want to ask her about it but I can't with J.D. standing there.

The back door is open and a patch of sunlight is streaming through the window of the screen door. Hoover is sprawled out in the light sleeping, his belly turned up like he's in a tanning booth.

J.D. walks over and rubs his stomach with a bare foot. Hoover twitches an ear but otherwise doesn't move.

I set the orange juice on the island. "I can't believe he's letting you do that. I'd have lost a foot."

J.D. grins. "Cats are smart. They know who to trust."

Can you believe it? I'm in love with a wiseass.

We sit across from Mom and have a bowl of cereal and I tell him about the photos. I tell her to show him the pictures and she hands them over reluctantly, like she was giving him a kidney. He studies them intently and asks questions about the other woman and the baby, and Mom tells us she's going to do some more digging today through old birth records.

"Don't you start teaching this morning?" I reach across J.D. for more milk and he jabs me playfully in the ribs.

"Only one class. I'll have time afterwards to go to City Hall."

J.D. asks her about her class and she says it's a contemporary poetry survey course. He asks if she likes teaching.

"Sometimes." She shrugs. "It pays the bills."

She asks for the photos and he passes them back to her. She can't stop staring at the one with the baby in it, and when I ask her what time she has to leave she doesn't hear me. I roll my eyes at J.D. and he smiles and puts his foot on mine under the table. There's a predictable reaction between my legs and somehow he knows it. His smile widens.

I can't tell you how much I hope Mom leaves the house this morning before we do.

She doesn't. We finish breakfast and she's still sitting there, staring off into space, so we put our dishes in the sink and go upstairs to brush our teeth before we have to go to school. He uses my toothbrush after I'm finished and I stand beside him at the sink and we watch each other in the mirror. When he bends over to spit I put my hand under his shirt and run my fingers up his spine. He turns his head and looks up at me, and there's white foam on his lips until he fills his hands with water and rinses his mouth. When he stands upright I drop my hand to his waist and he puts his arms around me and kisses me. He tastes like peppermint. I can feel him, rigid in his shorts against me, but then we hear Mom's footsteps on the stairs and we hurriedly pull away from each other before she gets to the top of the staircase.

We pass her on the way down. "Bye, Mom. See you tonight."

"Bye, Mrs. York," J.D. says.

Mom makes a vague gesture intended as a wave but doesn't say anything. She's still carrying the photos in one hand.

I grab my gym bag and we go out the front door and head for school. It's warm out, more like summer than autumn. We fall into step, neither of us in any hurry to get anywhere. Even though we're not touching, I can feel him next to me; I'm so aware of his body we might as well be Siamese twins, with one shirt and one pair of shorts for both of us. He's whistling some song I don't know and he times it to match the rhythm of our feet on the sidewalk.

When we pass his house, J.D.'s mom is out watering her begonias. Heather is standing next to her, chattering, her arms full of books and a sack lunch. Donna calls hello to me and tells J.D. to walk his sister to school.

J.D. frowns. "She's old enough to walk to school by herself."

I can't believe he's arguing with her. She might turn him into a toad or something.

She puts down the hose and walks over, her face full of threats, Heather in tow. "Don't you dare talk back to me. I won't tolerate it."

"I wasn't talking back. Noah and I just want to walk by ourselves."

Donna's eyes flit over me like I just threw dogshit on her favorite dress, then she snaps at J.D.: "I'll give you a choice: either take your sister with you, or Noah can walk alone while I drive you and Heather to school."

Heather watches them with a weird half-smile on her face.

"Fine, okay, whatever. Come on, Heather."

Donna bends to kiss Heather and tells her to have a good day. We start walking and she falls in behind us, dragging her feet. We go a couple of blocks like that, not saying anything, J.D. ignoring her even at intersections. We come up to a semi-busy street (as busy as a street in Oakland ever gets) and I ask him if we should wait for her and make sure she gets across okay.

"Fuck that. I hope she gets run over by a truck." But after a few steps he stops and turns around. "Hurry up, Heather. I'm tired of waiting for you."

She takes her time getting to us, her head down, but when she reaches us I can see she's been crying.

J.D. looks away. "Give me your goddamn hand," he mutters, and sticks his fingers out for her to hold before we cross.

When we get to school we leave Heather at the elementary and head up to the high school. The bell hasn't rung yet and Paul and Riley come over to say hey, and then Kristin and Melissa turn up, yapping like terriers. Kristin puts her arms around J.D. and he gives her a quick hug, darting an uncomfortable glance at me. She pulls away and frowns at him but he pretends not to notice.

Paul asks if I'm going to be in band this year and when I tell him yes he reminds me to bring my trombone to school tomorrow for the first rehearsal. God. Marching band. What idiot came up with that? Dress everybody up in foul-smelling, ill-fitting uniforms and make them tromp around on a football field, playing shitty medleys from *Cats* and *Les Misérables.*

Melissa tells me she plays the flute and she's all excited because we'll be in band together. Kristin says she's captain of the color guard, and looks at me expectantly, like she's waiting for me to lick her feet. I say wow and cover a yawn. Paul's a percussionist and Riley plays tuba.

We're all standing in a loose circle and J.D. is next to me. We try not to look at each other too much but I swear I can feel a static

charge in the air between us. The hairs on my arm are like anten-
nae, groping in the air for him. Kristin is standing on his other side
and I see her studying him when he's not watching, as if her eyes
were nostrils and she's catching a whiff of something sour.

A big fat guy waddles by taking mincing steps and keeping his
gaze on the ground. We all fall silent as he passes us and I hear
Riley mutter "faggot." I ask who that was and Paul tells me the
guy's name is Louis.

"The school fag," laughs Kristin. "I pledge allegiance to the
fag."

Everybody laughs except Melissa and before I can help it I join
in. J.D. is laughing too but it sounds phony, and from the corner of
my eye I see him glance at me to see how I'm reacting. We're such
assholes.

Melissa frowns. "I don't think that's funny, you guys."

Riley rolls his eyes and turns to me. "Melissa's our resident fag-
hag."

Her temper flares. "And Riley's our resident redneck." She
clutches her books closer to her chest. "Louis is a really nice guy."

Paul changes his voice to a flutey lisp. "A really nice guy who
sucks cocks."

Kristin and Riley howl with laughter, and even though this time
J.D. and I don't join in I have the same sickly smile on my face that
I see on his. Jesus. What cowards.

The bell rings and we all move toward the building. J.D.'s first
class is upstairs and mine is in the basement, so we split apart at
the landing. For a second our eyes lock and I can tell he's as
ashamed as I am. He gives a slight, helpless shrug before we turn
away from each other.

High school is a farce. For every good teacher there are five
shitty ones; for every meaningful assignment there are twenty
brain-numbing, time-killing, stupor-inducing exercises in futility. I
know all the arguments about kids needing socialization and struc-

ture and a balanced curriculum, but that's all a bunch of pigeon shit. It's just theory. It's just four years of busy-work, teaching us what most of us could learn better in three months with a good tutor.

My geography teacher, Mr. Herbert, spends every class reading to us from the textbook, then has the balls to get pissed when someone dozes off. My math teacher, Ms. Cooper, hands out endless worksheets going over the same material day after day because "not everybody has understood the material yet and we can't move on until the entire class is ready." My genetics teacher, Mr. Pauling, prattles relentlessly about chromosomes and keeps forgetting what he's saying because he's too busy checking out Gina Klasson's tits in the front row. My health teacher, Mr. Bailey, lectures us about the importance of good nutrition with his mouth half-full of jelly beans and Hostess Ding Dongs.

What's the fucking point? I could be home reading, or painting, or listening to music. Hell, I'd learn more from *masturbating* than sitting in these goddamn classrooms day after day listening to these clowns drone on and on.

How about this? Why don't we take all the money we put in education and hire each kid a private tutor for two hours a day? Anyone can learn anything if it's taught one on one. Then for the rest of the day, let everybody do whatever he or she wants—music, theater, art, metal-working—hell, even sports. Whatever. If a kid needs more structure than that and starts to cause problems, lock him up in solitary confinement and make him listen to the soundtrack from *Annie* or *South Pacific* until he promises to shape up. It won't take long. A day of that and the worst delinquent in the world will do anything not to go through it again. (Come to think of it, it would probably work in prisons, too, except even the most hardcore wardens would probably shy away from that kind of cruelty.)

I'm not joking. Public education sucks. Modern high schools are really just drone factories, churning out legions of half-literate buffoons with every bit of creativity stamped out of them. (Please don't talk to me about exceptions to the rule. Show me one school that teaches kids how to think for themselves and follow their hearts.) And no one can do a goddamn thing about it because the whole society, hell, the whole fucking world, is only high school writ large, with the same skewed priorities and the same rigid adherence to someone else's mindless schedule. Put a bell in the workplace and ring it when it's time for recess, and I'll give you odds no one would make a fuss. The principal with his detention pad gets replaced by a boss with pink slips; the end of the workday brings the same sense of soul-consuming relief as the end of the school day.

Now that I think about it, it's all about that goddamn bell. At heart we're a bunch of cows, listening for the strident ringing that means it's time for supper. Television is the cud we chew until we go to bed, then we get up in the morning and do it all again. Ring, ring, ring. The cows are marching.

By the time I get to the cafeteria J.D. is already eating. Kristin is on one side and Melissa is on the other, but he's managed to save me a spot across from him between Paul and Riley.

The food, of course, is shit: soggy, bitter green beans, lukewarm applesauce, lumpy chocolate pudding with a glob of fake whipped cream on top, and a desiccated hamburger patty sprawled like a corpse over a stale white bun. I smother the burger with mustard and ketchup but give up after one bite and decide to make a meal out of the applesauce and a carton of milk.

Kristin's babbling about a dance next week and how she doesn't have anything to wear and J.D. should get a new suit and can he borrow his Dad's car and maybe Melissa and Noah can go with them too except J.D. and her will want the car to themselves later, of course, snicker snicker. I keep my eyes resolutely on my tray and wonder how Kristin would look with green beans jammed into every available orifice. J.D. abruptly changes the subject and when I lift my eyes Kristin is glaring at him but at least she's finally shut her goddamn mouth.

There's a clatter of a tray being dropped by the lunch line and everybody turns to stare. Louis is looking down at his food on the floor and there are four football jocks from my gym class standing behind him smirking. One of them pats another one on the shoulder and I see him mouth the words "Good job." There are guffaws from all over the cafeteria and someone yells out "Nice going, homo." A teacher shows up and asks what happened but Louis just looks at her, and there's something in his face I can't bear to watch, a kind of weariness that no one our age should know anything about. He quietly bends down and begins cleaning up the mess. The teacher glares at the jocks but they put on angel faces and one of them even offers to get a mop to help poor clumsy Louis. God, I hate high school. It's such a fucking cliché. If people are going to be cruel to someone else at least they could try to be original about it. I finish eating as quickly as I can and go stand outside until the bell for the next class rings. I find a spot in the shade and stay there even when J.D. and the rest come outside and I see them looking for me.

J.D.'s gym locker is next to mine. There's the usual homoerotic horseshit going on after class: half-naked guys pushing each other around, all the time spouting endless fag jokes and bragging nonstop about the size of their penises. J.D. and I quickly undress and go to the shower room, which of course is nothing but a big open space with a single drain in the middle.

Two of the muscleheads who fucked with Louis at lunch are already in here. Perry has white pasty skin and a ludicrously overdeveloped upper body, and the other one is Lester, who's more fat than muscle and has a forehead only a Neanderthal could love.

We're across the room from them but Perry yells out to J.D. when we turn on the showers. "Hey, Curtis. How about sharing

Kristin with me sometime? Let her see what a real man feels like."
He grinds his hips suggestively and grins. His pubic hair is dark
red. I hurriedly put shampoo in my hair and turn my back to him.

J.D. knows this game. "Sure, Perry. Since you were nice enough
to loan me your mom last night it would only be fair."

Lester and Perry both guffaw like J.D. is the reincarnation of
The Three Stooges. Probably the only thing that would make them
laugh harder is watching a cripple fall out of a wheelchair.

"Hey, York." It's Lester's voice.

I turn toward him and wince as lather gets in my eyes.

"I hear you've been dating Melissa. More cushion for the push-
in', huh?"

Why is it that fat, ugly, stupid guys feel they have a right to
make fun of fat girls? I don't even like Melissa but something
about this jerk ranking on her pisses me off. I roll my eyes and
don't say anything. When he realizes I'm not going to answer, his
face darkens and he frowns like I've just violated a cardinal rule of
locker room etiquette.

Other guys start filing in. I finish rinsing off and get my towel
from the rack in the corner. J.D. follows me and as we dry off we're
alone for a few seconds.

"Be careful with those guys, Noah," he whispers. "They're
dumb as stool samples but they'll kick the shit out of you if you get
on their bad side."

Somebody comes over before I can answer. We go to our lockers and start to get dressed. I watch him from the corner of my eye.
It's humid in here and there's already a light sheen of perspiration
on his chest. He knows I'm watching him; he darts a quick glance
at me as I'm pulling on my shorts. I have to think about things like
cat vomit and Melissa's sagging triceps to keep from getting an
erection.

There's riotous laughter from the showers. We look over and
Lester's standing in the middle of the room with his chubby little
dick in his hand, peeing into the drain. Ha ha ha. How very droll.

* * *

Billy Otis is a pain in the ass. He starts class by telling everybody my mom's a famous poet and maybe she'll be coming to talk to us sometime this semester. He asks if I asked her about it and I lie and say yes, but I don't think she'll be able to. He gets a look on his face like I just told him Santa Claus isn't real. I can't stand it. I tell him I'll ask again and maybe talk her into it.

Scott, the grease-boy, is sitting directly in front of me. He's finally washed his hair and looks halfway respectable, even though he's got a bad case of acne. He turns around to stare at me while I'm talking, and when class is interrupted by the principal at the door, he leans close so I'm the only one who can hear what he's saying. His breath smells like Oreo cookies.

"Tell him your mom is incontinent and can't leave the house without a diaper," he whispers. "Then maybe he'll leave you alone."

This startles a laugh out of me and everybody turns to gawk, including Otis and the principal. Scott faces front again and leaves me grinning at the back of his head.

J.D. has to wait after school to walk his sister home, so he tells me to go on ahead and he'll come over later. I ask him if he wants to spend the night again and his eyes flicker. "What do you think?"

I have to hold my books in front of my groin as I walk away. I can feel him watching me until I turn the corner at the end of the street.

Cars full of kids pass me and a few of them yell out the windows. Shannon Farnum from Otis's class calls my name as she slowly drives by and her dimples try to eat her face as she smiles. I wave and keep on walking.

When I get home Mom is on the phone in the kitchen. Her forehead is creased with concentration and she barely notices me. I raid the refrigerator and listen to her side of the conversation.

"I see. I didn't know that." A pause. "No, we've only found the one poem. There may be more of course, but so far that's the only sample of her work."

I unscrew a jar of mustard to make a sandwich and accidentally drop the lid on the floor. It rings loudly on the linoleum and Mom glares at me like I just farted in church. "Sorry," I mouth, but she's already forgotten me again.

"Absolutely. If anything else turns up I'll let you know."

There's another pause. "Oh, surely. But do you mind if I wait until we've gone through the rest of the house before I send them to you? There may be more and I'd like to keep everything together."

She twists the phone cord in her hands as she listens and I can tell she doesn't like what she's hearing. "Of course I understand. I'll send everything to you as soon as possible." She says good-bye and hangs up the phone.

I wait for her to acknowledge me but she just stares at the floor. "Mom? Who was that?"

"What?"

"Who were you talking to?"

"Nellie's younger sister. Elvin."

"Really? You found her?"

She finally raises her head and looks at me. "I called a colleague at Northwestern whose specialty is poets from Nellie's period. He put me in touch with Elvin. She lives in San Francisco."

"Did the Northwestern guy know that Nellie ended up here in Oakland?"

A faint smile. "No. You should have heard how excited he was. He said that for some reason Elvin has always refused to talk to anybody about her sister, and before now no one else has had any idea where Nellie finally ended up. He wanted to fly out here this weekend and see everything but I told him it belonged to Elvin and he'd have to speak to her first."

"So what did she say when you called? Did she have any idea what all this stuff is doing in our walls and floors?"

"None. She said she hadn't spoken to Stephen since Nellie's funeral. She didn't even know he'd died." Mom leans on the island next to where I'm sitting. The bags under her eyes are so dark they're almost purple. "She said she couldn't stand the son of a bitch and never understood why Nellie married him. That's why she's so stubborn about talking to people like my colleague, by the way. She associates all academic types with Carlisle."

"So why'd she talk to you?"

"I didn't bother to tell her what I do for a living. I just told her about the house."

Nice. That's vintage Mom. She never hesitates to withhold information when sharing it might damage her chances at getting something she wants. "Did you ask about the pictures?"

"I told her about them and described them to her. She said she thinks the other woman in the picture with Nellie is probably her because she remembers coming for a visit about the time it was taken."

It's like pulling teeth to get her to talk. "So how about the baby? Did you tell her about the dress?"

She straightens abruptly and runs a nervous hand through her hair. "She was completely taken aback. She said she didn't know whose it might have been."

I swallow some milk to wash down a bite of turkey sandwich. "So if it was Nellie's, she didn't even tell her sister about it. Why would she do that?"

She looks in my direction, but it's as if she sees two of me and can't decide which one to focus on. "Some things are private, Noah." Her chin starts to tremble.

"Mom? What's wrong?"

She rubs at her temples but doesn't answer.

"Every time we talk about the baby you get upset."

"I'm not upset." She crosses her arms over her chest protectively. The locket sticks to her throat like some kind of bloated insect. "You have mustard on your cheek." She walks out the door and goes upstairs.

Mom's still in her room when J.D. comes over. We head down to the basement to be alone. We close the door behind us and as soon as we get to the bottom of the stairs he puts his arms around me and buries his face in my neck. There's something a little desperate about how he's holding me, but when I ask him what's the matter he answers by stuffing his hands down the back of my shorts. Then I can't breathe and I can't think for quite a while.

Afterwards, we end up laying on a rug in the corner. There's an unpleasant moldy smell down here because it's been so humid and I must be allergic to mold because I can't stop sneezing. He's got his head on my chest and we're both still mostly dressed. Mostly. My shorts are around my knees but when I try to pull them up he won't let me. He runs his fingers over my exposed skin, again and again, as if he's reading pornographic braille. For once, my penis is too exhausted to care and lays there sleeping, acting like it just swam the English Channel or something.

His face is turned away from mine, so when he talks his voice comes out muffled. "My mom and I got in another fight this afternoon."

I stir and play with his ear. "What about?"

He shrugs. "The usual. Why am I so worthless, how dare I think I'm God's gift to the world, I better straighten up—stuff like that."

"J.D., your mom is fucked-up. She treats you like shit for no reason."

He says something I can't make out and I have to ask him to repeat it.

"I said, 'There must be a reason.' But when I ask her what I've done to make her mad all she does is walk away and slam the door in my face."

"Have you asked your Dad?"

He's tracing a circle around my navel and his hand pauses briefly as he sighs. "Yeah. He tells me it's between my mom and me then he mixes another gin and tonic and zones out in front of the television."

"That's fucked." I stare at the ceiling, which is still just rough boards and wires. "Maybe if you . . ."

"Can we drop it?"

His voice sounds so tired all of a sudden. I put my hand in his hair and don't say anything else. After a while he shifts his head onto my stomach, and when he talks I can feel his lips move on my skin. "Do you think your mom knows we're doing this?"

"I don't know. Maybe. I haven't thought about it much." I sneeze. "Probably not. She's too busy wrecking the house and chasing after jars to notice much else."

"She looked at us kind of funny this morning."

"I wouldn't worry about it too much. If she does know she won't care one way or the other. She'll just tell me to be careful and shit like that."

He raises his head for a second to look at me, then drops it on my stomach again. "My mom would go apeshit. Every time someone says the word 'gay' around her she goes off about perverts and sickies and how they should all be put on an island somewhere." He laughs a little. "Sounds fine to me. How about Hawaii?"

"Not nearly big enough. Let's hold out for a continent. How about Australia?" I raise up on my elbows. "When are you going to break up with Kristin?"

Believe it or not, I feel bad for her. She really loves him and it's not right that we're messing around when she thinks they're still officially together.

"I don't know. Soon."

"How soon?" I'm having trouble concentrating because his hand is doing something really distracting. "J.D.?"

He doesn't answer. He's way too polite to talk with his mouth full.

*   *   *

The Turtle River is just five or six miles north of town, hidden from the road by a thick wall of trees. There's a path leading from the road through the woods, littered with Budweiser cans and cigarette butts, but I'm so glad to get out of town I don't even mind the trash. We've only been in school for a little over a week but the routine is already getting to me.

Tom waddles up the hill in front of us on the way to the river, wearing a bright blue long-sleeved shirt, tight rubber wading pants and boots, and a Red Sox baseball cap. There are huge sweat stains under his arms and he's panting like a St. Bernard during a thunderstorm. He's carrying a net and a six pack of beer, and he's got a hunting knife strapped to his belt.

J.D.'s carrying the tackle box and I've got the poles. We're dressed in tank-tops and shorts and sneakers, and when the sun goes behind a cloud it's kind of chilly. J.D. stops for a second and bends down to tie his shoe and I stop to wait for him while Tom goes on ahead. I can hear the river now but I can't see it yet.

"Sorry about this," J.D. grumbles. "I don't know what put this particular burr up my Dad's butt."

"I don't mind. This is a lot more fun than cleaning up after Mom."

"I suppose." He grimaces up at me. "I wish you'd said no."

Tom surprised us after school today, pulling up to the sidewalk as we were walking home. He said he'd gotten the afternoon off work so he could "take my son and his best friend" fishing. J.D. stood by the passenger door and argued with him through the open window for a few minutes, saying how much he hated fishing and that "Noah promised his mom we'd be home right after school to work on the house," but Tom said he'd already talked to my mom and cleared my going "so stop bitching and hop in."

J.D. tried another tactic. "Don't you think we should ask Noah if he wants to go?"

I knew J.D. was expecting me to say no, but Tom looked so disappointed that J.D. didn't want to go with him that I couldn't do it. I said fishing sounded cool. Tom's face lit up with a big smile and when we got in the car he babbled happily about how much fun we were going to have and he couldn't wait to see my face when I caught my first trout. J.D. just sat there looking pissed off for a while but by the time we got out of town he seemed to be getting over it.

"I know," I tell him now. "But your dad had his heart set on doing this."

He stands and picks up the tackle box again. "He's only trying to prove to Mom that he's still this big fisher guy or something. He'd much rather be home drinking beer and playing stupid games on his computer." I'm surprised by the bitterness in his voice.

Tom pokes his head back over the hill and tells us to hurry up because "daylight's a'wasting," then he disappears again.

"He sure seems like he's really into it."

J.D. shrugs. "Whatever."

We come up over the hill and there's the river. Where we are it's not very wide, but downstream it spreads out quite a bit. It's fast moving and there are a lot of rocks and branches in it. Tom's standing on the bank with his hands on his hips and he watches as I bend down and put my hand in the water.

"Jesus." I yank my arm back. "That's freezing."

Tom laughs. "It sure is. I'm sorry I don't have any boots or pants for you boys. You'll have to do the best you can from here."

He gets everything lined up, showing me how to tie a fly and how to cast, but as he's demonstrating his line gets tangled up in some trees hanging over the river and he ends up having to cut it and start over. J.D. laughs and turns away to look upriver, and Tom stares at his back with a hurt look.

"I guess I'm a little out of practice," he says. His chubby fingers fumble with a knot in the line.

"It looks hard." I pick up my pole and give it a try. The lure doesn't get tangled up but it only goes about five feet in front of me and drops in the water with a plunk.

"Don't get discouraged. That's not bad for your first cast." He puts down his pole and helps me for a few minutes with mine, and eventually I'm doing a little better. Tom thumps me on the back and turns to J.D., who's been watching us without saying a word.

"Okay, son, let's get you fixed up."

"That's okay. I don't want to. I'll just watch you guys."

"Come on, give it a try. You used to like it."

"No, I didn't."

Tom frowns. "Yes, you did. You used to beg me to take you fishing."

J.D. sits on a boulder next to me. "That was a long time ago."

Tom sighs, frustrated. "Fine. Suit yourself." He pops open a beer and sucks it down, then he picks up his pole and slowly wades out into the water, stumbling once or twice in the strong current and nearly falling before he comes to a stop beside a large rock quite a ways downstream. He casts his line and starts to whistle, but every now and then he looks over his shoulder at us, and even though he smiles he doesn't look like he's having a lot of fun.

J.D. and I don't say much, but I kind of enjoy watching my lure sail across the top of the water. There's moss growing on the rocks, and the constant babble of the stream nearly hypnotizes me. I like the sound of the reel when I bring the line back in, and I like how the sun reflects off the river between patches of clouds, nearly blinding me when it hits directly in front of us. It's like sitting in a dark theater when a spotlight snaps on, flashing across costumes laced with gold and silver sequins and faces covered with glitter. But after about an hour without catching anything I'm starting to get bored, and both of us are cold. Tom's moved all over the place (coming back every few minutes to get another beer and to ask if I'm having any luck) but he hasn't caught anything either, so when J.D. yells that we want to go, he nods and slogs toward us.

"I can't understand it," he says when he gets closer. "The fish just aren't biting today. The last time I came here I caught half a dozen or more of the little bastards." He steps onto the bank, shivering a little. "Sorry, boys. We'll try it again soon."

"I can hardly wait," J.D. mutters.

Tom turns red. "What's your problem, mister? All you've done this afternoon is piss and moan."

"I'm not pissing and moaning. I told you I hated fishing before you dragged us out here."

Tom sets his pole down carefully. "Excuse me for wanting to spend some time with my son." His voice shakes a little.

I can tell J.D. feels bad but he's got this stubborn look on his face like he's determined to make his dad feel like shit at all costs. I reel in my last cast and try not to look at either of them. We gather everything up in silence, but when Tom starts to toss his empty beer cans into the woods J.D. gets really mad and calls him a slob, which sets Tom off and he starts yelling at J.D. about what a pain in the ass he's being. J.D. yells back that he might be a pain in the ass but at least he's not a fat, drunken slob. For a minute I think Tom's going to hit him, but instead he picks up the rest of the cans and one after another tosses them into the woods, never once taking his eyes off J.D.

"Oh, that's real mature, Dad. I'm sure Noah's really impressed."

Goddammit. Don't bring me into this.

Tom looks over at me and flushes. He's breathing hard but he slowly calms down. "I'm sorry, Noah. We shouldn't be doing this in front of you." He picks up the net and his pole and heads toward the car.

The river suddenly sounds loud in the stillness. J.D. and I look at each other.

"What?" he demands.

"You were being a little hard on him, weren't you?"

"That's easy for you to say. You don't have to live with him. All he does is drink beer and eat potato chips and do stupid shit."

I don't know what to say, so I pick up the other poles and he gets the tackle box. On the way toward the car he stops on the path for a minute and says he's sorry I had to watch them fight but he couldn't help it because his dad really pisses him off sometimes. "This is the first time in years he's bothered to spend more than fifteen minutes with me, and all of a sudden he wants to act like Super Dad." He kicks an empty bottle of peppermint schnapps off the path. "I guarantee as soon as I get home and Mom starts in on me again he'll be nowhere to be found."

I tell him I understand, but I can't say what I really want to, which is that he should be glad he's still got a father to be mad at. The whole time they were yelling at each other I was actually jealous of J.D. How stupid is that?

Dad and I almost never fought. He was a mild, easily distracted man who'd start to get mad and then something else would catch his attention and he'd wander off to look at it and forget all about what had set him off. For instance, when I was five I forgot to lift the toilet seat and ended up pissing all over it and probably the floor, too. Dad was the next one to use the bathroom, and afterwards he came tearing into my bedroom and was about two sentences into a blistering lecture about needing to be more considerate for the next guy when he saw a spider's web in the corner of the room and completely lost his train of thought. The next thing I knew he was holding me up so I could see the web better and he was talking about how misunderstood spiders were and how every time you killed one it was like snuffing the life out of an artist.

Sometimes his absent-mindedness made me want to knock his teeth out, one by one, but for the most part it was kind of endearing.

The only time he yelled at me, really yelled at me, was when I accidentally tore a page in his first edition copy of *Leaves of Grass*. I was thirteen at the time and just being clumsy like every other thirteen year-old you've ever met. I don't think he really cared that it was rare and expensive. I think he just loved that book, and it pissed him off that I'd damaged something he loved out of sheer carelessness. It wasn't like one of Mom's tirades about nothing; I felt terrible because he had every right to be mad. Once he saw how bad I felt, though, he stopped yelling instantly and tried to act like it didn't matter, even though I know he was probably still wanting to put my head through a wall. He was like that. He hated hurting other people's feelings, even when they deserved it.

God, I miss that man.

Mom is getting weirder and weirder. For the last couple of weeks—whenever she's not at the college—she's spent the days sleeping in her room, and then late at night she wanders around the house staring at the walls. I came downstairs around four in the morning last night to get something to drink and found her standing with her forehead on the big plate glass window mid-staircase. The moonlight was so faint I could barely see anything except the flimsy white cotton chemise she was wearing. I asked her what she was doing and all she said was "I can't find her anywhere."

Goose bumps ran up my back. "Find who?"

Nothing.

"Mom? Find who? Nellie?"

She shook her head and wouldn't say anything else. I went back upstairs without my drink and crawled back in bed with J.D.

I don't know what to do. When I talked to her this morning she seemed mostly normal—exhausted and cranky, but sane. I asked her if she remembered last night and she told me I must have been dreaming. I told J.D. about it and he thinks I should call someone, but who can I call? My grandparents are all dead. I could call Aunt Cindy, I suppose, but I barely know her, and even if I do call, what can she do? She lives in Los Angeles, and as far as I know, Mom and she haven't spoken in years. Besides, Mom would fucking kill me if she found out I talked to her baby sister. She doesn't have any close friends, either, and if I tell people she works with, someone like Walter the Icky Poet, she'd tear out my heart and eat it while I watched.

Shit. What do I do?

I don't really know why Mom doesn't have any friends. The easy answer, I suppose, is she's always working, and any spare time she gets she prefers to spend alone. Dad was really the only other person besides me she let get close, and I can't think of a single female she knows that's more than a passing acquaintance. She's social and everything, but she'd sooner share her underwear with someone than let her guard down and tell someone what she's really thinking or feeling. Dad told her once that she should get out more and do stuff with other people besides us, but she told him to shut up because he was just as much a loner as she was.

Being a loner is fine, I guess, and I'm kind of one myself. But Mom has turned her need for solitude into a religion. She quotes Thoreau all the time by saying "I never found the companion that was so companionable as solitude." But I've seen how her face used to light up when she was talking to Dad, and I doubt very much she ever looks like that when she's alone.

I'm only beginning to understand how good a relationship my parents had. They were never touchy-feely in public or anything, but anybody with eyes could see how much they loved each other. It was mostly the small stuff that gave it away—you know, things like how they'd listen to each other without interrupting, or the way they fixed a meal together without ever needing to say a word about who was going to do what. I haven't been around a lot of other married couples, but I have a hard time believing that Mom and Dad didn't have something going on that most people never figure out.

I have a tape of a party they gave one New Year's Eve when I was probably eight or nine. Some bozo friend of theirs was wandering around the house all night with a video camera, and while most of the tape is shit—drunken English professors and administrators making small talk around the punch bowl and blinking owlishly at the camera whenever the focus is on them—there's a great couple of minutes where Mom is talking and Dad is off to the side, leaning against a door frame and watching her. Mom was really animated that night, waving her arms around like a conductor on crack and fuming about some biography of Keats she'd just read, and Dad was his usual low-key self, sipping at a beer and rarely talking. When the camera first catches them it looks like Mom doesn't even know Dad is there, but as the seconds pass she gradually turns toward him and by the end they're face to face, and both of them are reaching out a hand toward the other and smiling.

It doesn't sound like much, does it? Just the kind of thing two people in love do all the time. But I swear to you, if you could see that tape, you'd know what I'm talking about. Most people would rip out a lung to have someone look at them that way. It's something I've wanted my whole life.

Mom didn't cry at Dad's funeral. (I tried not to, but tears kept leaking out of my eyes like a bad case of post-urinal dripping.) She just sat there, staring straight in front of her like she was watching a boring movie and would rather be at home shelling beans or manicuring her toenails. People who came up to talk to her must have thought she was a cold, heartless bitch who didn't give a crap about losing her husband.

But I know better. I've never heard her crying at night and she's never said a word about missing him. She can try to act like she's fine and maybe she'll even manage to convince herself and other people that she is.

But I'm not buying it. I've seen the tape.

J.D.'s folks are leaving town tonight for the weekend, and Heather will be staying at a friend's house, so J.D. and I can have his house all to ourselves for a couple of nights. Mom says it's okay as long as I'm at our house working during the days. (I'm a little worried about leaving her alone at night, but it's been over a week since I caught her wandering around the staircase mumbling to herself, and she's seemed a little more stable recently—and yeah, okay, I want to be alone with J.D. for once without having to worry about being quiet while we're fucking. That may be selfish of me but Jesus Christ, Mom's a little old to need a babysitter.) I hurry home after school and get a bunch of crap done in the basement before supper so she'll let me go for the rest of the evening. I can't wait to see J.D. because he said he was finally going to dump Kristin this afternoon.

Kristin's been driving me nuts. Every time I've seen her the last couple of days she's been hanging onto J.D.'s arm like a ferret, and when she sees me she clutches him even tighter. I don't think she has any idea what's really happening between him and me, but she's definitely figured out I'm the enemy. I told him this morning he had to break up with her and he got mad.

"What's the big deal? You know I'm not doing anything with her."

Sometimes he's as dumb as a handful of gravel. "It's just wrong not telling her. She already knows something's going on."

"Are you crazy? You want me to tell her about us? It'll be all over the school in an hour."

"Just tell her you want to break up. Tell her you want to date someone with a personality for once, or something."

"If we break up people will get suspicious about you and me. Paul and Riley were already blowing me shit this morning about how much time I've been spending with you."

"So?"

"So I don't really want people thinking I'm a homo."

He saw the look on my face and his voice softened. "It's not like I'm ashamed of you or anything. But if people find out about us our lives would turn to shit overnight."

"I know. But it's still not fair to Kristin to keep lying to her."

He finally agreed to dump her today. I acted like it doesn't bother me if people are suspicious of us but of course I'm worried about it. I'm not stupid. I see what happens to guys like Louis, and I don't need that kind of shit in my life. But as long as we're careful it doesn't have to come to that. We don't touch each other in public, and both of us pretend to be typical teenage boys perpetually lusting after tits and pussy. I hate the lies, but what are our options?

Anyway, Mom is in the living room when I come upstairs to clean up before supper. She's sitting in the chair Dad died in, with her legs curled under her. It's an old brown leather armchair with imprints where he used to rest his elbows, and a big butt-shaped dent in the seat. Mom's too small for the chair and looks like a little girl. When we moved I tried to get her to throw the damn thing out, because neither of us can look at it without remembering Dad's body slumped over in it. She wanted to keep it, though, so here it is.

She's got a stack of papers beside her on the floor, and she's holding a red pen over some pages in her lap. She's a terror with that pen. I've read some of her comments on student papers before, and the red might as well be blood for the wounds she inflicts. But it must work: her students write a hell of a lot better at the end of a semester than they do at the beginning.

She looks up when I come in the room. "Are you eating here tonight or over at J.D.'s?"

"At J.D.'s. He's got some pizza we can heat up."

She nods. For once she's looking at me like I'm actually in the room with her. "You guys are pretty inseparable these days."

I listen for disapproval in her voice but don't hear any. All of a sudden I wish I could tell her about what's really going on, but I don't know where to start so I just shrug.

She studies me as I sit down on the couch. There's a softness in her face I haven't seen in a long time. "I'm glad. He's a good kid."

"Yeah." I look at the floor. "I think so, too."

"I know."

She says it gently, and somehow with those two simple words I know for a fact she's already figured out exactly what's going on, and she's telling me it's okay. I glance up guardedly at her and she smiles, and the sweetness of it takes me so much by surprise that my throat closes for a minute and I have a hard time swallowing.

There are times I love her so much I can't stand it. I may bitch about her a lot, but whatever else she is, she is also this. I try to tell her how I feel, but no words come out. Is there anything harder than telling somebody how much they mean to you? So, of course, I can't, and I get up in a minute and tell her to have a good night and please get some sleep for once, and I'll be back first thing in the morning.

She's already got her head back in the papers when I walk out of the room.

How many parents could handle having a gay son or daughter without showing at least a twinge of disappointment or sadness? Especially if that son or daughter is their only kid? Let's face it: heterosexuality is the societal norm and most people can't stand being perceived as abnormal. I was watching some show on television recently where parents of gay kids were interviewed, and I couldn't help noticing that all of these folks, despite protestations of unconditional love and their kid's sexuality not making any difference, sounded a touch defiant, like a part of them knew that no matter what they said no one would believe them.

I've been trying to figure out why people get so freaked out about gays. Especially people who aren't religious. (I understand the objections fundamentalist Christians have; the Bible says homosexuality is wrong, so by God, it's wrong, no matter what— even if the same part of Leviticus that calls homosexuality a sin punishable by death also says it's a sin to wear two different fabrics of clothing at the same time or sleep with a woman while she's going through her period. Hell, there are places in the bible that endorse slavery, for God's sake, but apparently that's okay, let's just ignore anything inconvenient and embarrassing, shall we?)

I mean, what's the big deal? Some people use the argument that 'if everyone was gay the whole race would die out,' but come on, does anyone seriously think that's ever going to be a problem? Most men love women, most women love men, forever and ever, world without end, amen. Other people say the ass is made for shitting, not fucking, but if the sex magazines and talk shows I've seen are right, then there are a buttload of heterosexuals who get into anal sex, too. Why that's okay between a man and a woman and not between two men (or two women with a strap-on) has yet to be explained to me.

But as retarded as these arguments are, I prefer the jerk-offs who spout them to those who quietly disapprove of people like me without any justification. Most people don't even have reasons for opposing homosexuality. They just do. Because if it's not right for them, then it must not be right for anybody else, either. And by God let's make sure them fuckin' queers don't get too uppity and start thinking of themselves as normal human beings. (To be fair, I never really thought much about this stuff either before J.D. and I had sex. I guess some things have to slap you in the face before you'll deal with them.)

Anyway, all I'm saying is I'm pretty lucky to have the mother I have. Without a doubt, she'll piss me off royally tomorrow or the next day. But today, at least for this one nanosecond, she rocks my world.

J.D.'s family is gone when I get to his house. After he lets me in and closes the door he kisses me, but I can tell he's in a shitty mood.

"What's wrong?"

He turns away and leads me into the living room. "I just got home a few minutes ago. I was with Kristin."

"Did you dump her?"

He nods. We sit next to each other on the couch, and he takes one of my hands and starts to trace the lines on my palm with his finger. His hands are bigger than mine, and always a little sweaty. "She didn't take it too well."

"What'd she do?"

"She cried a lot at first, and she kept asking why." He lets go of my hand. "When I told her I wanted to be free to date other people she asked who."

"What'd you tell her?"

"I told her there was no one in particular right now." He lifts his legs onto the couch and hugs his knees to his chest. He's wearing jeans and white socks, and a preppy button-down shirt. I reach out and touch his hair and he leans into the touch. "When she heard that she started to get mad. She said it seemed stupid to break up if there was no one else I wanted to date. I told her that wasn't the point and that our relationship wasn't working for me and then she got really pissed. She said maybe it would work a lot better if I wasn't always with you."

His hair is short and soft and thick, and when I run my thumb through it I can see his scalp under the roots. He's so blond there's almost no difference in color between his scalp and his hair.

"I asked her what she meant by that and she said it was really weird how you and me were always together. She also said . . ." He trails off.

"She also said what?"

"She also said she thought you were a queer. She said anybody could see you were in love with me by the way you look at me."

"Oh." I guess Kristin's not as dumb as she looks. My heart starts pounding a little faster, but only a little. I'm kind of proud of myself for hearing something like this and not letting it upset me too much. "What'd you say?"

"I told her that was stupid because I knew you'd slept with a lot of girls. She said that didn't prove anything." He takes my hand out of his hair and holds it again in his lap. "We're going to have to be really careful."

I'm worried too, but I try and joke. "I'll make sure to leave my pink jockstrap at home."

"I'm not kidding, Noah. If anyone finds out, we're fucked."

"That's a little dramatic isn't it? It's not like we're living in Nazi Germany or something."

Neither of us says anything for a long time. It's kind of funny that Kristin would tell him I love him before he ever heard it from me, and even funnier that he already seems to know it. Maybe everyone in Oakland is psychic.

Dad never told Mom he loved her, at least not when I was around. I'm sure he must have when they were alone, but I never heard him say the words. Come to think of it, I don't remember him saying it to me, either. I know he loved us, though.

I remember one time when I was about nine or ten and Mom was sitting on my bed, reading to me. The book was either *A Tale of Two Cities* or *David Copperfield*—she was always stuffing my head with Dickens even before I knew most of the words. I remember leaning my head on her shoulder and watching the words as she read them; once in a while I'd point at one of them and demand to know what it meant. She was usually willing to explain, but that night I think I must have interrupted her about fifty times in five minutes and she'd about had enough.

"Just listen to the story, honey. You can get the gist of the words if you just listen."

"What's 'gist'?"

She sighed. "Do you want me to read to you or not?"

I grinned. "What does 'read' mean?"

She finally figured out I was fucking with her and she laughed. "You stinker." She elbowed me lightly in the stomach. "Just shut up and listen."

The floor creaked by the door and we both glanced up at the same time. Dad was standing there, watching us with a big smile on his face. I don't know how long he'd been there, but he looked like he was seeing the face of God.

Why would a poet marry a critic who hated her work? There's nothing more personal than what you write; if someone sees no worth in your poems, they sure as shit don't see any worth in you, either.

So was Nellie's marriage only about sex? That's hard to believe, considering the ghastly wedding photo Mom found. Nellie's cute enough, but I'd rather sleep with Elmer Fudd than with Stephen Carlisle. I guess he's not physically ugly, but by all accounts he had all the personal charm of a rabid rottweiler. Yet even if she did have the hots for him, how could she stand to wake up in bed day after day next to someone who didn't respect her? How could she deal with his contempt for her work? Could she have hated herself that much?

And how about him? How do you fuck someone you don't admire? I'm not being stupid; I know some guys will fuck anything with a hole in it. But how do they look at themselves in the mirror afterwards? How do you roll over in the morning and face someone you loathe? Call me old-fashioned, but like it or not, the body's connected to the soul. What you do to one, you do to the other.

I came across another of Nellie's poems in that collection:

Myopic

I am full of judgment
damning all I see—
I lavish scorn on everyone
and most of all on me.

Is this what makes a poet?
A distaste for the world?

The oyster is an eyesore
if the search is for the pearl.

I've got a theory. I think most people hate themselves. They may not know it, but they do. I have yet to meet a really secure human being; by secure I mean someone who doesn't need constant maintenance on his self-esteem, usually from outside sources. I know all the self-help books say we don't need other people's positive feedback to like ourselves, but that's bullshit. It's been my experience that self-love only becomes possible after receiving an inordinate amount of external validation, usually from a person who adores you. And that's a best-case scenario. I think instead most people get saddled with someone even more bogged down by self-loathing than they are themselves, and the relationship turns into an unconscious, morbidly dysfunctional, please-bring-your-own-nails crucifixion party.

So maybe that's why Nellie married Stephen. Maybe she didn't think she deserved any better. It's a half-assed assumption, but it's the best I can do.

I wake up Sunday morning in J.D.'s bed. He's still asleep, with one leg over my legs and his arm across my chest. His cheek is against my shoulder and he's snoring lightly, like a purring cat. I kiss him on the head but he doesn't wake up. I glance at the clock and see it's only eight-thirty; his folks aren't due back until this afternoon, and Mom's not expecting me home until lunch.

I can't remember ever being happier.

He helped me all day yesterday in the basement at our house, and even though Mom was back to hiding out in her room again for most of the day, we had a lot of fun and got a shitload done. The basement is almost completely finished, and the rest of the house should be done in a week or two. Mom seems to have given up on finding more jars, and she hasn't knocked a new hole in the wall or the floor for at least a week. It will be nice to be finished with everything, and maybe I can even get an after-school job or some-thing. J.D.'s says he's going to apply for work at the local grocery store and says I should try there, too.

How has this thing between him and me happened? What did I do to deserve this kind of miracle? I glance over at the bulletin board above his desk. Janis Joplin is still neighbors with Buddy Rich and Leo Tolstoy; Al Einstein still hovers over all of them, giv-ing me the raspberry with his tongue. But Kristin's school photo is gone, leaving a blank space. When did J.D. take that down?

I shift a little because one of my legs is going numb, and his cock and pubic hair press tighter against my hip. I turn a little more and in his sleep he rolls on top of me, just like I wanted him to, chest to chest, groin to groin. It's a perfect fit, like two hands pressed together in prayer, especially when he breathes in and his stomach pushes into mine. He's heavy and warm and I think I could stay like this for the rest of my life.

How in God's name did I ever sleep alone? Is this something my parents experienced? Did Mom used to lay next to Dad in the mornings and hold him while he slept? In some ways, I hope not, because if she did I don't know how she can bear not to have him next to her anymore. How do you give up something like this?

J.D. stirs against me and I think he's waking up, but then he set-tles down again. I stroke his back with my hands and stare at the ceiling, watching the sunlight play over the rough white paint. His skin is warm and his breath tickles my neck, and even though I try to stay awake so I can keep on feeling this good, I can't stop my eyes from closing any longer and I doze off.

We both wake up when we hear footsteps. The bedroom door swings open and Heather's standing there. The sheet only covers our legs and she can see way too much. Her eyes are enormous. I try to pull the sheet up but it's too late.

Her voice comes out as a squeak. "I got dropped off early."

"Get the hell out, Heather!" J.D. yells.

She covers her mouth with her hand and pulls the door shut

with a bang, then we hear her running down the hall. J.D. rolls off me and puts his hands over his face.

"Shit. Fuck." He slams his head into the pillow again and again. "Fuck! Goddamn son of a bitching fuck!"

That about says it all.

We get dressed in a frenzy and he tells me to go home for a while until he can talk to Heather and make sure she keeps her mouth shut. On the way to the front door we see her in the kitchen, holding the phone in her hand and whispering. J.D. runs over to get the phone away from her but he looks like someone who's just heard a click under his foot while walking through a minefield.

When I get home Mom is in the closet under the staircase. She's pulled out everything we've got stored in there—board games, puzzles, clothes, boxes of dishes—and she's ripping into the back wall with a hammer. She sees me looking in at her and stops for a second.

"It just occurred to me we haven't looked in here yet." She says it reasonably, as if it's a perfectly normal thing to pick up a hammer and tear up a wall that doesn't have anything wrong with it. She's already filthy, and she's blinking and coughing from all the dust.

"Great. Perfect. Good thinking, Mom." Predictably, my voice skirls up about four octaves. "In fact, let's get a bulldozer and do it right." I squeeze in beside her and yank the hammer out of her hand. There's barely enough room for both of us, and we have to crouch down to keep from hitting our heads on the underside of the staircase. I can't stand this any more. I start beating the shit out of the wall and lose track of how many times I hit it. I don't quit until Mom is shaking my shoulders and yelling into my face.

"Stop it, Noah!" Her fingers are digging into me and it hurts. "That's enough!"

I yell back at her. "Isn't this what you want? I've got a great idea. Why don't I play the whacko for a while and you can clean up after me! Doesn't that sound like a fun game?"

She lets go. "What on earth has gotten into you?"

I drop the hammer. "Nothing. Forget it. Do whatever you want."

The front doorbell rings and both of us step into the hallway as J.D. lets himself in. He stares at us for a second, then says he needs to talk in private. Mom asks if something is the matter and he tells her no. She knows he's lying, of course, but right now she's in Ahab mode and not interested in much else besides capturing the Great White Mason Jar, so she gives up on us and goes back in the closet. I lead J.D. into the kitchen, and before we step out the back door we hear more hammering behind us.

I sit on the cement steps outside and lean against the screen door, and J.D. sits beside me. His chin is trembling and his eyes are wet, but when I reach for him he shies away. I put my head against the door and close my eyes.

It's not even ten in the morning. Just a little while ago life was about as good as it gets. Now look.

He can't talk for a while. One tear after another runs down his face, and he keeps wiping his nose on his shirt sleeve. He finally swallows a couple times and tilts his head to look at me. "Heather called her friend Jenna and told her about us before I could stop her. Jenna is Perry White's little sister."

Perry. One of the cavemen in our gym class. Fabulous. Just fabulous. "Maybe she won't tell him." My hands start shaking and I can't stop them.

He snorts and some snot escapes onto his upper lip. "Yeah. And I believe in the Easter Bunny, too."

"What did Heather tell her?"

"Before I got the phone away from her I heard her saying she saw us naked."

I drop my head on my knees. "So what do we do? We can say she made it all up."

"It won't matter. No one will believe us." He sobs. "Christ. She'll tell my folks when they get home today."

I can't help it. I start to cry too. My stomach is in knots and I'm having trouble breathing. I keep my eyes closed but the tears leak out anyway and soak into my pants. "There has to be something we can do." The words come out muffled because I'm talking into my legs, so I lift my head. "Maybe we could . . ." I run out of steam and slump back against the door.

"We could run away." He says it bluntly, like it's our only option.

"Where would we go? And what would we do for money? Give head to homely old men on streetcorners?"

"Goddamnit, Noah. How the hell should I know?" He sounds more tired than mad. "But do you really want to stick around here and deal with this? Do you have any idea what's going to happen? Do you think people are going to walk up and congratulate us and buy us champagne and wish us good luck? Jesus." He's looking at me like I'm all ten of the stupidest people who ever lived. "We are so fucking screwed and all you can do is sit there and be a smartass."

I don't know what to say. He looks so scared and I want to tell him that everything will be all right, but I can't. He's right. Life just got supremely fucked up for both of us. I'm as scared about his parents and the assholes we'll have to deal with at school as he is. White's going to be a major problem, and as for Donna, she'll probably cut off my dick with a machete.

I take a few deep breaths and try to calm down but my heart is flopping around in my chest like a spastic fish. What can we do? Once the word gets out that we're sleeping together it will be open season on us all the time just like it is for Louis. Christ. My whole upper body starts shaking.

All of a sudden J.D.'s holding me. I wrap my arms around him so hard I'm surprised he doesn't snap in two, and I cry into his shirt. He's still crying, too; his breathing is ragged, and his face is wet on the back of my neck. It takes a long time to cry ourselves out, and even then we don't let go of each other. I listen to his heart and try not to think for a while.

The unmistakable yowl of a cat fight starts somewhere in the neighborhood; Hoover's probably kicking some other cat's ass. The noise builds to a deafening pitch and ends abruptly, as if someone turned a hose on them. It's completely silent for a while, then finally a few birds begin to chirp. A few minutes later I can hear some kids batting around a whiffle ball; even from down the street I can hear it humming through the air when somebody smacks the shit out of it.

J.D. clears his throat. "What are we going to do?"

"I don't know. Nothing, I guess." I lift my head to look at him. "What else can we do?"

"Mom will try to keep me away from you. She'll probably chain me to the radiator when she finds out." He sees the look on my face and kisses my forehead. "Don't worry. We'll think of something." Unbelievably, he starts to laugh.

"What?"

"It's stupid. I was just thinking of how I could sneak out to be with you, and that made me start to feel like Romeo or something. Then I started wondering which of us is Juliet."

I can't help but smile. "We're both Romeo. Juliet didn't have a penis."

"Says you." His smile fades. "I can't believe we're joking about this."

I finally let go of him and both of us lean against the door. I'm starting to feel a little better. Not much, but a little. The sun is warm on our faces, and the breeze is cool and clean, and in spite of everything, he's still sitting here next to me. "You're going to think I'm nuts, but in some ways I'm glad this happened."

"You're right," he says bleakly. "I think you're nuts."

I don't know how to explain it to him because I don't really understand it myself. But part of me feels relief. I don't know why. Maybe it's because I don't have to pretend anymore I'm something I'm not. I still feel like shitting my pants, but at least I can stop lying.

And besides, what's the worst that could happen?

I reach for his hand. "It's going to be all right." I'm almost as calm as I sound. "Everything will be okay."

J.D. gets a phone call mid-afternoon from his mom, telling him to come home immediately. I don't hear from him for the rest of the day, and when I try to call no one answers. Mom and I have a silent dinner together, the kind where the only sounds you hear are chewing noises and silverware clinking on plates. I ask her later if she unearthed anything new in her archaeological dig in the closet and all she does is shake her head. She waits a while then asks if anything is the matter between J.D. and me. I want to tell her but there's a clump of words caught in my throat that not even the Heimlich maneuver could dislodge. We go to bed early, but I can't sleep. I sit on my mattress with a sheet around my shoulders and stare at the walls, and sometime around one in the morning I hear her get up and pace through the house, her feet unsteady and slow on the floorboards in the hall and down the stairs.

The sky is thick with black clouds in the morning, and you don't have to be a meteorologist to know that rain is coming. I try to call J.D. again, but the line is busy, and when I walk by his house the shades are pulled and no one answers when I knock. When I get to the school I don't see him anywhere.

A few people say hello to me outside the building, just like normal. I guess news doesn't travel as fast as I thought it might. Melissa comes up and chirps good morning, and I can tell she hasn't heard anything yet. Maybe this won't be as big a deal as I thought.

Somebody shoves me from behind. "Hey, faggot."

I turn around and Perry and Lester are standing there in their letter jackets. Something in their faces scares me; no one has ever looked at me like they're looking at me. Perry steps close. "I hear you like to suck cocks, Noah. How about a blowjob before the bell rings?"

Lester guffaws. "Did you drive this morning? How was traffic on the Hershey Highway?"

"Leave him alone," Melissa says.

Perry glances at her. "Didn't you hear? Your boyfriend here and J.D. are buttfucking each other."

"I don't know what you're talking about." My voice is shaking.

Perry does his best fag imitation. "Oh, J.D. Bend over and let me ride you like a pony!" He leans over and points his butt at Lester. Lester eagerly complies and grinds his pelvis into Perry's ass. They both laugh like retarded hyenas.

Melissa's staring at me with a confused look on her face.

I force myself to keep my voice calm. "Wow. It looks like you guys have been practicing."

The smiles fall from their faces like the curtain at the end of the play, and Perry abruptly straightens and grabs the front of my shirt.

"If I were you, you fucking queer, I'd watch my mouth."

Melissa takes hold of his arm and yells at him to let go of me. He shoves hard and when I fall backward, she falls on top of me. Her white purse lands on the sidewalk next to my head and makes a noise like it's full of surgical instruments and marbles.

People are gathering around to watch. I see Paul and Riley in the crowd, and Scott the Grease-boy, and all of a sudden, Kristin. They're all gawking at Melissa and me like we're the main attraction in the freak show at the circus.

Perry raises his voice so they can all hear him. "Hey, everybody." He's enjoying himself. "You're all invited to J.D.'s and Noah's homo wedding. Bring your own condoms." He giggles.

Melissa and I get warily to our feet. Kristin's mouth is twisted like a cellophane wrapper on a gumball. Paul steps forward to help us, then gets an uncertain look on his face and stops. The bell rings and the mob starts to break up.

Perry backs off and grins at me. "See you in gym, cutie."

Melissa glares at their backs as they walk away. "Jerks." I head for the door and she grabs my arm. "Is it true? Are you and J.D. to-gether?"

I pull away without answering. It's starting to rain.

I finally see J.D. at lunch. He looks like shit. He's got a black eye and his cheeks are puffy and pale. When he sees me his lips tremble a little, but he makes room for me next to him. I'm sur-prised to see Paul and Riley eating with him, because by now I'm sure the whole fucking school has heard the story. They look un-comfortable when I sit down, but Paul says hi under his breath and Riley nods at me.

"Hey," I say.

"Hey." J.D.'s food is untouched on his tray. I'm sitting on his right and it's that eye that's black and swollen shut, so he has to turn his whole head to see me. "How are you?" he whispers.

"I'm okay." I want to touch him so badly and I can't. Not here. "Who did that to you?"

He doesn't answer, which means, of course, it was probably his mom. He picks up his fork and pushes some beanie weanies around on his plate. "Paul said you had a run-in with Perry and Lester this morning."

I shrug. "Yeah. We had an intellectual debate." I smile in spite of myself. "Melissa was on my team, and her closing argument was to fall on top of me. It made quite an impression."

Paul and Riley are listening to us and trying to act like every-thing is normal, but I can see they're having a rough time. They're probably trying to figure out if the rumors are true or not, but either way they're decent guys, I guess, to still be sitting with us, since anyone who hangs around with us now is suspect.

Kristin walks by, tailed by Melissa, and sits at another table, completely ignoring us. Melissa says hi and stands still for a minute, trying to decide where she should sit. She finally puts her tray down next to Kristin. J.D. looks at their backs for a second, then drops his gaze back to his plate.

Paul clears his throat. "Those assholes will be after you guys in the locker room today. Maybe you should go home sick or something."

J.D. shakes his head. "If we did that they'd just make up more shit about what we're doing when we're not in class. Things would be twice as bad tomorrow."

Riley lifts his head and looks at us directly for the first time since I sat down. "So it's all just bullshit, right?"

J.D.'s fingers tighten on his fork. "Of course it's bullshit. My little sister got mad at me and told all her little friends that Noah and I are homos, just to get even."

He lies well. I need to remember that. He looks straight at Paul and Riley, and keeps his eyes wide open, and manages to put just the right amount of indignation and fury into his voice. I don't blame him, I guess. How can I? I don't say anything, which makes me just as bad.

Riley looks relieved, like he just passed a kidney stone, but Paul's got a slight frown on his face as he studies us. He knows we're lying, and it makes me feel like shit.

This whole thing sucks. This is exactly the kind of crap I was going on about earlier. When a guy humps a girl, his buddies clap him on the back and God's in His heaven and the whole fucking world is just hunky-dory. But if a guy gets his rocks off with another guy, then let's pretend it never happened and beat the shit out of him just in case it did. Who gives a rat's ass about the truth or what's right and wrong? I can't stand it.

Riley says that he and Paul will stick close to us in the locker room in case there's any trouble. J.D. says thanks, but he doesn't think there'll be a problem after he tells Perry and Lester what really happened. I don't say a word. I chew my rancid beanie weanies and stare at the salt shaker, wishing I had enough balls to reach over and unzip J.D.'s fly right here in front of the whole goddamn cafeteria.

Maybe in the next life.

* * *

J.D. and I wait until the last possible moment to go into the locker room before gym class, so Perry, Lester and the two other football morons whose names I don't know are already dressed and out in the gym. It's a day of introductory gymnastics, which we start off by sitting in a circle on a wrestling mat while Mrs. Chapman explains how to do a back flip. When she's done yapping, we go up one by one, and she has the two biggest boys—Perry and Lester, of course—stand on either side of whoever's doing the flip and physically spin the poor bastard end over end to get the feel of it.

J.D.'s sitting a couple of bodies away from me, and it's my turn before his. Lester gets an evil little smile on his fat stupid face as I walk up to them. It's hot and I'm nervous and I'm sweating like a German housewife, and I know every kid in the room can see the dark patches under my arms and the wet spot on my ass where my shorts are sticking to me. Sure enough, some horse's rectum asks if I've pissed myself and several other mindless numbnuts titter their appreciation for this priceless witticism.

Then I'm standing between Perry and Lester, and Lester leans close to whisper in my ear. "Hey, faggot. It would be too bad, wouldn't it, if we dropped you on your head and snapped your little faggot neck."

Mrs. Chapman doesn't hear him, but she senses something is up. She frowns and tells them to be careful, and she tells me to just bend my knees and relax. J.D. is sitting upright, his lips pressed together, watching. Each of them puts a hand on one of my arms and his other hand on one of my legs, and Lester digs his fingers into my bicep and thigh so hard I wince. Perry counts one, two, three (I have to fight the urge to tell him I didn't know he could do that without stamping his foot on the floor), then I'm spinning through the air, landing awkwardly and tumbling backward with the force of all my weight and all their strength. I sprawl on my tailbone and the air gets knocked out of me with an audible whoof. Perry and

Lester guffaw like baboons, and Mrs. Chapman yells at them for being too rough. She asks if I'm okay and Perry gives me the finger while her back is turned to him.

As soon as I get into the locker room after class and begin to undress, Perry starts in on both J.D. and me.

"Hey, Curtis. I've always heard that fags like violent sex. Is that how you got that black eye?"

"Good job, Noah," Lester lisps. "Did you spank him afterward, too?"

J.D. is standing next to his locker. He's got one shoe and a sock off and something about that single bare foot makes him look more vulnerable than I've ever seen him. He ignores Lester and turns to the marginally smarter Perry. "Fuck off, Perry. My little sister lied to your sister about Noah and me to get even for something I did to her."

Perry snorts. He's got his shirt off by now and he struts toward us, swinging it lazily at his side. His pale body has a dull shine. "Bullshit. If you're not queer, why are you hanging out with York all the time? Anybody can tell he loves to suck cocks." He winks at me. "Isn't that so, sweetie? You're probably getting a hard-on just hearing me talk about it." He winds the sweat-soaked shirt up and snaps my bare stomach with it, and he grins when I cry out. A red welt blossoms on my skin.

"Leave him alone." J.D. steps between us. "He isn't gay."

Lester and the other two assholes immediately come up behind Perry. He winds the shirt up again. "Isn't this sweet?" he says over his shoulder. "J.D.'s protecting his little lover."

J.D.'s hands are balled into fists. "Are you deaf or just stupid? I told you he isn't queer."

Suddenly Paul and Riley are beside J.D. The smile leaves Perry's face. "So you two are homos, too?"

No one says anything, no one moves. The door bangs open and the football coach, Bubba (I'm not kidding) Ellis, waddles into the room on his way to the toilet. He eyes the eight of us until Perry and his goons back off. Perry makes a kissie face at me, and says he'll see me soon. The coach takes a piss then comes to stand by the showers until we're all finished and dressed and the bell rings for the next class.

J.D. meets me outside of Otis's classroom right after school. Scott the Grease-boy nods at us as he walks by; Shannon the Dimple-girl waves at me like I'm her long-lost twin. Some of the other kids smirk when they see us together, but no one says anything.

"Come on," J.D. says. "Let's get the hell out of here." He takes off down the stairs like there's a doberman at his heels.

I run after him. "What's your hurry?"

He stops at the front door and looks before going outside. "There's no football practice today."

I feel like throwing up. I thought Perry White and his fun-loving friends wouldn't be a problem after school because they're always in practice at this time. "How come?"

"Coach Ellis had to go to a funeral or something. Didn't you hear the announcement?"

I didn't. The yard in front of the building still has a lot of people milling around on it, so we go on out and walk as fast as we can down the street. Kristin and Melissa drive by and J.D. tries to flag them down for a ride, but Kristin doesn't even look at him.

We keep going without saying anything. J.D.'s face is expressionless except for the tears in his eyes. I know we should talk, but I'm just concentrating on getting home and forgetting this miserable fucking day, and besides, I don't have much to say.

He swallows hard a couple of times. "God. What a shithole of a day."

"Yeah." I take another couple of steps then stop. There are puddles everywhere from the rain this morning. "Just imagine how bad it would have been if we really were gay."

He flushes. "What did you expect me to say? You're the one they seem to be after. I thought maybe I could stop them."

"You said it yourself yesterday. People are going to believe we're lovers no matter what. So what's the point in lying?" I start walking again. "We're not doing anything wrong. We shouldn't act like we are."

He laughs like I'm a little kid that just said the stupidest thing he's ever heard. "What planet are you from? This isn't some liberal rich kid suburb in Chicago where homos are everywhere you turn. This is Bumfuck, New Hampshire."

Before I can answer, a Plymouth Fury from the Stone Age screeches up next to us. We gape at each other as the doors pop open. Fabulous. Just fucking fabulous. It's White and his three braindead buddies. They pile out of the car and come running.

J.D. grabs my arm and we tear off town the street, but within a few steps one of them tackles me. My books go flying and my right elbow smashes into the sidewalk, tearing the skin. I bite my tongue and taste blood in my mouth. When I look up J.D. is kicking who-ever's on top of me, but then I see Perry hit him in the side of the head and he starts to fall. Lester and another kid catch him from behind and hold him while Perry hits him again and again, in the face and stomach. Mostly in the face. His nose disappears behind a red smear, and something in me snaps. The bastard on top of me is hitting me, too, but I scream and twist and finally manage to jab a finger into his eye. He rolls off, howling, and I jump to my feet and land on Perry's back. He tries to throw me off but I get a hand in his hair and yank as hard as I can. A fistful comes loose in my palm and there's blood all over his scalp.

"Get him off me, goddamnit!" he bellows, and before anyone can get to me I grab his cheek and dig my fingernails in with a strength I didn't know I had. I feel his flesh give way. He starts screaming and falls to his knees. Lester drags me off, holds me by the collar and hits me in the face three times before he lets me fall.

One of my eyes is stuck shut, but with the other I see J.D. lying next to me and they're still kicking him. I hear a siren and then I see a foot coming at my face.

"Don't move, son." I cry out when a hand lightly touches my face. "It's all right. There's an ambulance on the way."

I open the eye that works and see Officer Ganski kneeling next to me. It's starting to rain again and the drops sting when they hit my skin. I try to talk but nothing comes out except a croak. I lift my head frantically and try to look around.

"Lie still," he says. "You'll be okay. Your friend will be, too. He's right here. But both of you need to go to the hospital and get fixed up." He takes my hand and gives it a squeeze, and suddenly I can barely see at all because my good eye fills with tears. He looks away, embarrassed. "They ran off but we'll get the punks who did this to you. Someone across the road saw the whole thing and called 911." He studies me carefully. "You're the York boy, right? I met you a few weeks ago."

I nod. He nods back. "I thought so. I'll find your mom as soon as the paramedics get here."

I must look bad. In spite of what he said he looks worried. I wish I could talk. I wish I could tell him not to worry. I hurt all over, but I'm still here, and so, apparently, is J.D. They did the thing we were most scared of, but we're still here. When Ganski drops my hand I hold it up and flex my fingers. They're sticky with Perry's blood, and I feel enormously pleased with myself because that son of a bitch will carry scars for the rest of his life for what he did today. Maybe I shouldn't be glad I hurt another human being, but I can't make myself feel sorry when I don't. Fuck him.

I may be just a faggot, but this faggot has some claws. It's good to know.

CHAPTER SIX

I wake up in the hospital with Mom sitting next to my bed. She looks truly awful, but she tries to smile when she sees I'm awake. I've got some kind of bandage over my left eye.

"Noah." She gets up and kisses my forehead. I can smell coffee and cigarettes on her breath.

"Cigarettes?" My voice sounds like my throat's been scraped raw. "Since when do you smoke?"

"Ever since my son's been in the hospital." She pushes the hair off my forehead. "I used to smoke a long time ago, before I met your dad. I didn't think I'd ever want another one but as soon as I saw you lying here it was like I never quit." She drops her hand. "You've been asleep for almost two days."

If she thinks I'm going to live with a smoker she's out of her goddamn mind. "Where's J.D.? Is he okay?"

"Stay still. He's going to be fine. They released him yesterday but they wanted to keep you here for observation." She straightens and walks to the window. "He looks terrible, but the worst that happened to him is a broken nose and some bruised ribs. He'll heal."

I'm so relieved I can't talk for a minute, but eventually something occurs to me. "So what's wrong? Why am I still here?"

Her back is to me. "Your eye may be permanently damaged. They're waiting for the swelling around it to go down to see if they need to do surgery or not."

"Oh." I reach up to feel the bandage. "Oh."

It's silent for a long time, then she finally turns around. Her face is bright red and her jaw muscles are clenched like a fist. "If you lose your eye, I'll kill those little fuckers, Noah. I swear to God."

It might be worth an eye to see that. "What happened to them?"

"They were arrested but they're all out on bail except for the one you got hold of. He's here in the hospital somewhere recovering from plastic surgery. For some reason they won't tell me which room he's in." She smiles grimly. "Next time don't just tear off his face. Tear off his whole goddamn head."

"I tried my hardest." I'm really tired all of a sudden. "Has J.D. been in to see me?"

She shakes her head. "No. I stopped by his house this morning to see how he was but Donna told me to get the hell off her property or she'd call the cops."

I'm not surprised. The stupid bitch probably beat him up again for not getting beaten up in a way she approved of. "What else did she say?"

She purses her lips. "A lot of very unpleasant things. Our conversation ended with her slamming the door in my face."

I shift my head so I can see her better. "You know why we got jumped, don't you?"

"Yes." She comes and sits on the bed and her face softens a little. "I'm so sorry, Noah. I wish . . . I don't know what I wish. I've been wondering for years who you'd first fall in love with." She picks up my hand. "I know that first loves are notoriously difficult, but this seems a little extreme, even for you." She looks at me closely. "You do love him?"

I nod and manage a feeble grin. "So much that it feels like I've been kicked in the head."

She grimaces. "I'd always hoped a good beating would improve your sense of humor. I guess not." She squeezes my hand and I squeeze back.

The door opens and Officer Ganski comes in. He's getting fatter by the second.

Mom manages to smile warmly. "Look who's here. The Seventh Cavalry."

The Seventh Cavalry should cut back on the donuts, I almost say, but then I remember how nice he was and how he probably saved J.D. and me from much worse than we got.

He asks me how I'm doing and stays to chat for a minute, and then, unbelievably, starts to flirt with Mom. Jesus Christ. Apparently they've gotten to know each other over the last couple of days. I tell them I should probably get some sleep, and they both go out in the hall.

My whole body hurts. Especially my head. They've got me on some kind of pain killer but it's not helping much. I asked the nurse for a morphine drip but she thought I was joking.

I'm not too good with pain. Some people seem not to mind it much, but I don't do so well. I can't think of anything except what hurts, and all I can do is lie here and fixate on what part of my body is throbbing the most. I try to watch television for distraction but soap operas and game shows are my only choices, so I eventually get tired of flipping channels and turn the damn thing off.

Mom finally went home for a few hours to get some sleep. I made her promise not to smoke anymore and I was surprised when she didn't argue with me. She even took the pack out of her purse and tossed it in the trash before she left. She said she wasn't addicted; she'd just needed something to do to keep from going crazy while she was waiting for me to wake up. I told her she should have tried a crossword puzzle or a game of solitaire instead because the last I'd heard neither of those made your breath stink or gave you cancer. She got a little pissy and told me I was a lot more pleasant to be around when I was unconscious.

She left me a book to read *(The Farthest Shore,* by Ursula Le-Guin, one of my all-time favorite fantasy novels) but I haven't even tried because my head hurts too much and reading with one eye out of commission doesn't sound appealing. But after another hour of trying to sleep, I get bored and restless enough to give it a shot.

You'd think I'd get tired of the story after reading it so many times, but I never do. It's about this old wizard and a kid my age chasing down an evil freak who's destroying the world. I don't know why I like it so much. I mean, the writing's great and I get off on all the magic and dragons and shit, but I think maybe the real appeal of the thing is the relationship between the two main characters. The old guy and the kid piss each other off now and then, but in spite of their age difference they basically treat each other with love and respect, as equals. Now that's what I call a fantasy.

I prop my pillows up behind me and try to get comfortable, but just when I start to read, there's a knock on the door. It's Donna Fucking Curtis. What the hell does she want?

"Come in," I tell her.

"I won't be staying." She stands in the doorway and studies me, her eyes taking in the bandages and the hospital gown. She's wearing a red raincoat, and she's got the ugliest purse I've ever seen, a white corduroy thing with green and blue beads she holds in front of her like a chicken she's getting ready to behead. "I just came to tell you to stay away from my son." Her voice is dry and cold.

I can't believe this woman. I'm half-blind in a hospital bed and my head feels as if someone's squeezing it like a tube of toothpaste and she's actually threatening me. I put the book down on my stomach and I make my voice offensively pleasant. "Hello to you too, Mrs. Curtis. Nice weather we're having isn't it? That's a lovely purse. Did you make it yourself or did you find it at a garage sale?"

She looks mad enough to shit a fireball, but she pivots neatly and leaves without another word. I stare after her for a long time.

"Thanks for stopping by," I mutter.

*   *   *

My eye's okay. The whatchacallit got something or othered, but it's going to be fine without surgery. My vision will be blurry for a while and I'm supposed to use these eyedrops that make me feel like I'm squirting hydrochloric acid directly into my pupil, but there's no permanent damage. On the drive home Mom tells me she's got a surprise waiting for me but she won't tell me what it is. I get excited because maybe she found a way to sneak J.D. over to our place.

We pull up in the driveway and I hobble as fast as I can to the front door. I turn the knob and charge in, expecting him to be standing in the foyer. It's empty. I stop still and Mom accidentally collides into me from behind.

I can't believe it. I just can't fucking believe it. There are several new holes in every wall I can see. I stop counting at eleven. There are piles of debris under each hole, and the air is thick with heavy white dust. Welcome home.

I turn around and raise both my hands in a *What the hell?* gesture, and Mom stares around at the mess like she's as perplexed as I am.

She smoothes her blouse nervously. "I guess it does look kind of bad. But wait till you see what I found."

She scampers up the stairs like a deer with a firecracker up its ass. I hear her run down the hall to her bedroom, then she comes pelting back down the stairs. In her hands she's got another mason jar. She holds it out to me like she's Oliver Twist asking for more gruel.

I should have stayed in the hospital. "Just one jar? You did all this for one jar? Goddamnit, Mom, are you nuts?"

Her face flicks through emotions like it was one of those kid's books you fan with your thumb to create an illusion of a moving picture. I see anger and disappointment and sadness before it settles on impatience. "Just look. I'll clean everything up later."

I take it from her and open it. There's a single stiff sheet of paper inside, folded twice to make it fit, and the creases make it hard to read. I scan it once, and then, against my will because I shouldn't give a shit, read it more carefully.

It's a birth certificate, saying that Maria Louise Carlisle was born on January 21, 1953, and that her parents are Stephen Wesley Carlisle and Nellie Mitchell Carlisle. I look up and stare at Mom. "Okay. So they had a baby. Was finding that out worth trashing our house?"

"There's more. Look where the baby was born."

I read again. " 'St. Luke's Hospital in Boston.' So?"

"So I've been asking myself why they went to Boston to have the baby when there are any number of hospitals closer."

"Maybe they were sightseeing at Old North or something. Maybe one of them had a Paul Revere fetish. Maybe they didn't trust the local doctors."

She shakes her head. "I don't think so. I've been hunting for any other record of this person and can't find anything. No court records, no school records, nothing. Not even a death certificate or an obituary or any evidence at all that she was put up for adoption. That piece of paper is the only proof that my little girl ever existed."

"Your little girl?"

She looks away. "I mean their little girl."

Something in her voice chills me. I study her but she won't meet my gaze. "We also have the picture," I tell her.

"Yes. And it was taken in this house. So if the baby in the picture is the same baby, we know they brought her home."

"And then what?"

She takes everything back and puts the certificate in the jar. "Let's get you some food and put you to bed. The doctor said you still need lots of sleep."

The phone rings sometime in the afternoon and wakes me from a nap. I wait for Mom to answer it, but when it keeps ringing I roll out of bed and stumble down the hall. I'm still a little dizzy. I get to the phone and say hello.

"Noah? Are you all right?" It's J.D. He's whispering.

I can't talk for a second. I guess I didn't realize how worried I've been about him. "I am now. I thought your mom may have put a stake through your heart, or something."

"Just about." There's a long pause. "She won't let me come see you. She told me if I leave the house or try to talk to you that she'll pack my bags and send me off to military school or something."

"I figured." My heart's doing weird things in my chest. It feels like one of those oxygen bags they hook up to people in intensive care, filling and emptying, filling and emptying. "Are you okay? The last time I saw you, you didn't look so good."

"You weren't so pretty yourself." He makes an odd noise, like he's got something caught in his throat. "It's good to hear your voice." And then, choking on the words, he tells me he loves me.

Neither of us can talk for what feels like an hour. I swallow a few times and manage to grunt out how much I miss him. He grunts back.

Goddamn his mom. The words spill out of me. "J.D., come live with us. Your mom acts like she doesn't want you living with her, anyway."

He starts crying audibly. "Do you think I haven't thought about it? She'd be glad to get rid of me, but there's no way she'd let me live with you."

"Why not?"

"Because I want to."

I hear Donna's voice calling for him in the background. "I gotta go." He hangs up.

I went to a music camp once in Virginia. The resident artists were from some hotshot brass quintet out of New York, but in spite of that they were also really nice people. If you don't play an instrument, you might not know how rare that is. Virtuosos are usually the biggest pricks you'll ever meet, with egos the size of Canada and personalities like sandpaper. But these guys were still human beings.

The camp was on the grounds of some remote rural college, and it was mid-July. Virginia in July is pretty fucking muggy, and every time I stepped outside, my clothes immediately soaked through with sweat, even at night. One evening after rehearsal, some of the other kids and I went for a walk with the french horn player and the trombonist from the quintet, and all of us ended up sitting on the bleachers by the football field. It was dark, and quiet, and we talked and passed around a bottle of whiskey the trombonist had with him, and we gawked at the stars like we were looking through the window of some giant mansion where there was a huge party going on none of us were invited to.

Voices in the dark, whiskey burning in our throats, shirts sticking to our backs. Subdued laughter, wild talk, easy conversation about simple stuff like music and life. I'd never felt so grown-up, so welcome in adult company, and I could tell from the quality of the other kids' voices they felt the same. It was one of those times when you feel like you've arrived, like you've finally figured out what life is supposed to be about.

We found out later that both the trombonist and the french horn player were gay, and we all acted appropriately horrified. After all, God only knows what those perverts were thinking about us. And, Holy Mother of All That's Good and True, our lips had touched the same bottle as theirs did. We all felt like puking.

What assholes we were, every one of us. Decent human beings and perfect summer nights don't come along all that often. Only an ingrate or a retard shits on a good memory.

Mom brings home my homework assignments so I won't get too far behind, and she says that the principal, Jack Warner, told her when she was at the school that J.D. and I probably shouldn't come back for another week or so. He said the school board had already brought in some counselor to do a workshop on tolerance, but he wanted a few more days to let things cool down. I guess quite a few people are pretty bent out of shape about this—some are pissed at the Fab Four for beating us up and some, of course, are pissed that J.D. and I weren't killed and can't believe that the police actually think Perry and his buddies broke the law and should be punished.

I'm reading a book on the couch in the living room and she leans against the door while she talks to me.

"I also spoke to your English teacher, Mr. Otis. It seems I turned down his request to speak to your writing class." She raises an eyebrow at me. "He asked me to reconsider."

Fuck. "What'd you tell him?"

"That I'd be glad to, and that my poor addled son must have somehow thought he'd asked me when in reality he hadn't."

"Thanks a lot, Mom. Now he knows I lied to him."

"Don't blame me for lying and getting caught. If you had asked me in the first place and told me you didn't want me to speak to your class, I wouldn't have come."

Yeah, whatever.

She leaves me alone and after a while I go upstairs to take a shower. I undress and study myself in the mirror. The eye that got hurt is pretty nasty. It's an angry red mess, with a bunch of crusty stuff at the corners. My other eye is black and blue. There are scratches and bruises all over my face and neck and upper body, and fingerprint marks on my throat from where Lester held me while pulverizing my face. I guess I'm lucky my nose wasn't broken and all my teeth are still in my head.

I get in the shower and let hot water run over me and try to figure out how I can get past Donna to see J.D. She'll call the cops if I just show up on the doorstep. Maybe I can wait until dark and then throw rocks at his window. Yeah. Great idea. When she hears me she'll beat me to death with a skillet on the front lawn.

Every part of me aches. I groan a little when I bend over to turn off the water, and I groan some more when I reach up to push the curtain aside.

"You sound like an old man." J.D.'s sitting on the toilet with the lid closed, grinning at me. I'm so startled I nearly fall down, then I bang my knee on the side of the tub in my rush to get to him. He pulls me onto his lap and puts his arms around me like I'm a small animal he's afraid of crushing. I bury my face in his shoulder for a second then pull back to look at him.

He looks a lot worse than me. His face is swollen, and he can barely open either eye. There's a vivid black bruise with flecks of gold in it running all the way from his left temple down to his chin, and his lips are puffy and sliced like he's been kissing the edge of a sharp knife.

He studies me as carefully as I study him. "Jesus," he whispers. "And I thought I looked bad."

"You do." I reach up to touch the bruise and he flinches. "Sorry."

"It's okay. Just hurts some." He kisses my neck and laughs a little. "You're getting me all wet."

His hair smells like papaya and coconut, so of course my penis lifts its head and starts to sniff the air, completely oblivious to how gross both of us look. J.D. stares down at it, then drops one of his hands from my waist to touch it. "Hmm . . ." he says. "You seem to be naked."

"Yeah, I take my clothes off when I shower. I'm weird that way."

He takes a shaky breath, then moves his hand back to my waist. "Maybe we shouldn't. We're both pretty sore."

I nod. "And Mom might hear us."

"She's not here. When she let me in she told me she had to go up to the college for a while." His hand returns to what it was doing a second ago, like it's got a mind of its own. I shift my weight to get more comfortable and we both watch his fingers while he talks.

"She gave me a kiss on the forehead when she saw me. That was sweet."

"I can't believe I didn't hear you come in." I unbutton the top part of his shirt and rest my hand on his chest. His heartbeat changes from a trot to a gallop. "How'd you get away from Demon Donna?"

"I snuck out."

"Shit." I start to rock back and forth and the toilet seat creaks a little in protest. My voice comes out husky. "What if she catches you?"

He shrugs. "I don't care. I had to see you."

"She might send you away."

"Let her try."

"But what about . . ."

"Shh." He kisses me on the lips and we both wince from the pain of it. His hand speeds up and slows down, speeds up and slows down, and it goes on forever and finally I can't stand it any more and I cry out and make a mess.

He cradles me as I collapse against him, and he rubs my back with his free hand. "Oops," he says, after a while. "I guess we need another shower."

I shake my head and feel my hair brush against his chin. "Not just yet."

Donna shows up on the front porch in a while and J.D. and I answer the door together. Her skin is splotchy and her eyes are bugging out, and her shoulders are so tense they're almost touching her ears.

"You're coming home right now," she says to J.D.

He shakes his head and takes my hand. "No, I'm not."

She looks at our hands clasped together and she starts to tremble. "Come home now, or don't come home again."

J.D. swallows hard. "Like you care one way or the other. You only came to get me because you're worried I might be happy here and that makes you sick to your stomach."

She lowers her voice. "I could call the police and have them bring you home."

"Why? You don't want me there."

"Don't be ridiculous."

"I'm not. You hate me. I don't know why, but you do."

There are some conversations not even a lover should be part of. I try to pull away but he's gripping me tightly, so I stay still.

Donna blinks but her face stays hard and cold. "That's absurd. I'm your mother. I want you home because this . . ." she gestures at me, "this is sick. Everyone in town is laughing at your father and me."

"Let them laugh. I don't care. Noah's mom is okay with it."

She smiles bitterly. "I'm not surprised. I'm sure she encouraged you. She's probably a lesbian herself. I'm told the disease runs in families."

"So who did J.D. get it from?" I blurt out. "You or Tom?"

J.D. flinches but stays silent.

Donna pales and raises her hand like she's going to hit me, then slowly controls herself and drops it. "Neither of us, I'm afraid."

What the hell does that mean?

She turns back to J.D. "Fine. If this is what you want, then don't bother coming home. I'll have your father bring over your things. When you and your little boyfriend have a falling out, don't blame me when you have no place to stay."

She turns and goes down the steps and across the lawn, and J.D. stares after her blankly, like someone just asked him the square root of a six-digit number. I hug him, but he keeps staring over my shoulder at her retreating back. "I guess that's that," he murmurs in my ear.

When Mom gets home we try to tell her what happened with Donna. We're both tongue-tied and stuttering like a couple of harelips in an ESL course, but we eventually get the story out. Mom listens without saying anything, then sits at the island and tugs her hair for a while in silence.

She glances up at J.D. Her eyes linger on the bruises and cuts, his blond hair and blue eyes. "Are you sure your parents won't let you come back?"

"I'm sure." He says it flatly, without emphasis, and the words just hang there like limp socks on a clothesline.

She chews her lip. "It's probably not the healthiest thing for you boys to live together. Isn't there someone else you can move in with? Grandparents?" Her hair is getting a knot in it from all the twisting. "This isn't really a good time for this. And besides, our house is a mess."

I roll my eyes. "I wonder how that happened."

J.D. pinches my arm hard. "Please shut up, Noah. Just for once." He turns to Mom. "There's no one else, Mrs. York. My mom will make sure no one in my family will take me in, and even if they did, none of them live in town."

She sighs. "And of course leaving town is out of the question?"

I sit across from her. "I don't want this to sound like a threat or anything, but if he goes, I'm going with him."

Her mouth twitches. "God, that's tempting." She rubs her eyes with her fists and gazes at me balefully. "What a pain in the ass you are."

She puts up a feeble resistance, but in the end she lets him stay. We all knew she would. She says she'll expect him to help with the house and to do his schoolwork, and she thinks both of us should get a job to help with the bills. She asks if J.D. wants his own room or if he'll be sleeping with me and both of us blush. Talking about this stuff openly is going to take some getting used to, I guess.

There's a scratching sound coming from the basement door and when I open the door Hoover jumps out of the dark and runs past me like I'm the angel of death. "Hey, moron. How long have you

been trapped down there?" He ignores me and makes a beeline for
J.D. We're all grateful for the distraction.

J.D. leans over to pet him. "What's he got in his mouth?"

On cue, Hoover lets go of whatever he brought with him and it
falls on the linoleum floor with a light click. J.D. picks it up and we
all stare at it.

It's a tiny bone, the size of a baby's finger.

Something's wrong with Mom. Seriously wrong. We're all in
the basement trying to find where Hoover found the bone, and
Mom's looking around wildly and trembling like she's got the flu.
All the lights are on, plus she's got a flashlight she's using to poke
into every shadow. I'm a little on edge, too, I guess; you don't
spend every day hunting for bones in the basement.

What's bugging me is that I know every square inch of this
place, and I don't have a clue where to look. The new linoleum and
carpet are untouched, and the paneling J.D. and I finished together
is intact and shows no sign of cat claws.

Mom's rooting around in the corner by the staircase in a pile of
paint cans. Her hands are shaking as she pushes the cans around.
"Where else could he have gotten it?" She gives up and stares at
me intently. "Have you seen anything while you were working
down here?"

"I probably would have mentioned finding a carcass."

"What about under the stairs?"

"All three of us looked. There's nothing there."

J.D. wanders over to the corner of the room by the water heater
and the furnace, but I'm sure nothing's there either, because the
floor in that part of the room is solid concrete.

I lean against the wall. "Maybe he found it outside someplace.
Under the front porch, maybe? He could have brought it in a while
ago and hid it someplace until tonight."

"Maybe." She twists the chain of the locket on her neck over
and over, and it gets so tight it starts to poke into her skin.

"Or maybe he found an unattended baby on a neighbor's porch and got hungry. Maybe he's sick of Meow Mix."

"Noah!" Both Mom and J.D. yell it at the same time and in exactly the same tone of voice. They stare at each other comically, then turn to glare at me. "That's not funny," Mom finishes lamely.

J.D. gets down on his knees by the furnace and asks Mom for the flashlight. She takes it over to him and I wander over to see what he's messing with.

The furnace is an old monster, a rusty, heavy, oil burner that's probably solely responsible for global warming. We haven't turned it on yet this year, and even though the realtor said it was fine, Mom's afraid we're going to have to buy a new one before winter. J.D.'s shining the light near the base of it and I finally see what caught his attention. There's a six-inch patch between the furnace and the wall where the concrete has cracked and turned to rubble, and underneath the crumbled cement is a dirt hole several inches deep. J.D. moves some of the debris out of the hole and reaches his fingers into the dirt. Mom and I watch without saying anything, but Mom's breathing sounds loud and strained.

"There's something here," J.D. whispers. He looks up at us, and the expression on his face makes my flesh crawl.

The front doorbell rings; we can hear it echoing through the house. J.D. jumps a little and bangs his head on a pipe.

Mom doesn't even glance at me. "Go get that, will you Noah?" Her voice sounds strained, disconnected.

I start to argue but J.D., watching her, speaks up. "Go on. It'll take a while to dig out whatever's here, anyway."

I nod and charge up the stairs.

It's J.D.'s dad. He's holding a big box in his arms, balancing it against his beer gut.

"Hi, Noah," he says quietly. Remarkably, he looks sober. "Is my son here?"

"He's downstairs. Do you want me to get him?"

"Please." He asks where he should put the box and I tell him to come in and set it on the floor. I ask if he wants to sit down and he says no.

J.D. comes upstairs when I yell for him. He's got cobwebs in his hair and his fingers are dirty, and he looks excited. He starts to say something and then he sees Tom. They stare at each other.

"Hi." Tom gestures at the box. "I brought your stuff."

"Thanks."

They just stand there. I excuse myself and head for the basement, but J.D. grabs my arm as I go by and asks me to stay.

Tom objects. "This is kind of private. No offense, Noah." He says it quietly, without heat, and he even smiles a little at me. Weird.

I try to pull away and leave them alone, but J.D. won't let me. "I want him here."

Tom frowns but there's no anger in it. Just sadness. "If you want. Can we sit on the porch?"

We follow him out. He sits on the wooden railing, and even though it's sturdy it creaks a little under his weight. J.D. and I sit in the porch swing facing him. Before anyone says anything J.D. pulls his legs up to his chest protectively and the swing rocks slowly in response.

Tom looks around the porch like he's trying to avoid looking directly at us. "Nice night," he mumbles.

J.D. just stares at him, waiting, but Tom doesn't say anything else. A minute passes, then another. We all hear a couple of muffled pops coming from the basement, like someone's throwing a baseball against the wall or something. "What do you want, Dad?" J.D. blurts out. "We're helping Noah's mom with something."

I don't know why, but I want to tell him to go gently. Something's strange.

Tom clears his throat and looks at him. There's enough moonlight to see that his eyes are full of tears. J.D. swallows hard and shuts up. Tom blinks rapidly and uses his sleeve to wipe his face.

"I told your mom she was wrong to kick you out." His voice sounds muffled, like he's talking through a blanket. "She can be a little headstrong, sometimes."

J.D. snorts. It's the most eloquent snort I've ever heard.

Tom's mouth twitches a little with bitter amusement. "All right. She can be a world-class bitch. Is that what you want to hear?"

J.D. doesn't answer.

Tom pauses again. A breeze blows across the porch and messes up his hair; a bald patch gets exposed for a second and then a few strands fall back in place over it. I can hear some creature stirring in the rosebushes beside the house, and the swing squawks when J.D. shifts closer to me.

When Tom starts to talk again the words get snagged in his throat every few syllables, like leaves floating on a river full of roots and branches. "There's a reason she is like she is . . . Something happened to her a long time ago she wouldn't want you to know about . . . I know it seems like she hates you but it isn't you . . . It's this thing and it's not your fault and she knows that but she can't help it . . . It's gotten harder since you got older . . . She does love you but you remind her of . . . And you know how she feels about this . . . gay stuff . . . so put the two together and . . ." He sputters into silence.

J.D. drops his legs off the swing and sits with his hands clasped tightly in his lap. "What are you talking about, Dad? What happened to her?"

I shouldn't be here. I stand up abruptly and tell him I'll be inside if he needs me, and this time he doesn't try to stop me. Tom looks at me gratefully, and even though I think he's a fat pile of shit for letting Donna treat J.D. like she does, I can't help but smile at him reassuringly. At least he's trying, which is more than I can say for the troll he married. Still, it kind of pisses me off that he's here trying to make J.D. feel sorry for her. No matter what might have happened to her, what gives her the right to be such a loser?

I go back inside and have to force myself to walk away from the open door so I can't hear what they're saying. Then all of a sudden I remember Mom, and run down to the basement to see what she's found.

Jesus, what a night. She's sitting on the floor with her face in her hands and she's sobbing. I've never heard her cry like that, not once in seventeen years. I walk up to her slowly.

"Mom?"

She doesn't hear me. I can see she's been pounding on the cement with a hammer to make a bigger hole by the furnace. On the floor in front of her is a dirty rag, piled high with small, slightly yellow bones. There's part of a rib cage, and a spine that's only a few inches long, and there's a little skull, too, about the size of my fist, grinning up at us.

The rag was probably a man's white dress shirt, but now it's almost brown from the soil, and riddled with holes. The front of it is still neatly buttoned, though, and the collar has somehow managed to keep its shape, as if somebody took it fresh from the closet before burying it in the ground. It looks like one of those horribly uncomfortable, insanely over-starched things only old men wear. The sleeves are close together and twisted at the wrists; Mom must have had to untie them to open the bundle.

The shroud, I mean. That's what it is, I guess. A shroud. I've been trying not to look at the bones, but now I make myself.

The skull is the worst of it. It looks fragile enough to crush without even trying, and there are dark shadows in the eye sockets. Involuntarily, I remember the real estate agent telling us about Hoover eating Carlisle's eyes, and that gets me thinking about what got to the baby's eyes and I almost gag. There's a clump of dirt in the nose hole, and a tuft of fine yellow hair next to where the left ear would have been. The crown has an unnatural flat spot that's darker than the rest of the skull, a dent about the size of a quarter. Something hard must have hit it.

The rib cage is hovering over the spine like a giant spider feeding on a knobby white worm, and the leg bones look like thick chopsticks resting beside the plate of the pelvis. I can't stop the wretched puns that flit through my head: bone china, *bon appetit.* It's not even remotely funny, but for a second I have to cover my mouth to keep from braying laughter. Then I shudder and my eyes fill with tears.

Mom's sobs are coming out in some kind of dotted rhythm— short-long, short-long—and echo around the basement. Hoover comes over to sniff at the skeleton and without warning she slaps him hard enough to knock him across the room. "Get away!" she screams, and he bolts up the stairs, claws skittering wildly on the steps. When he reaches the kitchen I hear him smash into the wastebasket hard enough to topple it. There's a crash, and an empty aluminum can rolls down the stairs, picking up enough momentum by the bottom to smack into the wall with a loud clang. Mom doesn't even glance at it. She reaches out to touch the shirt and where her hand comes to rest it dwarfs an ankle and a foot.

A couple of the smallest bones, probably fingers, are caught on the front pocket, and all of a sudden I'm remembering the last time I held a baby. Dad and Mom had a friend, Colleen, who visited with her ten-month-old daughter one time and Colleen asked if I wanted to hold her kid. I didn't really want to; I've always hated babies. But I said yes anyway and took the brat from her, and the first thing the kid did was grab my pocket in her fist like she had figured out there was a nipple hiding behind it, and for all she knew, it was full to bursting with juicy manna. I watched those puny fingers twist the fabric and her eyes looked up into mine and she smiled at me, trusting me absolutely. It was the first time I'd ever held anything so utterly helpless.

I look down at the bones again and it's like I can see them with flesh on them again. The empty sockets get their eyes back and the skull grows a fresh mop of blonde hair. That hideous toothless grin gets covered over with lips and a real smile and . . .

Oh, Jesus. I'm going to be sick.

I walk away from Mom and try to swallow. What the fuck happened in this house? Why is there a dead baby wrapped in a shirt next to our furnace?

There are too many lights on down here and my eyes hurt. I stare at the paneling J.D. and I put up not long ago. When we did it we were talking about how cool this basement would be when we were finished, and how we were going to hang out down here all the time. Fat fucking chance of that, now. I'd rather hang out in a morgue.

I slump down with my back to the wall and listen to my mother cry.

Dad found a bat one time hanging on the hall curtain. It was brown and black and furry and upside down, of course, and it was sleeping between the folds near the curtain rod. Dad trapped it against the curtain with a bucket and then smacked the curtain on the opposite side and tried to knock it loose, but the thing had claws like a pterodactyl and refused to let go. Dad dragged the bucket down the curtain, hoping that would dislodge it, but the handle on the bucket got in the way and a thin wing crept out under the rim and we could hear the bat hissing and mewling.

Mom and I were watching from a few feet away because both of us were grossed out by bats, but when it started getting away Mom jumped to her feet and ripped the curtain right off the rod, and Dad bunched it around the bucket before the bat could get out. We took it outside, Mom and I trooping behind him like an honor guard, and he turned it loose, shaking the curtain as hard as he could. The bat fell to the ground and lay in the snow, not moving. We watched for a while, waiting for it to fly away or at least crawl off, and finally Mom got stressed out and picked up a stick to poke it.

It was dead. Dad must have accidentally squeezed the curtain too hard or maybe it just died of fright. All of us stood there and stared at it, and Mom chewed Dad out for being too rough and Dad chewed Mom out for yanking the curtain around it in the first place and probably smothering the poor thing to death and it was one of the few times Dad was as mad as Mom. I was only five or six and I started crying and they both thought I was crying because they were yelling at each other and so they calmed down and tried to reassure me they were only yelling because they felt bad about killing the bat.

I didn't have the vocabulary to tell them that even though I knew what death was and had seen other things die (Mom accidentally ran over a squirrel once), I'd never really gotten it. It wasn't the bat's dead body that upset me. It was the abruptness of the transition. Something was alive and breathing, and then it wasn't. Even now it freaks me out.

When J.D. comes back downstairs Mom has sort of pulled herself together, even though she's still sitting on the floor with her arms around her chest. The whole time J.D. was talking to his dad, maybe half an hour, I just sat in the corner and watched Mom crack up in front of me. I've never felt so useless in my life.

I look up at J.D. and see that he's been crying, too, and he's in about the same shape as Mom. Great. Let's all fall apart at once. I want to ask him what Tom told him, but I guess I should wait until we're alone. He walks over to Mom and stares at the skeleton, but even though he flinches he doesn't look too surprised. Maybe whatever he just heard from his dad shocked him enough that nothing else can get to him. He reaches down and puts his hand on her shoulder, and she drops her head on his hand.

I suck as a human being. I really do. He's known her for maybe two months and I've known her my whole life. It should be me helping her, but I don't know how and he does. And you know what? I could just puke. Instead of being glad that he's comforting her, all I am is jealous. I feel like kicking his ass all over the basement, and hers too. What the hell's wrong with me?

I force myself to speak normally. "So what do we do? Call the cops?"

Mom pulls away from J.D. and shakes her head violently. "No. Absolutely not. I will not have this house turned into a circus."

I don't say a word. She's wrong but I'm sure as hell not going to argue with her tonight.

She keeps on talking. "Besides, what good would it do? This little girl has been dead for fifty years and the bastard who murdered her is dead, too."

I can't help saying something. Somebody down here needs to be thinking clearly. "That's kind of jumping to conclusions, isn't it? We don't know for sure this is the Carlisles' kid, or that she was murdered." She's glaring at me but I don't care. "For that matter, we don't even know she was a she."

"If it's not the Carlisles' baby, whose is it?" J.D. asks quietly. "And if they didn't kill her, why would they bury her in the basement?"

Jesus, whose side is he on? "I don't know. Maybe it's been here since before the Carlisles moved in. Maybe we're on an old Indian burial ground or something."

"Don't be stupid," he says.

I want to get mad but I can't. He looks so sad he'll probably dissolve into the earth if I say anything back to him. The expression on Mom's face is almost identical to his. What the hell is wrong with these guys? I'm upset, too, but as sick as this whole thing is, it's got nothing to do with us.

Mom rewraps the bones and gets slowly to her feet. "We'll bury these properly later. But until we find out exactly what happened in this house, neither of you is to say a word to anyone."

She glances at J.D. and he nods, then she turns to me.

"Noah?"

How the hell she thinks she'll figure out what happened fifty years ago between a bunch of dead people is beyond me. We should call Officer Fatski and get a coroner in here, but God forbid we do anything that normal people would do in this situation.

I shake my head. "Yeah, okay, fine, sure, whatever."

She heads for the stairs, cradling the bundle to her chest.

I wait until she's upstairs before I go to J.D. "What did your dad say?"

His face twists, and without knowing why I feel like I just stuck a screwdriver into his stomach. I try to put my arms around him but he pushes me off and tells me to please just leave him alone for a while.

Christ. I'm living with a couple of sob sisters.

What kind of twisted human being buries a baby in the basement, then covers the ground with cement and puts a furnace on top of it? What kind of mind says to itself that doing something like that is okay? Did whoever did it feel any guilt or sorrow? Or was it just something kind of unpleasant but not necessarily difficult, like burying your shit on a camping trip?

I can't get the image out of my head of somebody standing in our basement with a shovel, looking down at that small, white, trussed-up parcel lying in that shallow hole. Did he or she pray? Or cry? Or did they just toss the dirt over it without any ceremony, dust off their hands and then go upstairs and cook a nice dinner?

I guess when you think about it there's not a hell of a lot of difference, intellectually speaking, between a graveyard and a basement. Dirt is dirt. If the person being buried is loved, who cares where the body goes, so long as it's treated with respect. But it's hard to see love and respect in a secret, unmarked grave and a flattened skull.

I sometimes wish I was more religious. I'd like to believe there's a nice, grandmotherly God taking care of that poor little kid in a comfy nursery somewhere, playing peek-a-boo with it and feeding it all the pabulum it can eat. And I'd also like to believe there's a vengeful, cruel God, full of piss and vinegar, kicking the living crap out of shitty people who do terrible things. But I don't have much faith that the universe works that way. I think it's more likely that the Buddhists have it right: heaven and hell both exist simultaneously, right here on Earth, and all most of us do is step from one to the other, day in and day out, too damn stupid and mean to know the difference.

J.D. and Mom are still asleep when I get up. I try to wake J.D. but he just puts his head under the sheet and rolls over when I shake his shoulder. I get dressed and go downstairs, then make a cup of coffee and wander into the backyard.

It's really quiet this morning. All the kids are in school and most of the adults are at work, so I don't hear anything but birds. I stumble around, sipping my coffee and trying to figure out what I'm going to do today. Mom usually tells me before I go to bed at night what she expects me to get done on the house the next day, but after last night's macabre little drama she shut herself up in her room and didn't come out again. J.D. was still in the basement when I fell asleep, and he somehow managed to climb into bed sometime in the night without waking me.

I go from spot to spot, trying not to think too much about all the strange shit that's been happening. It's easier out here than in the house; everywhere I look inside I keep wondering what else is waiting to crawl out of the walls and floors. What other nasty little surprises are there? I feel like I'm living in The House That Stephen King Built. Now all we need is a vampire or two and somebody can make a shitty TV movie about us.

The coffee's bitter but I like it. It's a bad idea for me to drink it on an empty stomach because caffeine without food makes my heart spaz out, but I can eat something in a while. I take a big swallow while I'm walking and when I look down I'm standing in the middle of the filled-in fish pond I found the other day. I squat to study it.

The rim is about two inches wide but mostly hidden by dead grass and dirt. I don't think I would ever have noticed it if I hadn't seen the picture; I've mowed right over it half a dozen times, and even though I guess I knew there was some concrete there I never

thought twice about it. But now that I know it's here, I can make
out the outline of the pond. It's a big one, probably about twelve
feet long and shaped like a wineskin, about five feet wide at the fat
end and three at the other. I have no way of knowing how deep it is,
not until I dig it out.

I glance back at the house. I doubt J.D. or Mom will be getting
up anytime soon, and I've got nothing better to do with my time, so
what the hell. Mom may get pissed at me for messing up her croquet course, but considering her present mood I doubt she'll give a
shit. Besides, it's my yard, too. I stand up and go over to the little
stone tool shed next to the garage. I slide the door open and before
I step in something small and furry scuttles across the sudden
patch of sunlight and disappears into the shadows near the back
wall. This is obviously a Hoover-free zone: there are droppings all
over the floor and the place reeks of mice.

Most of the stuff in here was Carlisle's. Saws of all sizes are
hanging on the walls, and ropes and chains dangle from the ceiling. There's an ax in the corner next to the lawn mower, and the rest
of the place is stuffed with rakes and hoes, a wheelbarrow, a weed-
whacker, and nearly a dozen tin cans full of rusty nails and screws.
I poke around until I find the shovel, and only when I'm stepping
back outside does it occur to me that this might be the same shovel
somebody used to bury the baby. I drop it without thinking and it
clangs on the gravel of the driveway.

I'm being stupid. It's just a shovel. I bend down and pick it up
again, then head back to the fish pond. The wooden handle feels
cold and hard in my hands.

I stop digging when my stomach starts to growl. I've been at
this for almost an hour and each hand has a big blister on the palm,
my shoulders are burning, and I'm only about an eighth of the way
done. I started at the narrow end and I'm just now getting to the
foundation, about two feet down, and it looks like it's going to get
deeper as it gets wider. The digging wouldn't be so bad except

every time I stick the shovel in I hit another fucking rock. Maybe I should just give up and refill what I've done.

The screen door bangs open and when I look over J.D. is walking toward me, wearing a light jacket and carrying a piece of toast and a glass of orange juice.

"Hey." I jam the shovel in the ground upright and crawl out of the hole to stand beside him.

"Hey." He probably just got out of bed, but he looks like the guinea pig for a sleep deprivation experiment.

"What time did you come to bed last night?"

He shrugs. "I don't know." He kicks at the mound of soil and dirt I've piled beside the pond. "Why are you digging up the yard?"

"I don't know." I ask him for a bite of toast and he hands it over. It's smothered with butter and honey. I snarf half of it without thinking but when I look at him he tells me to go ahead and eat the whole thing because he's not hungry. He passes me the orange juice and climbs down into the hole. I squat on my haunches to eat and he pulls the shovel out like he's King Arthur laying claim to Excalibur.

"Is Mom awake?"

He shakes his head. He starts slow, grunting, but when he gets into a rhythm the dirt starts to fly. He's a lot stronger than me and the head of the shovel goes in all the way every time.

I want to ask him about what happened last night but when I clear my throat to say something he says maybe we should get the wheelbarrow and start dumping the dirt behind the garage so we won't mess up the yard. I get to my feet with a sigh and drag the wheelbarrow and a bucket out of the shed.

We trade off between digging and dumping, and pretty soon the pile behind the garage is about the size of a Volkswagen. Since he's a better digger I do most of the dumping. The grass between the garage and the pond is crisscrossed with tire tracks, and even though we've been trying to be careful we've spilled enough dirt to make the lawn look like a no-man's-land between enemy trenches.

I take another load to the pile and when I get back to the pond J.D. is bending over with one hand on the shovel and the other scrabbling near the foundation at the deepest part of the pond. So far the concrete is smooth and unbroken and there's a graceful slope from the narrow end to where J.D. is messing around.

"I've found something." His fingers are tangled up in some kind of black cloth. He lays the shovel down and tries to get a grip with both hands.

The temperature is only in the fifties but we're both sweating, and J.D. has taken off his jacket. I can see his shoulder blades sticking to his shirt. I climb down next to him and scoop out some dirt so he can get at the fabric. He gives it a yank and it tears.

"Dammit." He grabs the shovel again and tosses another few clumps out of the way. In the patch he clears I can see some white cloth next to the black. He keeps digging until we can get at whatever it is.

We pull the things out together and hold them up. The black one hangs to J.D.'s knees, and the white covers my feet. Both are tattered and filthy and nearly unrecognizable, but there's enough lace left on the white to know it's a wedding dress, and the forked material at the bottom of the black clearly belongs to a tuxedo.

I toss the dress aside. "I've had just about enough of this shit."

J.D. sets the tails carefully on the side of the pond and bends down to pull out a shredded set of pants and the remnants of a veil. He roots around for more and finally straightens with a grim look on his face.

"What?"

"Notice what's missing?" He dusts off his hands and steps out of the hole.

I shrug. "The minister? A brass quintet?" I start to giggle and he looks disgusted.

"There's no shirt for the tux. Guess where that ended up."

I stop laughing.

He walks back to the house and I watch him go. As he steps into the house the curtains move in one of the windows on the second floor. Mom is watching from her bedroom. Her face is as white as a wedding dress. For a second our eyes lock, then she floats away from the window, like a ghost.

We're going back to school today. The last few days have been the weirdest days of my life. Mom's called in sick to work four days in a row, and all she does is sit in her room during the day and wander the house at night. I opened her door one morning when she didn't come down for breakfast and found her sitting on the bed, staring at all the shit we've found. Everything was laid out on a table in front of her, like she was pretending to be the curator of a museum and the Carlisles' artifacts were her favorite exhibit. She told me to close the door and go away.

Bad as she is, J.D. isn't much better. He still hasn't told me what his dad said about his mom, and even though we're together twenty-four hours a day, he only talks in monosyllables and doesn't eat much and doesn't smile and doesn't get up until almost noon. We've only had sex once since he moved in, and even then I felt like he wasn't really in the room with me. It's like he's eaten something poisonous and can't find a way to get it out of his system. To be honest, I'm not sure I want to be there when he finally vomits it up.

I'm not doing so good. My bruises and cuts are healing and I'm done with the acid eyedrops, but the two people I love the most in the world are seriously fucked up and I haven't got a clue what they need from me. So day after day I work on the house (I had to finish digging out the fish pond by myself because even after I threw the tux and the dress away J.D. didn't want anything to do with it), and I listen to music, and I try to have conversations with people who don't answer me.

I also can't even imagine what this day is going to be like. Every single kid in this goddamn town knows by now that J.D. and I are queer, and I'm pretty sure the word's out we're living together, too. I'm not too worried about getting beaten up again, because Ganski called and said that White and Company are waiting for trial and have been warned by their lawyers to stay the fuck away from us. That doesn't mean some other butthead won't decide to work us over, but the principal, Jackass Warner, has promised to keep an eye on us during the day, and Mom is letting me take the car to and from school, at least until she's sure we'll be safe walking again. We can't hide forever, I guess, but I'd feel a lot better about this whole thing if J.D. weren't acting like a robot and Mom's new best friend wasn't a skull.

I eat breakfast alone but J.D. finally gets up and showers and comes downstairs. He won't eat anything but at least he's dressed and ready to go by the time we have to leave. I run upstairs and knock on Mom's door and as usual there's no answer. I poke my head in and she's on her back staring at the ceiling. Her hair is greasy and her room smells stale. God only knows when she last took a bath or brushed her teeth.

"Mom." She doesn't even look at me. "We're going now. Are you going to get up and go to work today?"

"No. I don't feel well."

"Maybe you should go see a doctor or something."

No response. This is getting really old. I pull the door shut without saying good-bye, and when I get back downstairs J.D. and I go outside and get in the car without a word spoken.

I can't take too much more of this. I'm sorry they're depressed and messed up, but my life isn't exactly peachy keen these days either. In a perverse way I can't wait to get to school, because at least there somebody might talk to me.

When we pull into the parking lot I cut the engine and turn to J.D. "Well, here we go."

He nods like he doesn't care about anything and all of a sudden

I'm pissed as hell. I get out and slam the door and get some satis-faction from the surprised look on his face through the window.

He gets out and faces me across the hood. "What's with you?"

"Wow. It talks."

He looks bewildered. "What's your problem?"

"Oh, I don't know. Living with two mental patients for the past week has me a little off my game."

"You try too hard to be funny, Noah."

That stings, but I keep my voice light. "Maybe if you hadn't for-gotten how to laugh you wouldn't think so."

"Sometimes there's nothing to laugh about."

"I'll have to take your word for that, since you won't tell me what's bugging you."

Another car pulls up in the parking lot and a couple of girls get out. When they see us they stare for a minute then walk off, whis-pering and giggling.

Words come bubbling out of my mouth like foam from a pop bottle. "What the fuck is going on? You won't let me help you and Mom's acting like a corpse and I'm scared and lonely and in about two seconds we have to go into a war zone and I feel like you don't give a shit about me."

His face softens. "It has nothing to do with you." He lowers his voice so kids walking by can't hear him. "You know how I feel about you."

"Then why won't you tell me what's happening? What did your dad tell you?"

He stares at the ground. "I can't talk about that." He looks up at me, and for the first time in days I feel like he's seeing me. "Give me time."

I nod. What else can I do? We head up to the school.

It's a fucked-up day but better than I'd hoped for. I hear the words "faggot" and "homo" more times than I can count, but I also have people I've never even met come up and say hi and tell me they're sorry about what happened. Melissa gives me a hug when she sees me, and so does Shannon Farnum, the Dimple-girl. Louis sashays up and greets me like his long-lost brother and says J.D. and I should come over to his house sometime. I put him off with a "sounds like fun" non-answer and I hope he forgets all about it. (He's a nice enough guy, I guess, but I don't think we have much in common except being gay. I can't see hanging out with him just because we share the same sexual orientation, but then again, I guess a lot of straight guys probably hang out with each other for no better reason. Whatever, it seems like a stupid basis for a friend-ship, if you ask me.)

Perry and Lester and their two sidekicks have been moved into another gym class, and even though a few jocks say some shit to us in the locker room (Hey, faggots, what are you staring at? If I catch you looking at my dick I'll cut your balls off), no one touches us. Paul and Riley say hey but keep their distance, and some of the teachers look at me like I'm a big turgid cyst taking up valuable desk space in their classes.

It's kind of funny that no one seems to have any doubts anymore about whether or not we're really queer. I mean, J.D. denied it be-forehand, but since we got beaten up, our bruises are somehow proof positive that we're sleeping together, like wedding rings or His and Hers matching towels. I don't get it. I guess it could be possible that J.D. and I are somehow different now than we were before White and his cronies redecorated us; maybe the beating made us more sure of ourselves. Can people actually see how we feel about each other now? Is love that obvious? I'd like to think so, but I'm too much of a cynic to believe it. I like thinking about it, though.

In the last class of the day, Billy Otis tries to act cool with me, but it feels like he's only doing it because he thinks of himself as a hip, artsy guy and hip, artsy guys are supposed to be cool with fags. He tells me he's glad I'm back and how thrilled he was to meet my mom, then he gets the hell away from me as fast as he can.

If it gets people like Otis to leave me alone, maybe homophobia isn't such a bad thing.

Halfway through the class, Scott the Grease-boy turns around in his seat. He's the only person all day to look at me normally. "Those black eyes make you look like a raccoon," he whispers. "Maybe you should have gone to a vet instead of a doctor."

I manage a grin. "You should see my vestigial tail," I whisper back.

He smiles, too, and all of a sudden I'm so grateful I could cry. Not because he smiled at me—lots of people did that today—but because he smiled without a trace of pity or discomfort in his eyes.

"Maybe that's why fundamentalists hate homosexuals," he says. "Not only are you funnier than they are, you're also the missing link in evolutionary theory."

I laugh out loud for what feels like the first time in years, and Otis tells Scott to turn around. He grins again before facing the front of the room.

In a better world, I'd lean forward and kiss him right on top of his beautiful greasy head.

Can anyone explain sexual attraction to me? Why is it that J.D. trips my trigger and Scott doesn't do anything for me at all, except as a potential friend? I mean, sure, Scott has zits and J.D. is beautiful, but Scott's not ugly or anything. He's got a good smile, and he looks like he's in pretty decent shape, and he's funny and kind, and from what I can tell he's also smart as shit. You'd think I could at least work up a good fantasy about him, but I look at him and feel nothing beyond simple affection.

Is my lack of interest because he's straight? That doesn't seem likely, because if I wanted to fuck him, his unavailability would probably just make him more attractive. Is it because I'm in love with J.D.? Maybe, but when I saw an old River Phoenix movie the other night I almost drowned in drool. So what causes desire? Why lust after one person and not another? And don't give me any shit about pheromones and past lives. There's got to be a better answer than that.

Is it brains? I don't think so, because to be completely honest, J.D.'s not smart in the same way I am. We both know it. It doesn't matter to either of us, but you'd think we'd be more comfortable with someone who shared the same kind of intelligence. His is musical and mechanical, mine is mostly book smarts. (I have no idea what my IQ is because my parents have always refused to let me be tested—they told me there was no point, since if it was high it would just make me cocky, and if it was low it would just give me an inferiority complex, and if it was average it would just give me an excuse not to excel. God bless Mom and Dad. That was one thing they got right. What the hell's the point of labeling someone with a number when people with genius IQs are more often than not total stuck-up assholes who might be able to decipher hieroglyphics but are utterly helpless when it comes to tying their shoes or frying an egg?) So it's not about brains. Scott and I are probably smart in the same way, but I could care less.

Is it a sense of humor? Sort of, but not really. Even though J.D. makes me laugh, my sense of humor lines up more with Scott's than with his. J.D.'s too fucking nice to be really funny. But so what? If I want a good laugh I'll watch *South Park* or *The Simpsons*.

Looks? There are a couple of guys in the school who are better looking than J.D., but when I look at them all I feel is clinical admiration. I suppose if one of them groped me it might change my mind, but I doubt it. Looks are just the most obvious of the initial factors. Sweetness and vulnerability? Those may be part of it, but if they were all I'd just get a puppy.

J.D.'s an athlete, I'm not. He's twice the musician I am, I'm twice the artist he is. He's got morning breath sometimes; I've got foot odor all the time. And I'm finding more differences between us every day. So what's the big draw? Why him and not Scott?

I haven't got a fucking clue. My body likes what it likes and has absolutely no qualms about dragging my mind and soul along for the ride.

I meet J.D. after school and we head for the parking lot together. A car peels out next to us and sprays gravel all over the place, then some moron I don't even know sticks his head out the window, calls us buttfuckers and flips us off. We watch him drive away in a cloud of dust.

"J.D."

We turn around and see Kristin. J.D. says hi.

She comes up to him with her purse clutched to her chest like she's afraid he's going to try and steal it. They stare at each other for a minute while I stand on the other side of the car.

She pushes her hair behind an ear. "Are you okay?"

He shrugs. "More or less." He waits for her to say something else but she seems to have exhausted her conversational gambit, so he finally asks her how she's doing.

"I'm okay."

Silence. God, this is like watching golf on television. I open my door as a hint that I want to go but both of them ignore me.

J.D. asks if she wants a ride and she shakes her head. "No. I just wanted to tell you I'm not mad at you or anything."

That's big of her. J.D. mutters thanks.

"I mean, it's not your fault you think you're gay." She pointedly avoids looking at me. Guess whose fault she thinks it is.

J.D. sighs. "I don't just think I'm gay, Kristin. I know I am."

"I've been reading some literature at my church. There are counseling programs for people like you. My pastor says he'll be glad to help you. He says you'll go to hell if you don't stop what you're doing."

Keeping my mouth shut has never been harder. Goddamn Christians. Apparently 'love thy neighbor' and 'judge not lest ye be judged' are parts of the Bible you can just ignore when you're dealing with homos. I swear to God, where do people like this come from? What rock have they crawled out from under? I don't know much, but I have a hard time believing Christ would put up with the bullshit these dumb bastards do in his name.

J.D. opens his door and puts a foot inside the car. "No, thanks."

She turns and glares at me and suddenly her face turns ugly. "I wish you were dead, Noah." She spits the words out. "You're a pervert and what you've done to him is just gross."

I want to say something really witty and devastating, but I've never had anybody stare at me with so much hatred in their eyes. I just stand there like I'm paralyzed.

J.D. steps back from the car and slams his door. "You shut up, Kristin. Noah's not doing anything to me I don't want done." He starts moving toward her threateningly. I've never seen him so mad. He stops about a foot away from her with his hand raised and she cringes.

I come running around the car and grab his shoulder. "Stop, J.D. Please."

He lowers his arm, and there's part of me that's sorry I stopped him. He puts his face right up next to hers and lowers his voice. "Maybe if you weren't such a cunt I'd still be with you." The smile he gives her reminds me of his mom.

Her face turns ashen. As we drive off she's still standing there, tears dribbling off her chin and falling onto her purse.

In case you haven't noticed, I'm not the most compassionate person in the world, especially when it comes to dealing with a priggish sow like Kristin. She's stupid and she's petty and she deserves everything she gets, but any idiot can see she loves him, and I wish he weren't sitting there looking so proud of himself.

I keep my eyes on the road and I can feel him watching me.

"What's wrong with you?" he asks after a couple of blocks.

"Nothing." I glance at him and he's still got this cold smile on his face. It pisses me off and words come out of me like a bad case of projectile vomiting. "I guess I'm a little freaked out at how ready you were to hit her. There's more of Donna in you than I thought."

He flinches like I just tossed a pot of boiling water on him.

Neither of us says anything until we pull into our driveway. When I turn off the car and look at him, his face is streaked with tears.

Jesus. Which of us is the bigger bastard?

He looks at me and tries to talk but nothing comes out. He coughs a few times and swallows, wipes his nose on his sleeve, then tries again. "She was attacking you. I got mad. That doesn't mean I'm like my mom."

Suddenly it's me who can't talk. I never used to cry and now I can't seem to get through a day without imitating Niagara Falls. "I know. I'm sorry. I shouldn't have said that. You just scared me a little, that's all. Will you talk to me like that some day?"

He shakes his head. "You're so dumb, Noah. Don't you get it? Kristin and I had sex but that's all it was. I didn't love her. You're so stupid."

Usually I don't like it when people call me stupid, but I guess I'll let it slide this time.

When J.D. and I get in the house we just stand in the doorway and gawk like a couple of gargoyles outside a public library. The whole goddamn wall separating the study and the living room is a pile of rubble, and there are huge jagged holes everywhere: the floor, the ceiling, and every single fucking wall in sight.

We gape at each other, then we hear banging upstairs and I go running up to see what Mom's destroying now. J.D. follows me and catches up at the top of the stairs. It's even worse up here than it was downstairs. There's dust and it plaster and holes and nails and exposed wires everywhere and looks ten times worse than it did when we first moved in.

We follow the noise into our room, and there's Mom standing on a chair, pulverizing the shit out of the ceiling above the bed. My books and furniture are covered with chunks of insulation and enough white powder to go sledding on, and Mom looks like the Abominable Snowman. Her eyes are yellow because of all the dust on her face, and you can't even tell what color her hair is supposed to be.

"Mom!"

She jumps a little and glances at me, but then keeps right on battering the ceiling. She's swinging as hard as she can and nearly falls every time the hammer bites into the plaster.

"Mom! Stop it!" I walk toward her and get torpedoed by flying debris, but I manage to grab her arm before she can swing again.

"Let go, Noah," she says calmly, and she sounds so normal I take my hand away. She immediately bashes the ceiling again, but this time she loses her balance and I have to catch her. J.D. comes up and supports her on the other side of the chair, and we set her down on the floor.

I get the hammer away from her and start screaming. "What the fuck do you think you're doing? Jesus, Mom, you're a psycho, you're a fucking psycho!"

She looks at me with a puzzled, irritated expression on her face, like I'm a rude stranger yelling at her in a foreign language. "I'm looking for something to explain the baby in the basement." She sounds absolutely reasonable, but her eyes are darting around the room. I glance at J.D. and he looks back helplessly.

I force myself to calm down. "Mom, this . . . this is crazy. You know that, don't you?"

"I don't expect you to understand." She reaches for the hammer and I yank it away from her. She glares at me and tries again, and when she can't get it she starts to yell. "You fucking little cock-sucker, how dare you? Give me the goddamn hammer before I tear your fucking head off and shit down your queer little throat!"

She keeps swearing and swearing, but it's like her tongue is on auto-pilot. She finally runs out of words and sputters into silence.

The blood has left my face and, of course, I've got tears in my eyes again, but I take a deep breath and make my voice come out evenly. "Feel better?"

The wildness leaves her face and she seems to realize what she's been saying. She looks around the room like she's seeing the rubble for the first time. If she'd tossed a grenade in here it couldn't look worse. She stares at a big wad of insulation on my pillow and a pathetic laugh escapes her. "You expect an allowance when you keep your room looking like this?"

I don't know what to do. I let go of the hammer and it falls at my feet with a thump. She stares at my face, then at J.D., and she starts to cry. "I'm sorry, I'm sorry, I'm so sorry, Noah, J.D., I don't know what's the matter with me. I'm just tired, that's all."

She walks out of the room and down the hall. We hear her close her bedroom door, and we stand still, staring at each other.

"Cindy? It's Noah."

"Noah? Noah who?" She sounds a lot like Mom.

"Your nephew."

"Oh!" She says my voice has changed a lot and she's sorry for not knowing who I was and what's it been, eight or nine years since we saw each other? All of a sudden she seems to realize something must be wrong if I'm calling. "Where's your mother? Has she been hurt?"

"She's fine. I mean, she's physically fine. She's upstairs in her room."

I tell her Mom will kill me if she knows I'm talking to her, and then I prattle on about the house and the Carlisles and the dress and the pictures and Mom's recent bout with a hammer. (I want to tell her about the skeleton, but I can't because of the stupid promise Mom made me make.) I tell her I don't know what to do and J.D. said I should call her.

She asks who J.D. is. I tell her.

There's a long, uncomfortable silence. "Wow." More silence. "Wow."

I try not to get irritated. This poor lady hasn't heard a word from us in years and all of a sudden she finds out her sister is whacked and her nephew who she remembers as a sweet little nine-year-old has a live-in boyfriend. But I didn't call to hear her say Wow.

I ask her if she has any idea why Mom is so freaked out about this baby thing.

More silence. I guess they don't talk much in California.

But then she tells me some things. After a few sentences my legs feel weak and I sit on the floor with my back against the wall. She talks for a long time.

There's no way to say this and make it sound nice. Cindy says Mom is so fucked up because their father, my dear old granddad, got Mom pregnant when she was twelve years old.

Jesus Fucking Christ.

CHAPTER SEVEN

om won't get out of bed. She won't eat, she won't speak, she won't look at me. The only time she gets up is to use the bathroom, and when she does that she trundles down the hall like a sleepwalker. For three days she's in bed when J.D. and I leave for school in the mornings, and she's in bed when we come home in the afternoons. Her room smells bad, like her body is starting to feed on itself.

The dean of faculty at Cassidy College called this week and I told him Mom was still sick, and even though he pretended to be sympathetic, I could tell he was pissed when I wouldn't let him talk to her. I don't blame him; she's already missed so many classes this semester her students probably don't remember what she looks like. I told him I'm sure she'd be better soon and I hung up. That Walter Danvers guy I met in Mom's office during the summer called too and sounded worried about her, but at least he didn't get mad. He just sounded hurt that she wouldn't talk to him.

I can't take it any more, so I finally go in and pull the covers off her. She rouses enough to reach for them, but I don't let her have them. She's dressed in rumpled black sweats, and her hair hangs limply over her face. She's still wearing the locket around her throat, and the baby's skeleton has a prominent place in the exhibit on her table.

"Get up, Mom." I try to sound firm and angry. "Enough is enough."

It's probably the wrong approach, but I don't know what else to try except some of this tough love shit. After talking to Aunt Cindy the other day I haven't had the heart to speak roughly to her, but something's got to give and she's obviously not getting any better with me just leaving her alone. Cindy volunteered to fly out and try to help, but I told her I didn't think there was anything she could do. She seemed relieved.

It's late in the afternoon. J.D. is downstairs practicing his trumpet, and even though he's got a mute in the damn thing it's still too fucking loud. Mom doesn't even seem to hear it.

"Go away, Noah," she mutters. She tries to glare at me but she doesn't have the energy to keep it up so she drops her head on the mattress and puts a pillow over her face.

I wrestle it away from her. "You need to get out of bed and clean yourself up. You smell like Hoover's litter box."

She blinks at me listlessly. "I'll get up in a while. Let me sleep."

"No. You've slept enough." I try to pull her up by the wrist but she yanks her arm away with surprising strength and turns her back to me. I walk over and open the blinds and the windows to get some fresh air. Sunlight floods in with the cold air and she starts to shiver. J.D.'s playing some jazzy triplet thing over and over.

"Mom. I talked to Cindy the other day."

The shivering stops and her body tenses but she doesn't say anything.

"She told me about what happened with your dad."

Doo ba da Doo ba da goes J.D.'s trumpet. Mom just lays there.

"Come on, Mom. Say something."

A strong wind slices through the screen and rustles papers on her desk like it's looking for something. *Doo ba da Doo ba da* says J.D.

"Mom?" I walk around the bed so I can see her face. She's biting her lip, again and again, and blood is all over her chin and soaking into the sheet. I rush forward and put my hand on her shoulder, and she opens her mouth and starts to scream.

We're at the hospital. We got here about an hour ago, after both of us carried Mom out to the car, bleeding and screaming but not fighting us. I probably should have called an ambulance, but all I could think of was getting her to the hospital as fast as I could. I'm still shaking all over and I want to throw up. I keep remembering J.D.'s face when he came running upstairs and saw Mom on her bed, screaming her throat out; I was sure he was going to turn around and run for his life. But he helped me pick her up, and he sat with her in the backseat while I drove, holding her so she wouldn't hurt herself.

They've got her sedated now and we're in the hall outside her room, waiting for the doctor to come talk to us. J.D.'s biting his fingernails and staring at the floor and I've got an unbelievable headache. He still hasn't told me what his dad said about his mom, and I haven't told him what I found out about my mom, either. Sounds weird, doesn't it? We're living in the same house, sleeping in the same bed, going to the same school, but for some fucked-up reason we can't talk to each other about Virginia or Donna. I want to tell him what Grandpa did to Mom, but every time I try, my tongue just lays in my mouth like a lump of road kill. Maybe it's the same for him; maybe something just as bad happened to Donna and he can't get the words past his lips because there are no words for shit like that. So for the past week we've been talking about school and music and books, and we've watched television, and we've eaten breakfast and supper together, and we've fucked like bunnies. And the whole time we're holding secrets in the back of our throats, dangling there in each of us like a second epiglottis, and it's a wonder we haven't choked to death.

I reach over and pull his hand away from his mouth while he's still got some fingernails left. He looks at me and manages a weak smile.

The doctor comes out and frowns when he sees us holding hands. I let go and stand up to introduce myself. His name is Doctor Cromwell and he's got a spotty bald head and bad teeth. His glasses are crooked and they keep sliding down his nose like they're trying to get as far away from him as they can. When he shakes my hand his palm is cold and damp, and when he talks his breath smells like garlic and cheap breath mints. He tells me Mom is going to have to stay here a while for observation, and a psychiatrist has been called in who will need to talk to me. He asks me if I know what's caused this "episode" and I lie and tell him no. J.D. looks at me funny but I don't care. I'll tell the psychiatrist what I know but I'll be damned if I'm going to tell anybody else.

Cromwell asks if I have anybody to stay with and I tell him yes. He says he's called Children's Services and they'll need to talk to me too. Great. Fucking great.

He bustles off down the hall.

I turn to J.D. "We better get ready to do a lot of lying."

"Why?"

"Think about it. My mom's nuts and your folks have thrown you out and we're a couple of faggot teenagers living in a house with the skeleton of a mystery baby and about a million holes in the walls and floors. There's no way they'll let us stay together."

He starts to argue but stops abruptly. He knows I'm right. I turn eighteen in a couple of months and he's only a year younger than me, but no one besides Mom will treat us like adults and leave us alone.

By the time the lady from Children's Services comes to talk to me we've got our lies ready. The whole time I'm talking to her I can't take my eyes off a mole on her chin. It's got hairs on it long enough to comb. I tell her that Aunt Cindy is flying out to take care of me until Mom gets better. She asks me what if Mom doesn't get better which all of a sudden makes me feel like shit because the possibility of her not getting better in a few days hadn't even occurred to me. I choke up for a minute and finally manage to tell her I'll be eighteen soon and I can continue living in our house with or without Mom, at least until I finish school. She gets our phone number and asks when Cindy will be arriving and I make up something to get her to shut up and leave me alone. She seems satisfied and wishes me luck.

Then the psychiatrist comes and I tell him about everything except the baby's skeleton. He says he knows my Mom's poetry and he's a big fan and I stop listening because I've heard it all before. I ask him when she can come home and he says he doesn't know but he hopes soon, that she's suffering from severe depression and who knows what else and might be a danger to herself and others. I tell him that's ridiculous but even as I say it I know he's right. She was out of her mind this afternoon and we both know it. He tells me he'll call my principal if I want and explain what's going on in case I have to miss some school, but I lie and tell him I've already called. I don't want him talking to Warner because Warner probably knows that J.D. is living with me, and I don't want that getting around. The fewer people in authority who know about us the better because all it takes to mess up our lives more than they already are is some nosey right-wing asshole throwing a shitfit. Jesus. All these lies. We're not doing anything wrong, so why should I have to lie about everything?

Mom and I always teased Dad because every time he was introduced to another man his voice would drop about an octave when he said hello, like he thought the guy with the lowest voice got to be Alpha Male for the day, or something. Mom said it was the last acceptable vestige of male head-butting left in him, and she said she didn't mind because at least it kept him from clubbing some poor sap to death on the street with his bare fists.

One day a grad student of Mom's came over and Dad did the

voice thing as he shook the guy's hand. When I got introduced I de-
liberately dropped my voice as low as I could, and the sheepish
look on Dad's face got Mom laughing so hard she was stumbling
around the hall like a drunk, walking into walls and stuff. Dad was
embarrassed and the student was confused, but Mom couldn't stop.
It was the first time I ever made her forget everything except the
need to laugh, and I can count on one hand the times I've done it
since. What I wouldn't give to be able to do it for her again.

When we walk out of the hospital it's early evening and the
streetlights have just come on. There's a light, chilly breeze blowing leaves down the street and a full moon is coming up and people
are scurrying by wearing jackets and flannel shirts.

J.D. walks beside me silently and I don't much feel like talking
either but I'm glad he's with me. I know at some point we're going
to have to have a heart to heart about all this shit, but not tonight.
Tonight I just want to go home and have some dinner and go to bed
and make love.

When we get inside the house I don't even bother to turn on the
lights in the foyer because there's so much moonlight streaming
through the windows we can make our way to the kitchen without
tripping over anything. It's weird knowing that tonight will be our
first night alone here, and I get a shiver up my back looking at the
shadows inside all the holes on the walls. Christ. Mom's turned this
place into a haunted house just in time for Halloween.

J.D. sees me shiver and puts his arms around me. "Are you
okay?"

"Yeah. I was just thinking how big a hit we'll be with the trick-
or-treaters. Maybe we can bring down the skeleton and hang it on
the porch or something."

He shudders. "Don't joke about that."

"Do you think we should call the cops and tell them about the
baby?"

He pulls back and searches my face. In the dim light his eyes are like melted chocolate. "You've already said that if people find out what's going on in this house they'll use it as an excuse to separate us."

"I know. But it doesn't seem right to keep this to ourselves."

He doesn't answer, which frustrates me a little. Why should I have to make all the decisions around here? Then again, what do I expect him to say? We talk for a while and decide to keep looking for more stuff that might tell us what happened with the Carlisles. It doesn't seem likely we'll find anything Mom hasn't since she's torn the whole goddamn place down, but I guess she didn't exactly use the scientific method in her search. Maybe we can turn something up.

J.D. rolls over in bed and puts his head on my chest. "My dad's not my father," he says quietly.

I was almost asleep and it takes a minute for the words to register. "What?"

"Mom was raped seventeen years ago by some guy she went to college with." I can feel his breath on my skin. "She was two months pregnant when she and Dad got married."

I put my hand in his hair and move my fingers through it like I'm petting Hoover. It's stupid, but when you can't think of anything to say the only thing to offer is animal comfort.

"Your dad knew?"

"Yeah. They never told anyone else. She never even told anyone she was raped, and she wouldn't let Dad do anything to the guy. He says Mom still refuses to talk about it."

"Your dad knew the guy?"

"Yeah. I guess they were in some classes together. He won't tell me his name."

The moonlight is making huge shadows all over the room. The jacket hanging on my chair swells into a black circus tent spread across the wall. "Why'd he tell you now?"

"He said it explained why she treats me like she does. He says that when I was little I didn't resemble my real father, but in the last couple of years I look just like him."

"That's not your fault."

He nods; he needs a shave and the stubble scratches against my ribs. "I know. But it's not her fault, either."

He says it without anger or drama or frustration. Just a statement of fact, something he wants me to know. I take a few deep breaths, then I tell him about Mom and Grandpa. Afterward, we lay on our backs and stare at the ceiling for a couple of hours like we've forgotten how to sleep.

I stare out the window at the stars, and remember something Dad once told me. He said that when you look out into space you're also looking back in time, so everything you see—all that light, all that drama—happened a long time ago. At first I found it comforting, maybe because it gave me a feel for eternity or something. Now it seems kind of terrible, because all I can do is look. There's not a damn thing I can do to change what I don't like.

Cindy couldn't tell me what happened to Mom's baby. She said it was born, and lived with them for a couple of months, then one day it was gone and neither Mom nor her parents would tell her where it went. She said Mom never mentioned it again. It was a girl, and her name was Carolyn.

Secrets suck. They're like cancer in the person who carries them around, and they grow and grow until there's not a single healthy cell left in the whole fucking body. Mom and Donna are suffering now not because shitty things happened to them when they were younger, but because they buried those shitty things deep inside and let them take root. That sounds harsh, I know, like I'm blaming the victims for the crime or something. I don't mean to. God only knows what I'd be like if something like that happened to me. But why do some people handle awful things better than others? Is it because they don't run from them?

Who knows what Donna was like before she was raped? Maybe she was a decent human being, even though that's hard to imagine. And what about Mom? What if her father had left her alone? Who would she be now? Would her poems be more powerful, or less? Would she even feel the need to write?

I once heard some idiot on the radio saying that all great art has suffering as its dominant theme, and that the greatest artists are only able to create because they suffer immensely in their own lives. What a bunch of bullshit. Look at Van Gogh's paintings: there's as much joy in them as there is pain. Suffering is only a single color, and by itself it's boring.

We all know the bromide about life being a hand of cards, dealt by God. Mom and Donna were dealt shitty hands, and that isn't their fault. But I can't help wishing that they'd somehow found a way to reshuffle the deck. I haven't got a clue how. I just wish.

Perry and Lester see me in the hall by my locker between classes but they smirk and turn away. Perry still has bandages on his face, so his smirk is a trifle less intimidating than it might be. I guess they've got a pre-trial hearing next week, and if they don't make a deal with the district attorney there will be a trial and J.D. and I will have to testify. I'd rather staple my scrotum to my thigh. I should probably be madder at them than I am, and more scared too, but I don't have time for these assholes and I just want everything to be over.

I head into the band room and see J.D. already in his chair with his trumpet in hand. He's talking to Riley and Paul and Melissa but the second I walk in he waves me over.

"Hey, Noah." Riley punches me lightly on the shoulder and Paul and Melissa smile at me. I have to hand it to them; I know for a fact all three of them have taken shit for staying friends with J.D. and me now that everybody knows we're queer. Life is pretty strange. Just a few weeks ago no one knew anything about us. J.D.

was still living at home and dating Kristin, and Riley and Paul were serving up homo jokes at lunch like hors d'oeuvres. Since then we've been outed and beaten up, and J.D.'s been booted out of his family. Yet here the five of us are, mostly comfortable with each other, just like normal high school kids. Weird.

Melissa puts her arm through mine and I don't even mind it. "Are you guys doing anything Friday night? I already asked J.D. but he said I'd have to ask you."

I tell her we don't have anything planned and she invites us over for pizza and a movie. She says Riley and Paul will be there too, and maybe a couple of other kids. I ask her if Kristin is going to be there and she makes a face.

"Kristin and I aren't doing much together these days."

I tell her we'll come if my mom says it's okay. J.D. and I haven't said anything about Mom being in the hospital, but in this silly-ass town nothing stays secret for long, so I'm sure they know we may have to be with her or something instead of going out. Melissa nods and says great and we can just let her know on Friday.

All of a sudden it occurs to me what just happened and I quickly turn away under the pretense of getting my trombone out of my band locker because I don't want them to see me fighting back tears. I'm turning into such a crybaby but I can't help it. Not only have the two of us just been invited to a party, but before I got there J.D. apparently told them, in front of God and everybody, that he wasn't free if I wasn't.

Jesus. We're a couple, just like that. Like I said, life is fucking strange.

I have a few vague memories of my grandfather. Mostly stuff like him holding me on his lap while we watched TV and half a dozen other scattered fragments like that. Now that I know what a bastard he was it grosses me out to think of it, but at the time he seemed like a nice old man. I think I only saw him two or three times even though he didn't live far from where we did, and in retrospect I can't believe I ever met him. How could Mom have stood to be in the same room with him?

If I remember right, there was a bad thunderstorm one time when we visited. I couldn't have been more than three or four and I was scared shitless, especially because some neighbor's dog was yelping through the whole thing. Grandpa carried me to the window and when we looked out we saw that the dumb mutt was on a chain and had tried to jump a fence to get away, and now it was tangled up and hanging, with only one paw on the ground to keep it from falling and choking to death. It was a big dog and it looked mean as shit, but right then it was frantic, scrabbling at the fence with its front claws while it made that awful sound.

The neighbors weren't home, so Grandpa handed me to Mom and told my dad to come with him. I remember her holding me while we watched them go out to help the dog. Dad lifted it up while Grandpa loosened the chain, and when they set it free, it just lay at their feet for a while, exhausted. Dad came back inside, but Grandpa stayed out in the rain with the dog, petting it until it got to its feet and ran off. He stood up and looked after it, and when he glanced over at Mom and me in the window, he smiled and waved.

That's what I don't get. It doesn't make any sense at all. I can't reconcile my memory of that event with the knowledge that the same man who performed this simple act of mercy was also the dirtbag who fucked his own daughter.

Mom is sitting up in her bed when they let me in to see her. They've moved her into the small wing that serves as the whacko ward but at least she's still got a private room and there are no bars on the windows or doors. Her face is as colorless as her sheets, and her eyes look like they've been sucked backward into her skull, leaving two dark pits for her to stare out of. She manages to smile a little when she sees me, and she reaches out to pull me toward her.

There's a faint smell of ammonia in the room, but Mom still

smells like Mom. I bury my nose in her hair and she kneads my back for a minute and lets me hold her.

"I'm so sorry," she says in my ear.

I let go and sit beside her. "What for? You didn't do anything wrong."

She sighs. "I suppose not."

"I mean, nothing besides trashing the house and going temporarily insane and scaring the living shit out of J.D. and me."

She smiles a little even though her lips are trembling. "I don't remember any of it. How bad was I?"

I shrug. "Remember Jack Nicholson in *The Shining?*"

She laughs in spite of herself, then she starts to cry. I start to get up to get a nurse because I'm afraid I've set her off, but she grabs my wrist and pulls me down again. "No, it's okay. They've got me so doped up I don't know what I'm doing. I've got to get out of here."

"The nurse said they can't release you until they get a thumbs-up from the head shrinker."

"I know." Her face turns hard. "You shouldn't have told them about my father."

I knew she'd eventually get around to saying that. "The only one I told was the shrink. Besides, what options did I have?"

She glares at me for a second but then drops her eyes like she doesn't want another fight. "It's not your fault. Cindy should have kept her mouth shut."

"Somebody in this family needs to tell me what's going on. I'm not a little kid anymore."

Her fingers are picking fitfully at her sheets and she's not looking at me. "Your age doesn't have anything to do with it. Your father didn't even know."

I start to worry that she's going to flip out again, so I change the subject abruptly and tell her about the work J.D. and I have been doing on the house and what's been happening at school and the job J.D. just applied for at the local grocery store. She calms down a little even though she's not really paying any attention. I babble on for a little while, then kiss her on the forehead and tell her I'll come back soon. She lays down and I start to leave the room.

"Noah?"

I turn around by the door. "Yeah?"

"You didn't tell anyone about the skeleton, did you?"

"No."

"Good. Don't." She closes her eyes.

J.D.'s waiting in the reception area for me. He's wearing one of my jackets and it's too small for him. "How is she?"

I shrug. "I don't know. Let's get out of here."

"Her psychiatrist came by a minute ago and said you should stop by his office and see him before we leave."

Why? I've already told him everything I know. We go downstairs to his office. His name is Clarence Clinton. (I know. I laughed the first time I heard it, too.) We go in and his receptionist tells me he's waiting for me. J.D. starts to come with me but the lady says he should wait out here with her.

In spite of his goofy name, Clinton is actually a pretty decent guy. He's got watery eyes and an epic paunch, but he seems to be a straight-shooter. He says hello and gets right to the point. He says Mom won't talk to him about anything and is being obstinate and he can't okay her release until he's convinced she's not going to have "another episode." He says he needs more details.

I ask him what kind of details. He says he needs to know what happened to her baby, and did my grandfather keep abusing her after the baby was gone and when did she leave home and did she ever confront her father as an adult?

I tell him I don't know any of that. He nods and says that's the stuff she won't tell him, and he can't help her until she opens up.

"And you won't let her go until she talks to you?"

"I'm afraid not."

* * *

When we get home there's some middle-aged guy I don't know waiting on the front porch. We walk up, kicking through the leaves on the sidewalk, and he comes down the stairs to meet us.

He looks at J.D. "Noah?"

J.D. shakes his head and points at me. The guy looks embarrassed and apologizes. "My name is Peter Thorpe. I believe we've spoken on the phone."

Mom's boss. Dean Thorpe. I shake his hand and introduce J.D. Thorpe is tall and bald, and his hands are huge. He's wearing jeans and painfully white sneakers, and he's got a tweed jacket on over a sweatshirt. He looks like an academic geek trying really hard not to look like an academic geek. I ask him what I can do for him.

"How's your mom? I tried to see her at the hospital but they wouldn't let me in."

Shit. I was hoping he hadn't heard about her breakdown, but I should have known better. "She's doing fine," I lie. "The doctor told me he was going to let her come home soon."

"That's good." He fidgets with his glasses for a second. "Forgive me for asking, but did he say when she might be able to return to work?"

"He thought maybe by the end of the week." Okay, okay, I shouldn't be lying like this, but the last thing Mom needs right now is to lose her job. I doubt this guy has the balls or the legal standing to fire Virginia York, but I'm not taking any chances.

"Really? That's quite a relief. We've all been worried about her." He actually sounds sincere. He studies me briefly, trying to think of something else to say. "And how are you doing?"

Fabulous. Never been better. "I'm okay."

"I know this must be difficult for you. Is there anything you need?"

He's probably only asking this because he's supposed to, but I pretend he's asking in good faith and tell him no, thanks. He shakes my hand again and says to call him if he can do anything for me.

We watch him walk to his car. He's got bad posture and a slight limp.

"You shouldn't have lied to him," J.D. says. "He'll be mad if he finds out the truth."

"How's he going to find out? Besides, Mom may get better faster than you think."

He doesn't say anything.

I wake up shivering in the middle of the night. J.D.'s taken all the covers again and left me lying here bare-ass naked in a cold room. I have to pee anyway so I get up and put on some sweatpants and   a T-shirt and I trek down the hall to the bathroom. I pass Mom's bedroom on the way, and for some reason decide to open the door and go in and turn on the light.

The sheets are still bloody from her little self-cannibalization routine the other day, and I stand there blinking, shifting from foot to foot on the cold floor. The baby's skull grins at me and the mason jars stand on the table at the foot of her bed, in an orderly row like a grocery display. I wander around aimlessly, looking at this or that until I end up by her desk. I pick up a piece of paper and read a poem she's scrawled across the top of it:

Main Street

There is an empty house
within an empty town
where everything that was spilled out
and ran into the ground.

Hers: the form that held the walls
still and firm, with grace—

until she lost her footing, too
and falling, lost the place.

Like a corpse face down in water
flips when tipped or spun,
the house rolls over on its back
and eyes the blinding sun.

What once seemed full (behind her shadow)
is revealed in the light
as bare, cold space devoid of soul
and stuffed with endless night.

Weird. Mom never writes rhyming poetry; it sounds more like Nellie Carlisle than her. There's a lot more and it's about as much fun to read as a bottle of heartworm medicine. Jesus. She makes Sylvia Plath look like Erma Bombeck.

I drop the paper back on the desk and stare around at the walls. She's got a picture of William Blake hanging directly across from a charcoal sketch of Elizabeth Bishop. The only poem I know of Blake's is that *Tyger, Tyger* thing, but I like Bishop a lot. She's one of the few poets Mom and I agree on. I especially love *Sestina*— that's the one that ends with *"Time to plant tears,* says the almanac / the grandmother sings to the marvelous stove / and the child draws another inscrutable house."

"Tell me about it," I mutter to Bishop's smudged face. "I know all about inscrutable houses."

With a jolt it occurs to me that this is the only room in our happy home Mom hasn't ripped to shreds. Bizarre. It's the place she's spent the most time in since we moved in, and in spite of her craze to find stuff she's left this room untouched, like a fastidious bird unwilling to soil its own nest or something.

I walk over to the wall by the door and thump softly on it, wondering if there's anything behind it, then I realize what I'm doing and laugh in spite of myself. Shit. Insanity apparently runs in the family. I'm actually thinking of ripping this room apart. Why the hell not? Mom's already torn down the whole goddamn house, so what will it hurt to check one more place and see if there's anything else to be found that might explain some of this? Maybe if I can find some answers about the Carlisles' baby girl it will help Mom somehow. I don't know how, but it might.

Yeah, I know, I'm full of shit. But I'm tired of being sensible. I want some answers too.

Do you remember when I told you about the rehearsal Dad was late getting me to? And how pissed I was at him, and how he almost ran down a paper boy because he wasn't wearing his glasses, and how he didn't get mad even when I spewed venom at him like a rattlesnake? I didn't know until now why it seemed important to tell you about that, but after staring at the baby's skull for the last five minutes the answer just occurred to me.

When I think of my dad, it's that memory that hurts the most. It's just one awkward moment taken out of context from our entire convoluted and mostly normal parent-child relationship, but it captures with appalling clarity the stark contrast between his gentleness and my spoiled stupidity. All he did was make me late for jazz band, and I treated him like he'd just dropped the A-bomb on an orphanage. Somebody should slap the shit out of me. What if my dad had been like Carlisle or my grandpa? What horror-story vignette would come to my mind about a father like that?

I forgot to mention Mom's reaction the night after the rehearsal when I told her how much Dad sucked. She said I shouldn't have lost my temper with him and that he deserved better from me than that. She said I didn't have a clue how lucky I was to have him for a father. She said that patient, kind men should be given a little leeway even when they were being stupid, because they were a rarity in the world and someday I'd understand that.

She was right. God knows my dad wasn't perfect. He was opinionated and snobby and a bit of a nerd and he dressed funny and he smelled like old newspapers. It's possible he was just as fucked-up in most ways as somebody like Stephen Carlisle or my grandpa, maybe we all are. But at least he lived his life in the open. What you saw was what you got, warts and all. I'm sure there were things he was ashamed of that he never told me about, but I'm relatively certain they were small, human things. Dad never had any reason to hide secrets in the walls, and I pray to God I never do either.

J.D. and I are skipping school today. I told him after breakfast what I wanted to do in Mom's room and without batting an eye he told me he'd stay and help. So we've moved all her furniture into the hall and we're trying to decide which wall to pull down first.

He's sitting on the floor between the windows, staring up at me as I pace. He's wearing a tacky flannel shirt with a frayed collar and he's got a bad case of bed-hair and he needs a shower, but he's still distractingly handsome. The bruises are fading and his lips aren't swollen anymore, and his eyes are astonishingly blue. I stop to admire him and he flushes self-consciously. "What's wrong?"

"Nothing. I'm just having trouble concentrating with you in the room looking like that."

He's got his elbows propped on his knees and his fists on his chin, and he grins at me over his knuckles. "You are the horniest human being I've ever met in my life."

I'd argue but he's probably right. I force myself to turn and study the room before I get more turned on, because otherwise we won't get anything done today.

Without the furniture in here it's a big room. The walls are white except for a dark blue trim on the wainscoting, shot through with small, frilly red birds, and there's also a thin line of the same trim running around the room next to the ceiling. While J.D.'s cracking the windows to let in some fresh air I walk up to the north wall, find a spot between studs, pull the hammer out of my tool belt and give it a wallop even my mom would be proud of. There's a satisfying crunch and plaster goes flying.

J.D. jumps about a foot in the air. "Jesus, Noah, warn me when you're going to do that."

"Sorry." I poke the claw of my hammer in the hole and rip out more stuff. "Okay. Let's be organized about this. One wall at a time."

Pretty soon the room is thick with dust and we've both got our collars pulled up to cover our noses and mouths. We work fast and before long the first wall is down and we haven't found anything except an old mouse nest. We move on to the east wall and start in, but when we're about halfway through it, J.D. stops and stares out the window. He pulls the shirt away from his face and puts his hand to his lips in a peculiar gesture, like he's hurt himself and is sucking on a knuckle.

"What's wrong?" I come up behind him and take his fingers away from his face to see what he did, but he pulls free and points down the street.

There's a big yellow moving van parked in front of his house.

CHAPTER EIGHT

I'm sitting on the floor in a pile of rubble with several sheets of paper on my knees and an open mason jar at my side. The paper is old-fashioned stationery with tasteful black and white engravings of various fruits in the margins, and the handwriting on the pages is neat and fills almost all the available space. At the bottom of the last page is a signature: *Stephen W. Carlisle.* The first page starts off with the line: "My wife and daughter are dead." God Almighty.

J.D. left about half an hour ago to find out where his family is moving to and why they didn't bother to let him know. Right after I heard him go out the front door I found this goddamn jar and I could just kill myself for being such a stupid putz. Why the fuck did I go looking for this? There's nothing served in finding it; it won't help Mom get better and it sure as shit doesn't do me any good. But no. I just had to go for one last scavenger hunt. Well, I hit the mother-fucking jackpot this time. Whoopee. My fingers are trembling as I read the note again:

> *My wife and daughter are dead.*
> *It is entirely possible no one shall ever find these pages, as I intend to conceal them where they are un-*

likely to be discovered until long after my death. Perhaps a fire will destroy this house before a future owner stumbles across these words; perhaps a bulldozer will raze this home to its foundations and no human being shall ever discover what has occurred here. Let fate decide.

My wife was Nellie Mitchell Carlisle; our daughter was Maria Louise Carlisle. Nellie and I were married on June 20, 1952, and at the time of our marriage she was nearly two months pregnant with another man's child. We had known each other for some time, and though our relationship was far from amiable (I had writtten several unfavorable reviews of her poetry), there had always been an undeniable sexual attraction between us.

While visiting Chicago in early May of that year, I was invited to a dinner party. Nellie was there as well, and, as chance would have it, we ended up sharing a cab, and, soon thereafter, due to a great deal of alcohol, the same bed. Upon waking the next morning, she seemed quite distraught, even though I was pleasantly surprised to find myself rather enamored of her. Over a period of several weeks, and with a great deal of effort and patience on my part, I finally managed to convince her of the sincerity of my affections. She eventually agreed to marry me, but only after I had agreed to raise the child she was carrying as my own. As soon as we were married, she left Chicago and came to live with me in Oakland.

The first weeks of our marriage were idyllic. We spent many pleasant summer evenings outdoors, talking quietly beside the goldfish pond or playing croquet in the backyard, and we also enjoyed rising early in the morning to sit together as the sun rose. It seemed to me we were smitten with each other, though in light of later developments I am forced to admit that I may have been

grievously mistaken. My contentment may have pre-
vented me from accurately ascertaining Nellie's state of
mind, yet surely I would have known had she not shared
at least some of my satisfaction.

The only bone of contention between us in the begin-
ning was her stubborn refusal to reveal the identity of
her former lover. My curiosity was not spurred by jeal-
ousy; indeed, it was merely practical. I believed then, as
I do now, that the child's true father should have been
held financially accountable for that child; I thought it
only fair he assume responsibility for his actions. Nellie
did not agree. She said we had more than enough money
and needed no aid from the father, and she wanted noth-
ing more to do with him. But beneath her surface show
of hostility toward the man, I always felt that her reluc-
tance to discuss his identity was nothing more than a
sham designed to protect him from repercussions. This
is, of course, perhaps nothing more than idle conjecture,
but whenever I broached the subject of her former lover,
her eyes would furtively avoid mine and her face would
flush.

Because of her "condition," I did not wish her to be
seen in public after she began to show. I would not allow
my marriage to be the subject of lewd gossip, as it most
certainly would have been had anyone realized how ad-
vanced her pregnancy was at the time of our wedding.
She argued bitterly with me about this, but as she grew
larger I refused to let her leave our house or, aside from
a brief visit from her sister early in the pregnancy, re-
ceive guests. She was quite willful and on more than one
occasion she defied me by appearing in town, waddling
about like an obstinate heifer, completely oblivious to the
impropriety of her actions. After several of these ridicu-
lous excursions, I had no choice but to begin locking her

in our bedroom during the day while I was at work. In spite of my patient explanations as to why she had made it necessary for me to confine her, she became belligerent and spoke quite hatefully to me, and she never seemed to understand how childishly she was behaving.

Her rebelliousness reached a peak one evening when she packed a suitcase and foolishly demanded that I release her. She was nearly six months into the pregnancy by this time, and I reminded her that she had no money and no place to go. She dared to threaten me with returning to her former lover and insisted that she was absolutely sure he would take her in. Her manner with me was utterly disrespectful, and, though I regretted it instantly, I could not contain my anger and I struck her. She fell and injured her head, and, while not a serious injury, it was sufficient to silence her. She complained of dizziness and allowed me to escort her back to our bed.

Over the next two months her health worsened considerably, but at least her infirmity seemed to bring her to her senses. She no longer had the energy to antagonize me—indeed, she scarcely had the strength to move from the bed to the bathroom. On good days, she would sit up in bed and attempt to write; she only managed a few trifling sentences but as writing seemed to make her happy I kept my opinions to myself as to the worth of these "poems."

When her due date grew close, I took her to Boston to insure our privacy. Maria Louise was born underweight but essentially healthy, and as soon as Nellie was able to travel, we returned to Oakland. I had hoped that with the arrival of the baby our marriage might settle into a more pleasant routine, but when I proposed we put it up for adoption so that there would be no tedious and embarrassing explanations necessary, Nellie became furious and once again threatened to leave me and return to Chicago. I tried to reason with her but she ignored me and began packing her things. I managed to restrain myself until she again went too far and actually marched resolutely toward the door, carrying Maria Louise. A struggle ensued and the baby was dropped; it landed badly on its head and was killed instantly.

Without a word, Nellie cradled the baby to her breast and, turning, walked upstairs and locked herself in the bedroom. When she didn't come out for hours and wouldn't respond to my demands to be let in, I was forced to break the door down. Nellie lay on the bed and was nearly catatonic, and the only thing that made her stir was when I tried to take Maria Louise away from her. But she was still weak from sickness and I prevailed.

Within a week she, too, was dead. Despite all of my attempts to succor her, she starved herself to death, refusing even water, and her heart stopped. She never once spoke to me.

There are no words to compass the difficulty of that week. Nellie would not leave the bed, even to use the toilet, and she continuously soiled herself. No amount of cajoling or threatening had any effect; when exasperation got the better of me and I carried her to the shower, she collapsed in the tub the instant I released her. It was as if she had become a rag doll. I had no option but to begin changing her linens and her underthings as if she were an infant, and as I did so, her eyes watched me, unblinking, full of accusation and loathing. By the third day I was reduced to pleading with her to forgive me, but she was remorseless and cruel, using her silence as a bludgeon.

As she began to fail, the stench in the room became

unbearable and I was only able to be with her for brief periods, covering my nose and mouth with a handkerchief. By the morning of the seventh day, dehydration and hunger had taken their toll; I am certain she was no longer aware of her surroundings. She passed away before noon.

Lest any reproach me for not seeking outside help, it must be understood beyond a shadow of a doubt that my hands were tied. Had I called a doctor for assistance with my wife, no justification I could have given regarding the manner of the baby's death would have sufficed. The resultant scandal would have ruined my career and soiled my name forever. I had no choice but to allow Nellie to take her own life.

Likewise, the only course open to me (however distasteful) regarding the disposal of Maria Louise's corpse was to bury it in the basement. A public burial would have served no purpose but to raise humiliating questions. My instincts have proven sound; aside from an awkward moment now and then with various people who had seen Nellie pregnant (all of whom readily accepted my explanation that our baby died in childbirth, and its death had been too much for my wife), the matter soon resolved itself without further complications. No one dared ask where the baby was buried; they assumed, quite rightly, that any such question would be inappropriate and intrusive.

Though I readily admit to feelings of remorse for many of my actions, I refuse to bear the full burden of responsibility for the tragedy of Nellie's and Maria's deaths. I believe now that Nellie deceived me when we married; I believe she was in love with the child's father, and secretly wished he was the man she had married, and any feelings she had for me were either feigned or

*fleeting. Her deceit was the catalyst for everything that
followed.*

*This missive, therefore, is not intended as a confession, but rather as a chronicle of what I am sure will be
rightly perceived as a series of unfortunate events. In addition to these pages, I have also deposited various articles throughout the house, to the purpose of providing
authenticity to my words. As Maria Louise has no tombstone, let these items also serve as a marker, if you will,
to honor her brief, hapless existence. Make no mistake:
had Nellie been more forthcoming before we took our
vows, or more pliable after, there would never have been
a need to try and physically restrain her, and the accident with the baby need never have happened. We are
both innocent; we are both guilty. Do not presume to
judge.*

—Stephen W. Carlisle

"Do not presume to judge." He keeps his wife a prisoner and he
drops a baby on the floor and then he has the balls to tell me not to
judge him. What an asshole.

I stand up and refold the sheets before putting them back in the
jar, and I look around at the wreckage of Mom's room. We've torn
our whole house apart and Mom's gone nuts and what have we got
to show for it? A few jars full of knickknacks, a baby's skeleton
and a fifty-year-old letter written by a whacked-out dead guy.
Fabulous. What a colossal waste of time.

The Auden poem Dad was reading on the night he died has a
stanza in it that I can't get out of my mind:

Evil is unspectacular and always human,
And shares our bed and eats at our own table,
And we are introduced to Goodness every day,
Even in drawing-rooms among a crowd of faults;

He has a name like Billy and is almost perfect
But wears a stammer like a decoration;
And every time they meet the same thing has to happen;
It is the Evil that is helpless like a lover
And has to pick a quarrel and succeeds,
And both are openly destroyed before our eyes.

I hate knowing there are people like Carlisle in the world. He was just another numbnuts bully like Perry White, but at least White has the balls to let his hate be out in the open and doesn't go around beating up people he's supposed to love.

Christ. What a mess. I'm so depressed I could puke.

I look out the window and see J.D. sitting on the front lawn, staring down the street at his house. The moving van is still there and I can see Donna standing by it, giving orders to two big oafs carrying her sofa.

The lawn is covered with leaves and the few patches of grass I can see are mostly brown. I usually love this time of year but today everything just looks dead and hopeless. J.D. barely glances at me as I sit next to him. His nose is running a little from the cold but he doesn't seem to notice. Heather's jumping rope on the sidewalk in front of his house by the moving van and he's watching her like he's hypnotized.

I pull a Kleenex out of my jacket pocket and hand it to him. "What's going on?"

He dabs at his nose. "They're moving out of town." His voice is flat and emotionless, like he's practicing to be a cyborg.

"How can they move? They haven't even put the house up for sale, have they?"

He shrugs. "I don't know. Mom won't talk to me and she won't let Dad or Heather tell me anything." He stares bleakly at his feet.

I pick up a stiff brown leaf and start tearing off small pieces of it, working in toward the stem. "Did she at least tell you where they're moving?"

"Not exactly. All Dad was allowed to say was someplace out west."

"Allowed? Christ, J.D., your dad needs to grow a pair."

His voice tightens. "Don't talk about him like that."

"I'm sorry, but he does. And what the fuck does 'someplace out west' mean? San Francisco? Tokyo?"

He gets up abruptly. "I need to be alone for a while." He stalks off down the street in the opposite direction of his house.

Good going. Next time maybe I should just pour some salt in his open wounds. I stand up and brush my butt off and realize I'm still holding the mason jar in my free hand. I meant to show it to him but I guess now's not the time.

I stare at the moving van again and see Donna and Tom staring back at me, and all of a sudden I'm mad as hell. This is bullshit. I walk directly toward them, expecting them to run and hide in the house, but I'm surprised when neither of them budges. I come within a couple of feet and we all study each other.

Donna's dressed in casual yellow slacks and has her hair pulled back off her forehead, and Tom's wearing jeans that are too tight around the waist and a big blue and white Boston University sweatshirt. He's also wearing a baseball cap on his head, and he's got it on backwards like he's a bad boy rap star or something. Heather's a few feet away, pretending to ignore me.

I don't bother to say hello. "It was nice of you to tell your son about your plans."

Tom drops his gaze but Donna just keeps scrutinizing me like I'm some kind of talking rodent. "J.D. is no longer a member of this family. Why should we tell him anything?"

I hate her. "Does it feel good to be such a dick? Are you enjoying yourself?"

I didn't think it was possible, but her lips get even thinner. "If it weren't for you, none of this need ever have happened."

"If it weren't for me, J.D. wouldn't know what it's like to be loved. How in hell do you justify the way you've treated him?" I should stop there, but she's just standing there doing her best iceberg imitation and I can't help myself. "It's not his fault you got raped."

Tom flinches and makes a noise in his throat and she turns white and starts to shake. She looks at her husband for a second then turns back to me and suddenly there are tears all over her face and Jesus Christ, will I ever learn to keep my fucking mouth shut?

"Get off my property, you filthy pervert," she whispers. "God will know what to do with you when the time comes."

Believe it or not, I want to tell her I'm sorry, but the words won't come out and I need to get the hell away from here before I do any more damage. I start walking home but stop when Heather yells my name and comes running up. Donna screams at her to get away from me but she holds her ground for a second. She looks up at me and her face is pinched and tired and sad and all of a sudden I wish I'd tried to be nicer to her. She actually manages a smile. "Tell J.D. I'll write to him, okay?"

Donna's coming toward us fast and all I have time to do is nod.

Who was Maria Louise's real father? What happened between him and Nellie? Was she in love with him like Carlisle thought? And if she was, then why did she marry Carlisle? I can speculate my ass off, but I don't think I'll ever know anything for sure.

I guess it doesn't really matter. Everyone involved in that particular hell is dead. But I can't seem to stop thinking about it. Was Nellie's lover married? Did she tie the knot with Carlisle to make the other guy jealous, or was she just destitute, with no other choice but to move in with somebody who said he'd care for her? Was she mentally unstable or something? I don't get it.

Some people's lives are so complicated. And do you know what

I've realized? That crazy bastard Freud was right. At the root of every major complication, festering beneath the surface like an ingrown hair, is sex. That's hardly an original revelation, I know, but there it is.

Nellie had sex with some guy and look how that ended up. J.D. and I had sex and he got thrown out of his house and we got beaten up. A couple of sex-crazed sickos raped Mom and Donna and it messed with their heads and their hearts in the worst way. And if there's anybody who thinks that only "immoral," "abnormal," or non-consensual sex leads to serious problems, take a closer look. Your garden-variety, run-of-the-mill, socially sanctioned sex may not cause as much of a stir, but it wreaks just as much havoc with the participants: possessiveness, power struggles, jealousy, guilt, insecurity, feelings of inadequacy, kids—the list is endless.

So what's the obvious conclusion? Simple. Consensual or not, steeped in love or distorted by hate, sex fucks things up. It's too volatile, too all-consuming, too emotionally and spiritually loaded for human beings to handle with any kind of grace.

That's not an indictment. It's just an observation. I for one have no intention of abstaining. Not ever. But I need to keep in mind that there's always a price, and the sex had better be fucking great to make it worth my while.

When I walk in her room in the evening Mom is tearing Dr. Clinton a new asshole. Her hair is stringy and she's pale, and she looks exhausted, but even though she's lying down on her side with her head on a pillow, she's still got some fight left in her.

"I am not crazy and I'm not dangerous and what happened between me and my father thirty years ago is none of your fucking business." She glances my direction. "Noah, leave this instant and go call my lawyer."

What lawyer?

She faces Clinton again. "When I'm finished with you, you silly fat quack, you'll be lucky to get a job flipping burgers."

Clinton is completely unruffled, like she's just commented on the weather. "You may call whomever you like. I'll make sure your nurse gives you access to a phone. But it's extremely unlikely that your lawyer will be able to secure your release."

Her face is bright red and she's starting to cry, but her voice is getting steadily louder. "You pompous, preening, son of a bitch. How dare you keep me here against my will! I have work to do, and a son to take care of, and you have absolutely no right to treat me like this."

The more out of control she gets, the quieter he becomes. "Virginia, you need to calm down, or I'll have you sedated again." He glances at me. "Noah, you should go home for now. Your mother is in no condition to receive visitors."

Mom shakes her head violently. "No! I want him here." She forces herself to speak reasonably. "Please."

Clinton waits almost a full minute before saying anything, like he's hoping for another eruption, but when she stays quiet he finally nods. "Fine. Just a few minutes, son." He leaves us alone.

"Son, my ass." Mom glares at the empty door after he's gone. "If he was your father I'd have you neutered to make sure his line died with him."

I sit on the foot of her bed. "How are you?"

"I've been better." She studies me suspiciously and slowly raises herself into a sitting position. "I suppose you think I'm crazy, too."

"No more so than usual." I squeeze her wrist and I'm shocked by how fragile it feels. "You need to start talking to Clinton. Maybe he can help you figure out what's going on and then you can get out of here."

"I already know what's going on," she snaps. "I'm being held prisoner by an officious prick who can't wait to dig up some juicy gossip about me and blab it to anyone who will listen."

I let go of her. "Who cares who finds out? Besides, if he says anything you can sue him for violating confidentiality or something."

She sighs. "It's not that simple. This is exactly the kind of thing that ends up in those ridiculous biographical sketches they put in things like *The Norton Anthologies*. I'll be damned if people a hundred years from now will get the titillation of reading about how poor Virginia York was sexually abused as a child."

She says it casually, like we've talked about her childhood a thousand times. I try to sound equally casual. "Since when did you start talking about yourself in the third person? Isn't it a little silly to be worried about what people are reading about you when you're dead?"

She surprises me by blushing. "I suppose you're right. It's just not how I want to be remembered."

Ordinarily I'd try to poke a few more holes in her ego but I guess she doesn't need me being a jerk tonight. I don't know why her vanity always pisses me off so much. I mean, I know she's already got poems in dozens of anthologies and she's probably right in thinking people will still be reading her stuff in the next century. I just wish she weren't so sure of it.

Neither of us says anything for a minute. I reach into my jacket pocket and pull out Carlisle's letter. "Look what I found."

She unfolds the papers and when she reads the first sentence her eyes get huge and she looks up at me like I'm God and I just handed her the Ten Commandments. "Where was it?"

"Your room."

"My room?" She actually has the gall to sound indignant. "You tore up my room?"

"You tore up mine first."

She ignores me and wolfs down the pages. She's a fast reader and it only takes her a minute or so, and by the time she gets to the end her hands are shaking and tears are streaming down her face. I try to take the pages back but she won't let me. "Dear God," she whispers. "Why did she ever marry the son of a bitch?"

"Who knows? Maybe he was hung like a horse."

She pulls the covers tightly around her legs. "The least she could have done was to kill the bastard before she starved herself to death."

This is probably something I shouldn't say, but I can't help it. "You didn't kill your dad."

She jerks her head up. "I was a child. Nellie was an adult. She had a choice."

She's crying hard and I don't know why the hell I showed her this. What was I thinking? I try to distract her. "I still can't figure out why he hid the stuff in the walls. If he wanted people to know about this shit, why didn't he leave things out in the open?"

She doesn't answer me. She just cries.

Officer Ganski is waiting for me by the nurse's station. His face is even ruddier than usual, like he's been pouring beef broth over his Cheerios. "Hello, son." He offers me his hand.

It seems I'm everyone's son today. I shake his hand and his palm is sweaty. He asks me how I'm doing and I shrug and tell him I'm okay.

"How's your mom? I tried to get in to see her but they won't let anybody but family talk to her."

I've got to give him credit, because he still wants to see her and I'm sure he knows she's had some kind of a nervous breakdown. I lie and tell him she's doing better and I expect her to be coming home any day now.

He gets this hopeful look, but then he studies me closer and doubt creeps across his face. "Really?"

I shouldn't trust him, but I do. "I guess not. She looks awful and she won't let Clinton help her and I don't know what to do."

He mumbles a few clichés about not giving up hope and these things take time, and even though I know he's trying to make me feel better I don't have the patience for it right now and I tell him I have to go. He nods and tells me to call him if I need anything, anything at all. I say thanks and head for the door.

"Oh, Noah," he calls after me. I turn and face him. "I'm probably not the one who should be telling you this, but I just found out that the D.A. is giving Perry White and the other three shitheads a break. They're getting off with three months of community service and some counseling."

"That's it? No trial?"

"No trial. I argued with him but he told me I was blowing things out of proportion. He said 'boys will be boys,' and he was sure they'd learned their lesson." He smiles faintly. "If it's any consolation, I've warned them to stay away from you and your friend and I wasn't exactly polite about it. White was trying not to cry and the other three almost shit their pants. I don't think they'll be bothering you."

He waits, expecting some kind of reaction, but I don't know what look to put on my face. I didn't want a trial, but the D.A. is either a fool or a mongoloid if he thinks someone like Perry or Lester is going to learn any kind of lesson from community service and a few sessions with some court-appointed counselor. And Ganski may have put the fear of God in the four of them about J.D. and me, but they're probably already back on the streets looking for other fags to beat up.

I make myself smile and I tell him thanks and good night. He's done what he can, and it's not his fault that it's not enough.

Tom's waiting for me on the porch when I get home. He's sitting in the dark on the swing and even from the lawn I can hear the chains clinking and the wood creaking as he rocks back and forth. There are no lights on in the house so J.D. still hasn't come home or he's pretending not to be there until Tom goes away. I walk up the steps slowly, dragging my feet. I'm too tired to deal with anything else tonight.

"Hi, Noah," Tom says. There's enough of a moon that I can see him when he tries to get to his feet and slumps back, giving it up. There's a bottle of Southern Comfort by his feet, half-empty.

I sit on the rail facing him. "J.D.'s not here. I don't know where he is."

Tom nods, then wobbles back and forth on the swing, then nods again like he doesn't remember doing it the first time. "That's okay. I wanted to talk to you alone anyway."

Great. This should be fun. "What do you want to talk about?"

"J.D. shouldn't have told you about my wife. All she's done all day is cry after what you said this morning." He's not slurring, but he's talking really slowly, like he's having to concentrate on each word to make it come out right.

I can't believe he's still trying to make me feel sorry for Donna. Her tears are probably acid, like the blood in those *Alien* movies. "I didn't mean to make her cry."

His jowls jiggle as he nods again. "I know you didn't." He's having trouble focusing on my face. His left hand is picking at loose paint on the seat of the swing, and his right is wrapped around one of the chains, like he's afraid of falling. "Look, Noah," he blurts out, "I know you hate my wife and you probably hate me too but there's things you should understand."

Like what? Donna's a creep and he's a ball-less wonder and the two of them have made their son feel like shit for years. What else is there to know? I don't say anything; the less I talk the sooner this will be over and I can get him off my porch.

"I know what you're thinking," he says. "You're thinking I'm a fat pile of shit and Donna's a bitch. Right?"

He may be drunk but at least he's not stupid. "I'm not thinking anything, Mr. Curtis."

"Yes, you are. That's okay. But you don't know what it's like for Donna. You don't know what that son of a bitch did to her."

For a minute I think he means J.D., then I realize he's talking about J.D.'s real father. "I know enough. J.D. told me . . ."

"J.D. doesn't know shit and neither do you. I only told him part of it. I didn't tell him everything because I didn't want him to have to hear what kind of a sick fuck his dear old dad was." He spits the word 'dad' out. "I didn't want him to know he was carrying around the genes of some psychotic fucking lunatic inside of him. I thought it was bad enough to tell him he only exists because his father raped his mother."

He sounds almost sober but when he lets go of the chain for a second to scratch his head he loses his balance and the swing lurches under him until he drops his feet to the ground to catch himself. He glares at me like he's daring me to laugh at him.

I wait for him to go on but when he doesn't say anything else I clear my throat. "What did the guy do to her?" What's worse than rape?

When he starts to talk again his voice comes out in a whisper. "She told me the plan was to go hiking in the woods and then come back to town for some ice cream. It was their first date." He licks his lips; I can see the spit glistening in the moonlight. "He got her out in the middle of nowhere and knocked her on the ground, then he pulled some rope out of his jacket and tied her up like a pig. She was wearing a pretty red scarf he'd complimented her for earlier. He used that to gag her so she couldn't scream. He held her throat as he fucked her, and the whole time he was fucking her he kept telling her he was going to kill her when he was done. Then after he shot his load he left her tied up while he walked around smoking a fucking cigarette." His hand pulls at the front of his coat and he looks down at it like he doesn't know whose hand it is. "She'd never even had sex before."

He's quiet for a while, then he looks up suddenly like he just remembered he was telling a story. "I saw her earlier that day. She was so happy. She had that red scarf on and a pretty little brown sweater and she was all excited about going on this date. She said she'd called her mom that morning to brag about this great guy who'd asked her out."

Jesus. I feel my eyes welling up in spite of myself. "How'd she get away from him?" I'm having trouble talking.

"He finally just let her go. He told her no one would believe her if she said anything and it was her word against his. He said he'd make sure everyone would call her a whore for the rest of her life." He pauses. "He must have had her figured out pretty good. He must have known she'd rather die than tell anyone what happened." His voice breaks. "Then before he untied her he took a piss on her, just to make sure she knew what he thought of her."

He puts a hand over his mouth to stifle a sob. I look away and wait for him to pull himself together. A wind blows across the porch and passes through the gutters, making them whistle like a flute. There are two distinct tones, both low, and they alternate back and forth mournfully, like a simple dirge.

I can barely hear him when he starts talking again. "She waited till dark then walked home, just to make sure no one saw her. That's the part I can't stand, you know? I can picture her hiding in the ditches from the headlights of cars and then sneaking around her dorm when she got back, with piss and mud all over her."

What can I say to him? What can I possibly tell him that won't sound like the stupidest goddamn thing he's ever heard?

He leans toward me, wiping his eyes. "She told me that while he was pissing on her he was laughing. She says that every time J.D. laughs he sounds just like him, and that every day he looks more like him."

I finally find my voice. "I'm really sorry. But it's not J.D.'s fault. J.D.'s nothing like that. Nothing."

"She knows that. She hates herself for feeling like she does about him. But she can't help it." His foot brushes the bottle and knocks it over, but the cap is on so nothing spills. He tries to grab it as it rolls under the swing but he misses. "Well, hell," he says. It comes to a stop against the side of the house. He stares after it but doesn't bother to get up to go after it. "Want a good laugh? Everybody on campus thought the guy was gay. I think that's one reason she's been so nuts about this thing with you and J.D."

"How come she wouldn't let you do anything to him?"

"I didn't know anything about it at first. We'd been dating for a couple of months when I asked her to marry me. That's when she told me she was pregnant." He accidentally whacks his funny bone on the back of the swing and he swears and rubs his elbow. "We hadn't had sex yet because she hadn't wanted to, so I got really pissed at her because I thought she'd been screwing around behind my back. I started to walk out on her and so she told me everything." He burps softly. "After she told me, I was going to kill the motherfucker and she said he'd done enough damage to her without causing me to go to prison for murder and we were never going to speak of it again. She said if I ever said anything to anybody she wouldn't be able to live with the shame and she'd kill herself."

"She won't try to hurt herself just because J.D. and I know, will she?"

"I don't know. I don't think so." He scratches his head, leaving a small tuft of hair sticking straight up in back when he takes his hand away. "That bastard was in one of my classes that semester. I had to see him every day, talking and laughing with his friends, flirting with girls, kissing the teacher's ass. And I had to just ignore him when all I wanted to do was cut his dick off and feed it to him."

"Why'd she have the baby?" It feels weird to talk about this as if it weren't J.D. we're discussing.

He snorts. "Take a wild guess. She was brought up in a strict Catholic home. She couldn't make herself get rid of it."

He leans forward again and reaches out to touch my knee. His breath grosses me out and I have to force myself not to pull away. "Every once in a while we get the alumni newsletter and there'll be a blurb in there about this fucker saying he's the chief mucky-muck of some computer company in New York and he's got a wife and three kids. Donna reads it and gets a look on her face like he just raped her an hour ago." His hand tightens on my leg. "I swear to God I'm going to kill him some day. I'm going to drive to New York and . . ."

His voice trails off and he lets go of me. "Who am I kidding? I won't do anything. Donna won't let me do anything. She calls me a weak, useless drunk but then she won't let me do anything." He swallows a couple of times and I have to strain to hear him. "You don't know what she used to be like. Even after . . . she didn't get mean for a long time. It kills me to see what she's turned into." His chin drops to his chest. "I wasn't always a drunk," he mumbles.

I shift uncomfortably and he whips his head up and grabs my leg again so hard it hurts. "Noah. You can't tell J.D. any of this."

I shake my head. "It might help him understand."

"No. Don't say anything. Promise me you won't. He's my son and I know what this would do to him. You guys might be banging each other, but he's my son and I still know him better than you do in some ways. Promise you won't tell him."

This is fucked, but I say I'll think about it and he says thanks and after a minute he asks me to help him stand up. It's obvious he can't get home by himself so I put his arm over my shoulders and walk him down the street. He's breathing hard and I can barely hold him upright. We wander under a streetlight and our shadows stagger along next to us.

The moving truck is parked in the driveway and the front porch light is on when we get there, and Donna's standing in the doorway waiting for Tom. I can't tell which disgusts her more: seeing me or seeing how drunk her husband is. She comes out and takes him away from me without a word, but before he lets go of me he gives my shoulder a hard squeeze and says " 'night, Noah." She slams the door behind them and leaves me standing on the porch steps.

I don't know what to feel. I know I'm supposed to feel some big upswell of compassion for Donna and there's part of me that does.

But there's another part that can't quite manage it. It's really hard to feel compassion for someone who hates me.

J.D. comes home about three hours later. He says he was out walking most of the day and just as he was coming home he saw his family pulling away in the moving truck. He says Heather and Tom both waved at him but Donna, who was driving, just stared straight ahead and pretended not to see him. He says he's okay but he's lying.

I don't know what to do for him. I don't know what to do for Mom. I can't fix their lives, no matter how much I want to. All I can do is love them, and wish the best for them, and hope things get better sometime soon. I know in my heart that's the sum total of my usefulness, and a fat lot of good it does either of them. So after I hold J.D. for a while I turn away from what I can't fix toward what I can:

Our house. Jesus, what a mess. Every single room is destroyed. There's not an intact wall, ceiling or floor in the whole fucking dump. But this is doable. This I can handle. It's dark and it's late and I'm tired but I'll be damned if I'm going to bed until this place resembles a home again.

I start by carting all the rubble out to the backyard. J.D. sits in the kitchen at first and watches me, then he slowly gets to his feet and starts to help. We don't talk for the first hour or so, but as we get more and more crap out of the house, a few words pop out—mostly stuff like "careful" and "watch that nail"—then pretty soon we're talking about what to do after all the debris is out of our way, and by the time we're patching the holes in our bedroom ceiling, we're even joking.

It's almost dawn by the time we go to bed. The place still looks like shit, but I sleep better than I have in a month.

I skip school for the next couple of days. J.D. wants to skip too, but we decide that's probably not a good idea, because if he gets in trouble with the principal it could open up a huge can of worms about where he's living. I spend the days working on the house, and when he gets home in the afternoon we work together until late at night. It's amazing how fast the repairs are going. Our room and Mom's are already back together, and the downstairs should be almost livable by the end of the week.

I feel like I'm in one of those "in-between times" Nellie wrote about in that poem Mom recited to me, except where Nellie was dealing with anxiety, I'm just resting. It's like my emotions are still there, but they're on hold, waiting patiently until I have the strength to deal with them again. I work until I get tired, then I sit on the porch and wait for J.D. to come home. I'm worried about Mom and J.D. and school and who knows what else, but right now my worries are someplace else. Nothing much is getting through.

I took a break around three yesterday afternoon and went to sit on the front steps with a thermos full of hot tea. It was kind of cold out, but warm enough in the sun that I didn't need a jacket. I had my eyes closed and was half-dozing when some instinct made me open my eyes. J.D. was walking toward me, but he was still about two blocks away and hadn't seen me yet. He had his head down and was kicking through the leaves on the sidewalk. I watched him come, and I sipped my tea, and I felt the sun on my face. And then he looked up and saw me.

Did I say that my emotions weren't getting through? That's not what I meant. It's only the bad stuff that's temporarily leaving me alone. Because when J.D. finally lifted his head and saw me, it was like somebody had just told him that Satan was finally in therapy and Evil was a thing of the past. I have never seen such joy on a human face, and it was directed at me. Even more than that, it was because of me. And for one eternal instant, I swear to God I swallowed the sun. It's a wonder I wasn't cooked from the inside out, like a baked potato in a microwave. The moment passed and everything went back to normal, but I know it happened and will probably happen again. I may have granted the rest of my feelings an extended shore leave, but I don't seem to need a break from love.

J.D. finally asks me what I want to do about all the stuff we found. Especially the baby's skeleton. I haven't wanted to think about that but I guess it's about time we deal with it.

Walter Danvers is at the door and he's carrying a big bouquet of red roses from the local flower shop. He's wearing a black knee-length coat and his pants and shoes are black, too. Why do pale guys always wear black? Don't they know it makes them look like cadavers?

He says hi and tells me the flowers are for Mom. He says they wouldn't let him see her at the hospital and he wanted to make sure she got them so he decided to leave them with me instead of some nurse.

I tell him I'll take them up with me later today and he says thanks but he just keeps standing on the porch with a befuddled look on his face. The last thing I want is some lovesick boob snooping around the house, but it's kind of cold out and Mom seems to like this guy so I ask him if he wants to come in for a minute and have some tea or coffee or something.

He follows me back to the kitchen saying stuff like "What a beautiful old house" and "Wow, look at this woodwork," and when I'm boiling the water he sits at the island and asks me polite questions about what classes I'm in and how I like Oakland. But when I give him his tea and sit across from him he gets quiet for a minute then says how sorry he was to hear about her getting sick and me getting beaten up, and he asks how I'm holding up with having my mom in the hospital.

It's weird, but I don't mind him asking. I can tell he's not just being nosey and he actually seems to care. "I'm doing okay. I'm worried about Mom but school's going okay and everything's all right."

"I heard your boyfriend was hurt pretty badly, too. Is he feeling better?"

It's the first time anybody has referred to J.D. as my "boyfriend" without intending it as an insult and it takes me by surprise. "He's fine. He's sleeping in this morning because we were up pretty late last night."

We chat for a while about Mom's poetry and my painting and other stuff like what books I've read recently, and I'm actually a little disappointed when he finally checks his watch and says he has to go. I walk him to the door and before he leaves he stops and turns around and looks at me. He's a lot taller than I am. "I'm glad we got to know each other better. I see why your Mom talks about you all the time."

"Mom talks about me?" If he'd told me that Jimmy Stewart was Mom's favorite poet I couldn't be more surprised. "The only stuff she says when I'm in the room is how I'm a poster-child for why people should use birth control."

He laughs. "She adores you. You must know that."

I guess I did. But I like hearing it. All of a sudden my eyes are wet.

He's watching me closely. I'm embarrassed but I thank him for stopping by.

"Your mom's a very special person, Noah. Tell her I'm thinking about her and have her call me when she gets home."

I say I will. It suddenly occurs to me that he and Mom may be shtumpfing for all I know, even though I'm not sure when they could have found the time. I fight the urge to fuck with his mind by telling him that a huge cop with a gigantic gun is also interested in Mom, but he's so serious and his eyes are so kind that I can't do it. I must be getting mellow in my old age.

I keep forgetting how much I miss my father. That sounds dumb, but all I mean is that we never had the kind of relationship where we hung out a lot or did a lot of things together, and with

Mom and me are moving and J.D. coming into my life and everything else that's been going on there hasn't been a lot of time to
dwell on Dad not being here. But when I meet someone like Walter
it reminds me what it's like to have an older man around who cares
about me and then I get this ache in my chest that hurts so much I
could scream. I hate that I'll never get to know my dad as a fellow
adult. I hate that I can't show him who I've fallen in love with and
see how he handles that. I hate that he's not here to help deal with
Mom and that all of a sudden I'm supposed to be a grown-up.

When I was fourteen I won some stupid art contest for kids in
my school. There was a big showing of all the paintings in the contest and there were ribbons and prizes and some guest hotshot from
the art faculty at Northwestern. Mom was out of town on some
book tour, so even though Dad loathed all art shows and contests
on general principle, he came and wandered through the rows of
canvases, avoiding as many people as he could and looking like
he'd rather be anyplace else. He never congratulated me. He never
said he was proud of me or that he liked my painting. But when it
was time to go he walked up to me for a minute and put his hand
on the side of my head. I could feel his thumb on my ear and his
big fingers on the nape of my neck.

I'll remember how that felt till the day I die.

Tomorrow is Halloween, and Mom is coming home.

Clinton says he hasn't got a clue what triggered it (and since he
doesn't mention Carlisle's letter, I don't bother to tell him about it)
but all of a sudden she opened up and told him everything she'd
been repressing about her relationship with her dad. He says she's
like a different person now, and she seems stable and calm, and he
thinks with light medication and counseling her depression will be
manageable and she'll be "ready to rejoin the world."

This will sound bad, but I'm pretty conflicted about her coming
home. I miss her, but J.D. and I have settled into a good routine.
We go to school, we come home, we work on the house, we clown

around, we have dinner, we go to bed. Then we get up in the morning and do it all again. He starts working next week at the grocery store, and I just applied for a weekend job running the cash register at a gas station. We're still getting pushed around at school by buttheads and that's probably not going to get any better anytime soon, but for the most part life is going pretty well for us. What if Mom comes home and goes apeshit all over again?

I know, I know. This is her house, and she's my Mom, and I should just suck it up and stop whining.

There's a small army of trick-or-treaters on the porch, which is kind of surprising since this whole backwards town knows about J.D. and me. Aren't they afraid of getting queer cooties or something? I tell Mom we should hand out scented condoms and bottles of mineral water and she just smiles and drops handfuls of Sweet Tarts and Milk Duds in their bags.

She's weirding me out. Even though she seems sad, she's quiet and relaxed, and I hardly know how to talk to her. She caught me staring at her and asked me why, and when I told her I was looking for the lobotomy scar she actually laughed out loud and hugged me. Who is this person?

Even though I know what brought about her "recovery," I don't have the faintest idea why reading Carlisle's guilt-ridden diatribe helped her. I mean, it's not exactly a fairy tale where everyone lives happily ever after. But something in it gave her some peace. Maybe just knowing what happened to Nellie and the baby was enough to let her move on.

There's stuff we need to tell each other. It's probably a good sign that she hasn't asked anything about what happened to all the stuff we found, but I imagine she eventually will.

I need to tell her that J.D. and I tossed Maria Louise's bones in the Turtle River two nights ago. We talked about it a lot before we did it, and even though we still feel sick about it we couldn't think of one good reason to tell Nellie's sister or Ganski about the baby. All the law could do at this point is come in, read Carlisle's letter and make a media event out of the whole deal; all Nellie's sister could do is grieve for a niece she never knew she had. So we packaged up the other mason jars with their contents and shipped them off to Elvin, then we drove out of town late that night. We both said a prayer beside the deepest part of the river and watched the bones sink, one by one, as far out as we could throw them. I suppose Elvin will always wonder who the baby in the photograph was, and why there was a pink and red baby's dress in a jar in her sister's house. Maybe there are times when it's better not to know the answers.

Mom needs to tell me what happened to the baby she had when she was twelve. Did she and her father put it up for adoption? Did it die in its sleep and end up buried in a cemetery, or a basement, or was it tossed in some river? Was my grandfather a murderer as well as a pedophile, or do I have a much older half-sister somewhere out there named Carolyn who has no idea I exist?

I assume Mom told Clinton, otherwise she wouldn't be home tonight with J.D. and me. Maybe she'll tell me at some point, maybe she won't. I'd like to know, but she might think I'm better off not knowing. I'm hardly in a position to argue with her, since I've basically decided not to tell J.D. what Tom told me either, at least not for a long time. He seems to be healing some and I don't see how telling him the rest of what happened would do anything but make him miserable all over again.

I just had a thought. Maybe Mom never knew what happened to her baby. Maybe her dad got rid of it and she has no idea what he did with it. Maybe she's been living with that fucked-up mystery all of her adult life and seeing Maria Louise's bones in our basement overloaded her.

But what if Carlisle's letter gave her some way to get her mind around things? What if it let her see that she wasn't to blame for something her asshole father did when she was twelve years old? Even if she never finds out what happened to her baby, maybe hearing what happened to Maria Louise is still some kind of an answer, some kind of balm to smear on old scars and make them stop aching so much.

I'm probably full of shit. But it feels right to me.

I need to tell her how much I love her, and I wouldn't mind at all if she told me the same thing. Some things aren't meant to be secrets.

I'm getting ready to patch up the last hole in the living room when Mom walks in, carrying a mason jar. I start to freak out and she puts a hand on my shoulder.

"It's all right."

She opens the jar and pulls out a wad of tissue paper. Lying on the bottom of the jar is Nellie's necklace. She repacks the tissue and screws the lid back on, then she reaches down and puts the jar in the hole.

I ask her why and she shrugs. "It belongs here." The front of her neck looks naked without the locket.

"Won't her sister wonder where it is?"

"I never told her about it."

Her face is solemn as I repair the wall, like she's watching me seal a tomb.

So what happens now? Who the hell knows?

The dean has given Mom a leave of absence until January, so she can have time to recuperate. She's not resting much, but she's started to write again and looks a hell of a lot better than she did. Her poetry is getting back to normal, too; I read some of it last night and was in over my head after the first line. I'd thought for a while that all of this trauma might have jolted her into trying a different style, but when I asked her about the poem I saw on her desk when she was in the hospital she said she didn't even remember writing it. I asked if I could have it and she got this horrified look on her face and made me promise to forget she'd ever written something that bad. We had a minor blowout then about what makes a good poem, which ended with her calling me an ignoramus and me calling her a snob. It felt just like old times.

The roof above J.D.'s and my bedroom closet sprang a leak the other day and when we were trying to fix it we found one more jar. This one had another of Nellie's poems in it and we almost didn't show it to Mom for fear she'd have a relapse but when she saw it all she did was sigh a little and ask us what we wanted for lunch. I suppose it's possible we'll keep turning stuff up for years but I doubt it. I have a feeling this is the last we're going to hear from the Carlisles. That makes me a little sad but mostly relieved. It would be nice if the next surprise in our lives came from somebody still living.

I guess I'm going to have to start thinking about college in the near future, even though I'd rather take a year off and stay with J.D. and Mom until J.D. finishes high school and the two of us can go someplace together. That is, of course, assuming we're still together by that time. Maybe we'll fall in love with other people, maybe we'll get sick of each other. It doesn't seem likely, but what do I know? I'm only seventeen.

I finally asked him what his initials stood for. He made me guess and then had the balls to get mad when I came up with Jimmy Dildo and Jupiter Dork. It took a long time to mollify him and get him to tell me his real name: Jason David. He asked me what my middle name was and I told him it started with an "A." He guessed, of course, "Asshole" and "Anus," within five seconds, and seemed unconvinced when I told him it was Allen. Noah Allen York. Mom heard the whole thing and laughed herself hoarse.

And that's more than enough for now.

Epitaph

The dead gray sky is full of snow
but not one flake survives the fall.
Each will leave a single tear
and Earth, wet-faced, must weep them all.
—Nellie Mitchell Carlisle
2/07/53